FULL OF GRACE

BETHANY SURREIRA

This is a work of fiction. Names, characters, places, and incidents either are the product of the author's imagination or are used fictitiously. Any resemblance to actual persons, living or dead, events, or locales is entirely coincidental.

Copyright © 2021 by Bethany Surreira

All rights reserved. No part of this book may be reproduced or used in any manner without written permission of the copyright owner except for the use of quotations in a book review. For more information, address: surreiraink@gmail.com.

First paperback edition June 2021

Cover design by Bethany Surreira

Editing/Proofreading by Amanda Cuff, Word of Advice Editing Services

Formatting by CPR Editing

ISBN 9798706138912 (paperback)

ASIN B08W5C2GJ4 (ebook)

www.bethanysurreira.com

❀ Created with Vellum

*For Dave.
Not all heroes wear capes.
I love you forever.*

1

LEAH

After four long months, the day had arrived. If you had told me a year ago that being back in Grace Valley was where life would have taken me, I never would have believed you. In fact, I probably would have laughed in your face and stormed off in the opposite direction. I was a bit childish back then.

When I found out my mom had died in a car accident and I wouldn't be able to reconcile with her, I thought my life was over too. The amount of pain and guilt I felt was debilitating at times, and I wasn't sure where my life was headed. Even though I thought I had it all, she was always in the back of my mind. And once she was gone, I couldn't comprehend how I had ignored her for all those years. It was nice having the memories, though. And the pictures. Thank God for the pictures.

I grabbed her old sweater off the back of my chair and shrugged it onto my shoulders, my auburn curls bouncing on my back. I closed my eyes and let out a long breath, feeling her love squeezing me tight. I knew she was with me. I took comfort in knowing she forgave me even when I couldn't forgive myself.

I looked around the room my dad and I had transformed from my mom's old art studio into my new travel agency. The back wall had a floor-to-ceiling rose gold decal of a world map. The wall my desk sat against was covered in black-and-white pictures I'd found in my mom's old things. They were mostly taken in the Italian village she grew up in, but some were from other travels she took as a child. Rome, Paris, Lisbon, Madrid. I planned on visiting every single city she went to.

The opposite wall was my favorite. I had my dad put in floating shelves, but instead of wood or metal, he used small vintage suitcases. It was beautiful. I used those shelves to hold travel books, brochures for my future clients, and various old clocks—each set with a different time zone.

I founded Abernathy Travel and Leisure shortly after my mom's funeral last year, and I had hoped it would become one of my more positive ideas. Actually, it was my dad's idea, but it was a great one. When I brought up the idea of leaving NYC to start my agency, my old boss, Cameron, was my first cheerleader. It was nice to have that type of support system when I was about to take a leap bigger than I ever had before.

"Hi, pumpkin. Are you getting ready for your big day?" my dad asked, walking in from the side door that connected to his grocery store.

It also helped that he owned the building and wasn't charging me rent.

"I think so. I'm a little nervous, but I'm excited. I just hope I'm able to get clients organically," I admitted. "Not that I'm not grateful for the clients Cameron sent my way. I just want to prove myself, ya know?"

"Leah, you have always accomplished everything you have set out to do. You shouldn't let fear impede your dreams. I have every faith this will become more than you could ever hope for."

My dad always knew the right things to say. And even as a grown adult, I valued his input in ways I never thought I would. He was my father first, of course. But we'd built such a wonderful friendship since we lost my mother. Before I could respond, the front door was thrust open and a gust of wind tore through, blowing all of my papers around the room. It would have helped to actually use the paperweight that was currently in my hand.

"Oh shit! I'm so sorry, Leah. Let me clean this mess up," Sara said as she scrambled across the floor picking up paper after paper.

"Sara! What are you doing here?" I asked, throwing my hands in the air and motioning for her to come in for a hug.

"I was just in the neighborhood and thought I'd drop by to say hi."

Winking, she plopped the papers onto the desk and hugged me back tightly.

Sara lived in the Upper West Side of Manhattan, and while she visited me in Grace Valley a handful of times, she'd never come unannounced. I didn't complain though. I was more than happy to have her here for my big day.

"I can't believe you're here," I said and hugged her back. "I thought you said you were going out of town this week for work?"

"I am. I'm here!" she admitted.

"Always so sneaky. How was your trip over? Was the train ride okay?"

"Yeah, it was fine. Same old, same old. Tell me about today, though! I'm so excited for you. I always said you were destined for big things, my friend," she said and gave me her megawatt smile.

I was a ball of nerves. I had been waiting for the grand opening of my own agency for as long as I could remember, and now that the day had finally come, I thought I was dreaming. As I filled Sara in on everything that had happened since we last spoke, I felt a sense of calm wash over me. She was the yin to my yang. The combination of having both her and my dad here with me was heartwarming.

"It's almost time, pumpkin," my dad said, tapping his watch. "Sara and I will be front and center cheering you on with everyone else. I am so proud of you, and I know your mom is too."

He gave me a quick kiss on the forehead and a long squeeze before he walked outside to gather with the crowd. Sara winked and followed him, and I stayed inside alone as I looked around one last time. I could feel my mother, her arms wrapped around me and hugging me tight. I could hear her soft voice telling me how proud she was of me, and she forgave me for what I put her through the last seven years of her life.

I palmed the clay heart she made me, then tucked it safely into my pocket before taking a deep breath and straightening my shoulders. The crowd outside was forming significantly, and I was ready to fully make this mine. I walked out the front door and smiled at the mayor, who was waiting on the other side of the ribbon with the biggest pair of scissors I'd ever seen.

The chatter quieted down, and I saw so many of the other store owners on the green. Mr. and Mrs. Kratz from The Kratz Outta the Bag, Becky Butler from The Flower Pot, my dad, of course, and Tammy Patterson from Tammy's Diner. Bill and Marina Palmer were standing to the right of my dad and Sara, while Dooley Butler and his and Becky's daughter, Jackie, stood to the left. I even saw that Matt, from the train station's coffee shop, was here to support me. I kept smiling and waving until the mayor cleared his throat, urging me to come closer to start the ceremony.

I blushed and moved closer to him. "Would you like to say a few words, Leah?"

"Yes, Mayor, thank you," I said and looked out toward the crowd once again. "As most of you know, I grew up in this town.

I ate cookies at the bakery across the street. I sang in that gazebo every single Christmas. I played tag in the grocery store, even though my dad yelled at me every single time. And I did my homework in The Flower Pot with Becky almost every single day. I've always known the importance of planting roots, and while it took me a while to figure it out, I'm so glad I was able to come back to Grace Valley and start over right where I left off. Thank you all for being here today and supporting me in this new venture. I hope I can be of assistance to all of you in one way or another."

I took a step back and looked at the mayor as he handed me the scissors that were almost half my size. In that moment, my dream became a reality, and it felt wonderful. I opened the scissors and held them at the ribbon while I smiled at all the cameras flashing in my face. I looked up briefly and gasped. My smile dropped from my face as I made eye contact with Caleb, who was directly across the street on the other side of the green.

What is he doing here? He lived in Tennessee, and I hadn't seen him in Grace Valley since the night of the Christmas Festival last year.

"Leah," Sara whisper-shouted and knocked me out of my confusion.

I regained my smile and cut the ribbon. The crowd erupted into cheer, and I'd never felt so loved. I looked back across the green but was greeted only by the lushness of the grass and the stillness of the air. Caleb was gone.

"Leah, I am so proud of you," Tammy said, giving me a big hug.

"Thank you so much for everything. It means a lot to have you here today," I said, hugging her back. "And thank you for donating all the snacks. I truly appreciate it."

"You know I would do anything for you, sweetie. Anything," she said in return.

I smiled and turned to go inside and start greeting everyone who had attended the ceremony, when I saw my old boss.

"Cameron! What are you doing here?" I exclaimed and rushed over to hug him.

"I couldn't miss your big day, now could I?" he said. "I truly miss you in the office, but I couldn't be happier for you. Are you excited about your new clients?"

"Thank you so much for being here. You know I wouldn't have been able to make this happen without your help," I admitted. "I'm very excited. I can't believe this is my reality after dreaming about something like this for so long."

"Big things are happening, and this is only the beginning. I'm here for you throughout this entire journey. Whatever you need," he told me and headed into the building behind Sara.

Funny how grief and anxiety can change your perception of reality. Lately, my reality far exceeded anything that I could dream of. Well, except for Caleb. I was still bitter that he was getting married to that wretched excuse for a woman.

Speaking of Caleb. I knew I'd seen him across the green. But why would he have been here? Had Tammy told him during one of their calls? When she asked me if she could fill him in, I told her I'd rather she kept it between us, but if he asked, then sure. The last thing I needed was to have to deal with his prissy fiancée ruining my day. You ready to go in and celebrate? I have a surprise for you," my dad said, wrapping his arm around me.

"A surprise? You just gave me an office space free of charge. What more could you possibly have to give me?"

"You'll see."

We walked in together, my arm hooked in his. It felt nice to see him every day and not have to worry about him from afar. He didn't show his pain, but I knew he was hurting. And I knew the only way to help him heal was to be with him.

He led me to the back of the room near where Tammy set up

Full of Grace

the food, and I saw a small bucket sitting on the side of one table. I smiled when I peeked in and saw the champagne and pink lemonade. I turned around to thank my dad and felt the color drain from my face. Caleb was standing in the agency's doorway.

"What the hell?"

2

CALEB

Well, here I was again—back in Grace Valley at the same time as Leah. Only this time, I was single. And she was . . . well, I didn't actually know what she was. My mom kept her lips sealed tight whenever I asked about her. She mentioned that Paul asked her if she wanted to move back home. And I hadn't even known the answer to that. I hadn't spoken to Leah since the night of the Christmas Festival, and even though I knew things had ended with that city boy, I didn't know if she had met someone new.

I sold my grandmother's house in Tennessee in less than a week and had been working at warp speed ever since. After I had finished unpacking my clothes at my mom's house, I decided I needed to take a long walk to clear my head. I needed to slow it down and take in the town I grew up in. I took my earbuds out as I made my way over to the gazebo to sit and think. That's when I'd heard all the commotion from the side of the grocery store. I'd walked over that way and made eye contact with her just as she was about to cut the ribbon. And I freaked.

I saw my mom front and center, and I instantly regretted not getting all the info when she first offered it. She'd looked perfect. So naturally beautiful. When she had looked back down, I ducked behind the gazebo. I was still so hopelessly and helplessly in love with this woman, and I didn't know how to act around her anymore, which meant I had to get out of there, and fast. I'd snuck a quick glance and saw she was facing what I assumed was her new store, so I'd turned around and walked toward my mother's diner. At least I'd be safe there.

"Hey, Dante," I'd said to my mom's line cook when I walked into the diner. "What's on the menu today?"

"What's up, Caleb? Nothing new today," he replied. "Happy to be back?"

"You could say that. Hey, what's going on down the street with that new store? I saw some sort of ribbon-cutting ceremony," I'd asked, hoping to remain under the nosy radar.

I was grateful that even though he'd worked here for a while, he hadn't started until after we graduated high school and more than likely didn't know Leah. At least not the way the rest of us did. And this was also good because I didn't need to worry about him running back to my mom to tell her about this conversation.

"Oh, yeah. Your mom catered for it. I guess some woman just moved back here and opened her own travel agency."

"That's cool," I'd said. "Yeah, she grew up here. We knew each other when we were younger."

"Oh, okay."

"Yeah. All right, man, I'm gonna head out, but it was nice seeing you. Tell Maria I say hello, and hug those kids for me. If it's okay, I'd like to stop by one of these days to see everyone."

"Maria would love that. Let me know what day so I can tell her. You know she'll lose her mind if you show up unannounced and she hasn't prepared a three-course meal for you," Dante had said with a laugh.

"Definitely."

I'd nodded to Dante and decided to go back to the agency to see if I could talk to Leah. Now that we were both back in Grace

Valley for good, it was important to get this out of the way. I'd rounded the corner and, feeling very underdressed in joggers and a T-shirt, I'd stopped and stood in her doorway. I had a split second to decide if I wanted to stay or turn around again. As soon as I lifted my eyes, my ears were met with *"What the hell?"*

And now, time was up.

I walked inside and toward her. "Hi."

Hi? Seriously?

"Caleb," she said and threw her arms around my neck before pulling back just as quickly. "Oh, sorry. I don't know why I just did that."

She backed up abruptly and brushed the hair out of her eyes. She licked her lips and looked down, smoothing out her sweater. Her mother's sweater. It looked perfect on her.

"It's okay. I just wanted to come and say congratulations. I'm happy for you," I told her, as I desperately tried not to grab her and pull her in for another hug.

I could see the embarrassment wash over her like a giant wave. She was still so easy to read. I nonchalantly looked around to see if that guy from the festival was there, even though I knew they were no longer together. My heart jumped at the thought of possibly being with her again. I couldn't help but think that was my chance.

"We broke up," she answered as though she were privy to the thoughts in my head.

"Oh, I'm sorry," I said. The embarrassment at being caught had shifted from her to me.

We stood in silence for a bit. It wasn't awkward, but something about it didn't feel right. I wanted to tell her about Brittany and profess my love to her right then and there, but for some reason, I couldn't.

"This may sound like an odd question, but what exactly is all this?" I asked her.

Full of Grace

"Abernathy Travel and Leisure. We can take you anywhere!" She giggled. "After my mom passed away, I felt like something was missing from my job in the city. At first, I couldn't put my finger on it. But after a bit, I realized that, while I loved what I did, I needed to be doing it here in Grace Valley. I missed so much already, and I just wanted to be back home with my dad."

"Leah, I didn't know any of this. I'm sorry I wasn't able to help you," I told her and then immediately regretted it.

She smiled. "My dad showed me this place before I went back to the city, and we talked about keeping it as it was for a while. Sort of as a way to preserve my mom's memory. But then he called me and said I should use the space to open my own agency. I hung up with him and gave my boss my resignation. Told him I was moving back home to be with my father."

"Just like that? Wow. That's impulsive and so unlike you," I said.

"I know! You should have seen me march up to my boss. You would have laughed."

"What did your boss say when you told him you were resigning?" I asked her.

An older man walked over and stood beside Leah, handing her a glass of champagne.

"I said, 'Leah Abernathy, there isn't any other person on this earth I would wish this for more than you. I want to help you get this new business up and running,'" he said, thrusting his hand toward mine. "Cameron Waterstone, President and CEO of World City Travel, and Leah's former boss."

"Very nice to meet you," I said and returned his handshake, relishing in the knowledge that he was her former boss and not a current flame. At least, that's what I assumed.

"Caleb Patterson. Leah and I grew up together."

"Nice to meet you as well. Leah, I must be going, but I trust we'll speak again very soon. Enjoy every moment," he said and gave her a quick hug. Turning to me, he added, "Caleb, pleasure meeting you."

"He seems nice," I said after Cameron had turned and walked away.

I hoped my jealousy was not easily read.

"He is. He's been very good to me. And Sara, too," Leah said, nodding over to another woman who was talking with Paul. "He's been a sort of father figure, so it was sad to leave his company, but it's gonna be great here. I can feel it."

"That's great," I said, ready to take my chance. "Hey, Leah? There's something I wanted to tell—"

"Leah Abernathy, my little sweetheart. Come here and give me a hug," my mother interrupted my impending speech.

I watched the two of them chat; they were both so comfortable with each other. They looked more like mother and daughter than two adult women. My mind went wild thinking about the future with Leah and how badly I wanted to make things work with her.

Looking at her was so painful for me, but seeing the effortless connection she had with my mother was worse. I wanted to be with her—I *needed* to be. She was my destiny. But how was I supposed to convince her of that? *Man, I'm a sap.*

I'd never been one to run away from my problems. I was always the kind of guy to stand tall and proud and not cower in the face of fear. But with Leah, things were different. *I* was different. And it scared me. Before I had the chance to figure out what was happening, I found myself walking out the door and heading back toward my house. I didn't know who I had become, but I wasn't liking it.

3
LEAH

"Tammy, thank you so much for everything. You have outdone yourself once again," I said.

"Anything for you, Leah," she responded, her hands squeezing mine gently. "You know that."

"I can't believe the day is finally here. I almost felt like it was never going to happen," I said, motioning around my new business. "One day it was just a thought, and now, it's a full-blown agency."

"I always knew you were destined for great things. I'm truly honored to be a part of this and watch you become who you were meant to be," Tammy said with a smile.

My hands found their way into my pockets, and I clutched onto the clay heart as if I were summoning my mom somehow. But I already knew she was there with me. I felt her in me, in the room, in the air. She was always around me, and I took comfort in knowing she would approve. In all the hustle and bustle, I almost forgot I was talking to Caleb before Tammy interrupted us. When I finally looked up, he was nowhere to be found.

"Tammy, would you excuse me for a minute? I was talking

with Caleb and he's disappeared. I want to see if I can catch up to him," I said.

"Of course, sweetie," she replied, her mischievous smile hiding nothing. "Go ahead."

"Thanks," I said, rushing through the rather impressive crowd.

I got to the door, and it was as if Caleb had vanished into thin air. The street was empty. Not even a squirrel could be seen. I continued to look in either direction, hoping to catch a glimpse of him somewhere. Why did he leave? And where the heck did he go? I couldn't leave my own ceremony, so the answers to my ever-growing list of questions were going to have to wait.

I reluctantly retreated inside and rejoined the party. Seeing Caleb was not what I had expected, but it also didn't surprise me one bit. It seemed that everywhere I turned in Grace Valley, I was bumping into someone or something from my past.

"Leah!" Sara called from the back corner. Also not surprising was the fact she was still by the mimosa bar.

"Hi," I called back and walked over to meet her.

"Where'd ya go?" she asked, handing me a champagne flute. "And who was that ridiculously attractive man you were talking to?"

"That man was Caleb," I said before taking a large gulp of the mimosa. The tartness of the pink lemonade made my mouth pucker.

"Caleb, as in your ex-boyfriend, Caleb?" she asked, her eyes widening. "Wow, he looks so different from your pictures."

"Sara, those pictures were from when we were sixteen. Of course he's going to look different," I said with a laugh.

"Well, you know what I mean." She rolled her eyes. "Why are you not all over him? Go get him."

"You know, subtly really isn't a good look on you," I said and smiled. "I don't know where he went. I tried to find him but he's gone. I'm not in the business of stealing another woman's man."

Full of Grace

"Please, that's not what I meant. And judging by the way he was looking at you, he's either not with her anymore or he's not *into* her anymore. Leah, my girl, that man has it bad for you."

"I should be heading back soon too," Sara told me. "I have dinner plans with Aiden tonight, and I don't want to be late."

"How are things going between you two?" I asked her, thoroughly invested in her happiness.

"I love him," she smiled shyly, though there was nothing shy about her. "He's the one. I can feel it in every fiber of my being. Crazy, huh?"

"Not at all. Nothing is crazy when it's true."

I was happy being able to witness her falling in love with a truly wonderful man. Lord knows her track record was anything but stellar, and Aiden seemed to bring out the best in her.

"Thank you for making the trip over to be here with me today. You're the best." I leaned in to hug her tight.

"I know," she teased and squeezed me back. "Next time I visit, I'm going to bring Aiden. Maybe we can have a little double date with you and Caleb."

"Stop it." I smiled and shook my head.

"Love you, girl. Call me this week and let me know how everything's going."

"I will. Love you too."

I stood in the corner of my new office and stared across the room, taking in everyone and everything around me. I hadn't regretted my decision a single moment since I told my dad I was coming home. This was it for me. My future was bright, hopeful. And it was right there in Grace Valley. Now, if only Caleb was in it.

Oh well, can't win 'em all.

Who was I kidding? I didn't have time for a relationship anyway. Starting my own company in a matter of months was enough to keep me busy. I surely didn't need to be adding any distractions to my already overflowing plate. Even if he did look amazing. *Enough, go mingle.*

I spent the rest of the afternoon chatting up my guests. It felt good to be ready to work again, and even better that it was on my terms. When the crowd started to disperse, I looked for my dad so we could clean up and head home for dinner. I couldn't wait to talk about the day and decide what was next. I found him in the corner talking to Dooley, who I hadn't even realized had slipped in.

"Hey, pumpkin," he said, his rosy cheeks plumping. "Dooley asked if I could help him close up the barn tonight before it gets dark. There's a storm brewing, and you know how easily those horses can get spooked."

"Of course," I replied. "Do you want me to come help too?"

"No, you don't have to," Dooley said. "It shouldn't take long. I just want to move the horses to the bigger barn and board up the windows and doors. Should be thirty minutes, tops."

"Sounds good. I'll get dinner started so it's ready when you get home," I told my dad. "Anything you're in the mood for?"

"Surprise me." He winked.

By the time we finished cleaning up and my dad and Dooley headed to the farm, it was almost dark out. The storm was close; it never got dark this early in May. It hadn't rained here in weeks, and the flowers were wilting, so it was welcomed. I just hoped it didn't dump too much on us at once.

I locked the doors and started my walk home. I wasn't afraid of being alone in the dark in Grace Valley. It was much darker than being in the city at night, but it was far more peaceful. I found myself thinking of Caleb again and wishing he were walking home with me. Before my mind could wander too far, I was home snuggling Gnocchi on the porch swing.

"Come on in with me, Gnocchi. I have to get dinner started," I said as he continued purring on my lap.

Full of Grace

I took my sweater off and gently draped it over what used to be my mom's chair at the table. No one has sat in it since she passed, and I can't imagine anyone ever will. I opened the refrigerator and looked around for something to throw together.

What to make? What to make? We haven't had meatloaf in a while. That's easy enough to prep and should be ready by the time Dad gets back home.

I quickly checked to make sure we had all the ingredients in the house, and luckily, we did. I definitely didn't have time to defrost anything. I chopped and diced, stirred and poured; and before long, the meatloaf was in the oven, cooking away. I loved being back in that kitchen. The food would take at least forty-five minutes to cook, and my dad wasn't due back for another thirty or so minutes, so I decided to call my grandmother in Italy to catch up. We were planning a visit for the summer, and I couldn't wait to meet her and my grandfather.

"Hi, Nonna," I said after her broken English greeted me from the other line. "How are you?"

"Leah, my dear, it is late. Is everything okay?" she asked.

"Oh, I'm so sorry!" I rushed to say. "I didn't even think about the time change. I was just cooking dinner and waiting for Dad to get home and thought I would call you to tell you about the ribbon-cutting ceremony."

"Don't you worry, my love. Nonna is a night bird. Is that what you call it?"

I giggled. "A night owl, Nonna."

"Ah, yes. A night owl," she said. "Now, tell me all about your day."

I spent the next forty minutes telling her everything that had happened, including my weird conversation with Caleb. She ended the call by telling me she loved me and that she had a vision I'd become romantically involved very soon. I told her to lay off the vino before bed.

4

CALEB

"Caleb," my mom called up the stairs.

"I'm up here, Mom."

"Caleb, what is going on with you?" she started in on me before her foot even entered my room. "You show up to the ribbon-cutting ceremony late—in jogging clothes, no less—and then you disappear?"

"I don't think that's fair, Mom. You never told me about the ceremony. I went for a run through town—like I always do—and everyone was standing around the grocery store. At first, I thought Paul expanded until I saw Leah standing there with the scissors. Why didn't you tell me?" I demanded.

"She didn't want you to know. She didn't think you needed to know about her life since you were engaged to someone else," she admitted, looking down at her feet. *I get that trait from her.*

"I'm not getting married!" I yelled.

"You may be a grown man, but you won't raise your voice in this house, especially to me," she snapped, and I quickly straightened up.

It didn't matter how old I was. When my mom told me what

to do, I listened. And I had a feeling she was about to lay some serious knowledge on me. I sat on the edge of my bed and waited for the other shoe to drop.

"Caleb, honey," she started. *There it is.* "You're right, you're not getting married. And she isn't dating anyone anymore. But you're also not telling her how you feel. Or that you're even home for good. You can't expect anything to come out of this if you're not willing to do any work to rectify it."

Remember how I just said when she spoke, I listened? I wish I didn't . . .

"I know, Mom. I don't know what to say to her, though."

"How about you start with an apology? Then tell her you're still head over heels in love with her and that the two of you should start over?"

Coming from her, it seemed so easy. But when I was around Leah, I felt like a seventeen-year-old kid again, and I didn't know how to be open with my feelings. I didn't know if she felt the same way, and I couldn't put myself through the pain of losing her again. I wouldn't go through that again.

"Caleb, just relax. Get your thoughts together, and when you're ready, talk to her. She's not going anywhere. You have plenty of time. I'm going to throw a pizza in the oven. I'm tired and don't feel like cooking. Is that all right with you?"

"That sounds perfect, Mom. Thanks. I'm going to take a quick shower, and then I'll come down and set the table."

"All right," she said and kissed my head. I guess you're never too old for your mom to love on you like you're a little boy.

The faucet in the shower squeaked, and as the water heated, I made a mental note to fix the noise. I stood in the shower and let the hot water rain on me before I lathered up. My body was sore, but I wasn't sure if it was from the long train ride from Tennessee back to Grace Valley, my jog, or my bruised ego from screwing things up with Leah for the millionth time. The lights started to flicker just as I was finishing up in the shower. I knew the storm was supposed to bring heavy rainfall, but there weren't any predictions for high winds. *Typical New England storms.*

I pushed aside the curtain in the bathroom to see what it looked like outside. Just as I peered my head around, the power went out.

"I'm sure that'll only last a few seconds," my mom yelled.

I wasn't too sure about that this time. Grace Valley had gone black, and the silence was deafening.

"I dunno, Mom," I replied. "Let me dry off and get dressed, and I'll set up the generator for you."

Thank God I filled the gas cans last week.

Three years ago, Grace Valley was hit so hard that everyone was without power for over a week. Trees were down everywhere. It was a mess. I'd decided to come home to visit during spring break, and I ended up staying for two weeks trying to clean up the mess. As soon as the roads were clear, I went out and bought my mom a generator. Thankfully, Dante knew how to get it started, and I knew he'd help her if I wasn't around.

"All right, Mom," I said, running down the stairs and handing her a flashlight. "I'll get the generator set up. I have a feeling it's gonna be a long night."

"Don't say that. I don't think this town can handle another bad storm," she said.

"We'll be fine," I told her. "I'm here and we'll have power back in no time. Just be thankful it's May and not the middle of August when the central air doesn't work."

"True," she agreed. "Be careful out there."

I shrugged my raincoat up over my shoulders and lifted the hood. *I really need to build her a breezeway to connect to the garage.* Grace Valley was full of old farmhouse style homes with detached garages. They weren't as equipped as the newer homes and tended to fail during inclement weather. I moved Mom's car out of the garage and wheeled the generator around to the back of the house where the hookup was. I was glad that I had kept in touch with old high school friends and was able to have my old buddy, John, install a transfer switch last winter. Times like these without a generator could be brutal. I moved Mom's car back into the garage before running back into the house, avoiding a branch that had fallen and was lying on the ground.

"Are you okay, honey?" My mom reached out to take my raincoat and hanged it up in the mudroom.

"I'm good, Mom. It sounded worse than it was," I reassured her. "I'll go flip the switch. Which rooms do you want to have power for now?"

"Kitchen. Family room. And bedrooms," she said. "That should be all we'll need."

"You got it," I said, extending my arm for her to hand me the flashlight. "Call down when the power turns on."

The basement steps creaked, and I made another note to get those checked out too. I didn't want to think about what could happen if one of us, more so my mom, tripped on one of the loose boards and tumbled down. I opened the subpanel and flicked the transfer switch, then slowly turned on the kitchen, family room, and bedrooms. I had to do it one by one so I didn't trip the system. The last thing we needed was for me to set the house on fire.

"We're good, Caleb. Thank you," my mom yelled down the stairs, while the beeping from all the appliances turning back on rang out. "Dinner will be just a few more minutes."

I set the table and my mom threw together a quick salad while the pizza baked. No exaggeration, but the last time I sat at this table with my mom, eating this exact meal, was the week before Leah left for college.

It was the same night I purchased the engagement ring I would never give to her.

"Dinner is served." My mom smiled as she placed the pizza and salad on the table. "Dig in."

I fixed myself a plate and carefully placed my napkin on my lap. That was always a crowd-pleaser when I was out eating. Growing up with a single mom who insisted on proper table manners was both a blessing and a curse. More so a blessing. I learned how to be a man from the stories she told me about my father and the small number of memories I could piece together. He was a man's man. A good friend, a great husband, an amazing father. My best friend.

"What's got you thinking so hard, honey?" my mom asked between bites.

I loved that she knew me so well, but her conversation made it hard to be alone with my thoughts. I couldn't lie to her; she'd just pick up on it and then be pissed I lied. But I didn't want to tell her I was thinking about Dad, and I sure as shit didn't want her knowing I was thinking about Leah. But she was going to guess it either way, so I might as well come clean.

I decided to tell her the truth but omit some rather large components. "The last time we ate this meal together at this table—"

"Leah was with us," she finished. "I thought about that as I was preparing the salad. I'm sorry if this is difficult for you, Caleb."

"No, Mom, it's fine. It was forever ago. It's just strange, that's all."

"Caleb, honey. You don't have to pretend to be strong in front of me. I'm your mother. I know you better than anyone, and you, my boy, are hurting," she said. "There aren't many men like you, Caleb. Embrace it. You are your father's son, and I couldn't be more honored to be a part of both of your lives."

Her words always knew how to leave a mark, and never in a way that was offensive. She was blunt and honest, but so unbelievably caring. She was the toughest woman with the softest heart. It was refreshing to see her kick ass and take names, whether anyone was around to witness it or not. Leah was so much like her, and it made me realize why the two of them got on so well.

"Mom?"

"Yes?"

"How do I get her back?" The question flew out of my mouth, surprising me.

"Oh, honey," she replied, stretching her arm across the table to hold my hand. "You can't get anyone back if they think you're still engaged."

Way to lay it on thick, Mom.

I rubbed my forehead and temples and looked back at her. "I tried to tell her today, but you interrupted our conversation."

"Oh no, Caleb. Don't you try to pin this on me," she said, looking me dead in the eyes. "You are a grown man, and you could have called her and told her sooner. Maybe instead of disappearing—again."

"You really know how to kick a guy when he's down," I teased. "My ego is bruised."

"If you want anything to change, you need to tell her. Find the courage and actually talk to her. If she still loves you, you'll know."

"That is far easier said than done," I countered. "And she is one stubborn girl, if you don't remember."

"The two of you have always been honest with each other. Best friends for as long as I can remember. Just let her know. And if she doesn't feel the same way about you, you'll be able to move on with your life instead of sulking in your mother's kitchen," she teased me and went back to eating her salad.

I looked down at my plate and then back up to my mother. I hoped she was right. I didn't think I could be in Grace Valley with Leah if we weren't together. It was one thing to live my life without her in it when we were thousands of miles apart. But being in the same town just minutes apart? That would be torture.

5

LEAH

It was so great to head into my first full official day at the office. The warm air was nice and definitely made the walk a bit more enjoyable. I brushed my hair away from my neck and smiled as I passed all the familiar sights between my house and the center of town. I'd never get over the small-town views.

I noticed the sidewalk needed repairing and sent myself a quick text to call town hall and let them know once I got to my office. I was just rounding the corner when I heard a familiar voice calling out my name.

"Hey, Leah!"

"Hi, Becky," I called back. "Beautiful morning!"

"Beautiful indeed," she responded, quickly making her way across the street to meet up with me. "How are you today?"

"I'm great! Thankful the storm was a small one and we didn't lose power for too long. How's the farm? Any damage?" Our steps were now perfectly in sync.

"Luckily, no. I was afraid we might lose some trees with all that wind, but we definitely lucked out," she said. "So I wanted to know how the plans were coming for Dooley's trip. I know it's still a ways away, but I thought I'd ask."

I smiled. She was one of the kindest people I knew, but she couldn't keep a secret to save her life. I don't know how she hadn't spilled the beans on Dooley's surprise yet. We had been planning it for almost three weeks. Dooley was turning fifty this year, and with a milestone like that, Becky wanted to make sure he knew just how loved he was.

"It's great. I'm just finishing up the last touches, but I need you to come in and fill out some paperwork. You won't be able to leave the ship when it docks until you have all this squared away."

"Sounds great," she said as we stopped in front of The Kratz Outta the Bag. "I'll be over around eleven a.m. if that works for you?"

"That's perfect," I agreed. "I'm heading in here for a latte. Would you like one?"

"I'm all set, sweets. I've got a busy morning ahead of me. Jackie isn't in until this afternoon and wedding season is upon us," she told me. "I'll see you in a few hours."

"Sounds good." I waved goodbye, heading into the bakery to grab my coffee.

"Hi, Mrs. Kratz. The usual, please," I greeted when I made it to the front counter.

She gave me a wide smile and said, "You got it."

The smell of the bakery always brought me back to my childhood, and I couldn't picture it ever not being in Grace Valley. I hoped Mr. and Mrs. Kratz's grandchildren would take over ownership one day. Their granddaughter, Millie, was already working here every day after school and during the summers. She was an amazing baker, and it made me happy to see her enjoying being part of the family business.

"Here you go, love," Mrs. Kratz said as she stretched her arm over the counter to hand me my latte. "French vanilla with almond milk and two sugars."

Full of Grace

"You're the best." I smiled and handed her a five-dollar bill. "Keep the change."

"Thank you. Have a nice day at work, now," she replied and snuck back into the kitchen.

I wondered if I would have had the same feelings toward this town if I had gone to community college in Connecticut instead of ending up in New York City. I loved it here, and I couldn't imagine living life anywhere else now, but I had been so desperate to leave before.

I inhaled the scent of the latte and unlocked my office door. Having the bakery only two doors down was going to be the death of me. That, or the fact I had a Nespresso machine at the office and my dad's grocery store connected by only a hallway. *Caffeine addiction is real, ladies and gentlemen.*

I took a big sip, placed my things under my desk, and booted up my desktop. Thank goodness we live in an era of technology, where everything syncs automatically and I don't have to worry about backing things up twice.

The phone rang off the hook and the morning flew by. Before I knew it, three hours had passed. Becky would be there any moment, so I decided to make us both a coffee to be ready for when she arrived. I knew she would need one after her busy morning. And let's face it, I was always ready for another cup.

The chime dinged on the door. "Be with you in just a second," I called over my shoulder, stirring the sugar in my cup.

"No problem," a deep, husky voice replied. "Take your time."

I almost dropped the cup on the floor. I didn't recognize the voice, and the gravelly tone caught me by surprise. Like a character from a mid-afternoon soap opera a nineties housewife would watch while she ironed her husband's work shirts. I turned around and my breath caught in my throat.

"Oh, hello, hi," I said, stumbling over my words as my cheeks turned several shades of pink. "I was waiting for someone. I thought you were her when you came in."

"Sorry to disappoint," he said, his eyes burning right through me. *Who was this man?!*

"No, I'm sorry. I didn't mean it like that. I was just making a coffee. Would you like one?" *How are people able to keep their composure around you? Oh my gosh! Am I stress sweating?!*

"I'm all set, thanks," he said with a smirk. "I actually wanted to see if I could speak with Leah Abernathy regarding a few properties I own in the Poconos."

A small bead of sweat dripped from the top of my hairline down the side of my face. *Shit, I am.* I tried to wipe it away nonchalantly, but I had a feeling I looked more like a drowned rat than the cute twenty-something who had waltzed into work this morning. I hoped he didn't notice, but when I saw the left side of his mouth raise ever so slightly into a tiny smile, I knew he had. I swallowed deeply as I stood frozen in front of him. He looked like a surfer in a three-piece suit with his shaggy, dirty-blond hair and piercing blue eyes.

I swear, this man is Hallmark meets Lifetime, and I AM HERE FOR IT! No, I'm really not, though. I don't even know my name right now. And I'm staring at him while he smiles at me, and I'm not saying anything. Speak, Leah. Jesus, say something!

"I'm Leah!" I blurted out like I was back in high school and the hot substitute was taking attendance before turning on some stupid film. *Oh. My. God.* I closed my eyes and took a deep breath before opening them again.

"I'm so sorry," I said. "Hello, I'm Leah Abernathy. How can I help you?"

"Well, now that we've established you're who I came to see, I can let you know that you come highly recommended by John Cole. He's an associate of mine, and we were discussing the work you did for him on his Vermont ski resort, and I hoped you might provide some assistance on one, or a few, of my properties."

"Oh," I said and instantly snapped back into professional mode. "I very much enjoyed working with John and creating a dream destination for him. I can help you out. Would you be able to answer a few questions so I can better assist you?"

"Absolutely," he said, then slowly licked the corner of his mouth. *What kind of business deal does this guy think we're making here?*

My nerves were getting to me, but I needed to remain professional. I quickly made my way to my desk and opened the side drawer to pull out the new client paperwork folder. I was about to hand it to him when the door chimed again. This time, it actually was Becky.

"Hey, Beck," I said quickly. "I'll be with you in just a minute. Let me just finish up here with Mr . . ."

"Dalton. Luke Dalton," that husky voice spoke again, and even Becky's eyes grew wide as she blushed.

"Thank you. Let me finish up with Mr. Dalton and I'll be right over," I told her.

She looked back at me and her eyes widened. "Who is that?" she mouthed.

I returned her question with an I-have-no-idea look, slightly shrugged shoulders, and a presumably hideous facial expression. A slight and almost inaudible laugh crept out of Mr. Dalton's mouth, and I knew he had witnessed the entire interaction. Mortified was becoming my newest everyday feeling.

"I have a conference call I can't be late to, so how about I leave you my card and you can get back to me this afternoon?" he told me. "I'll be available any time after four."

"That sounds great, Mr. Dalton. Would you like to take this paperwork with you? Or I can send a copy of the forms to your email."

"Email is fine. I'm only up this way for a few days, so I'd rather not hang on to too many things."

"Oh, where are you from?" asked Becky from the table in the corner. I shot her a why-are-you-so-damn-nosy look.

"I own a few resorts in the Poconos, where I also reside. I'm thinking about purchasing some land to build a second house, though. Do you know any good towns in the area?" He looked at her with those same flirtatious eyes, but this time, I didn't see any heat behind them.

"Southeastern Connecticut is beautiful, and there are a lot of great spots by the water. Or you could go up a bit more northwest, past Litchfield. There's a lot of land and it's gorgeous," she told him.

I quickly interrupted this little getting-to-know-know-you session. "Okay, Mr. Dalton, I'll get these sent over to you right away, and we can reconnect this afternoon to talk more in depth."

"Thank you, Ms. Abernathy. And please, call me Luke. I don't like to be overly formal these days," he said and winked at me.

My jaw dropped, and I quickly shut it before anything unnecessary flew out of my mouth. He reached out his hand to shake mine, and I felt an electric shock from head to toe. Becky's eyes widened and I knew she saw it, too.

"I look forward to hearing from you," he said and walked toward the door. "Pleasure meeting you both."

The door chimed again and quietly closed behind him. *Did that really just happen?*

"Oh my goodness, Leah. Can I take him on Dooley's trip instead?" Becky asked and laughed at her own joke.

"Seriously, Becky? You're a married woman," I teased. "I didn't think men like that existed in real life."

"He was into you, Leah girl. I'm telling you, it's not just your business expertise he wants from you."

"Oh stop," I said as the heat returned to my cheeks. "Here, I made you a coffee."

"Don't you dare try to change the subject," she said, her eyes glittering with mischief. "You need to tell me everything that transpired before I got here."

"Nothing *transpired*, Becky," I said, rolling my eyes. "He was only here for a minute, max, before you got here."

"Mm-hmm. Okay then. What do you need me to sign?"

I reached across the table and handed her a folder full of paperwork. I pointed to the yellow sticky arrows indicating each section that needed her signature and had her sign and initial. I laughed, watching her flick the end of the pen with each stroke of her last name. She laughed with me.

"What? We will never go on another trip like this again. I can pretend to be fancy with my little autographs here."

"You're a mess. Do you want to grab lunch with me at the diner after you're done with the forms? I have a busy afternoon, and I didn't bring lunch with me today."

"That sounds good, sweetheart. This old body can't run solely on coffee like some people," she said, winking at me before returning to her paperwork. "All this signing better be worth it."

"You know, my mom used to say the same thing anytime she had to sign more than one thing. How did you guys ever make it through college if you can't even sign one document without complaining?"

I loved to joke around with Becky, even more so now that my mom was gone. She was younger than my parents but still such a mature and strong maternal force for me growing up. I was thankful to have her here with me now and happy that we'd forged an adult friendship.

"Well, I hate to burst your bubble, but I never made it to college. I worked on my parents' farm as a kid and then grew a strong interest in gardening. One thing led to another, and here I am," she told me, standing tall as she spoke, proud of her accomplishments.

"How come I never knew that?" I asked her.

"I'm not sure anyone really knows that aside from Dooley. It's not something I ever deemed important enough to discuss. I am a firm believer in following your heart and mind. I'm not discrediting a college education by any means. I just think that some people's destinies are in the opposite direction of a college campus. Dooley never went either, but I'm guessing you knew that already."

"I guess I just always assumed," I said. "Is this why you always support Jackie's art and let her choose her own path in life?"

"Precisely," she said, handing me back the folder. "Now, let's go get some lunch before you wither away to nothing."

6
LEAH

What started out as a beautiful and cool morning turned into a humid afternoon, and I was definitely not dressed properly to be walking around. I peeled my sweater off, thankful I had thrown on a nice blouse instead of the dingy old T-shirt I had originally planned on wearing. I carefully folded my sweater and laid it across my arm, feeling tired and sluggish and hoping for a breeze. I was starving, and the heat wasn't helping.

When we made it to the diner, I went to push the door open, but it opened before I could manage. I took a step forward, welcoming the rush of cool air.

"Ladies," a familiar voice said.

Caleb. *Why does he keep showing up everywhere? I get we live in the same small town and this* is *his mom's restaurant, but, come on!*

"Good afternoon, Caleb," Becky replied, smiling at him.

"Uh, hi," was all I could muster, and I rushed past him before he could say anything back to me.

"Everything okay?" Becky asked after Caleb exited the diner.

"Yes, I'm just going to run to the ladies' room before we eat," I replied. "I'll meet you at the table in a few."

"Okay, dear. I'll grab some menus, then. Take your time," she said.

I smiled as she headed to the table in the corner. We'd labeled it "our table" many years ago, and it was nice to see that hadn't changed. It was a good thing it held eight people because our family consisted of me and my dad, the Pattersons, and the Butlers, and it was rare to see less than five people here at a time.

I turned and continued on to the bathroom, heading straight to the mirror to examine my ridiculousness head on.

"Excuse me, miss," an older woman said gently as she walked around me to the other sink.

"Oh, I'm sorry," I said and smiled politely back at her.

I quickly finished up at the sink, threw my purse over my shoulder, and went to find Becky at our table. I was definitely hangry at that point, and I needed that feeling to go away fast. Tammy was sitting across from Becky when I reached the table, and she quickly stood up and hugged me.

"I'm so glad you two came for lunch today," she told us. "Leah, your usual?"

"I think I'm going to change it up a bit today, Tammy," I told her. "What's your soup of the day?"

"New England Clam Chowder," she replied.

"Hmm. I think I'll go with a cup of the chowder and the crab cake sandwich with extra sauce on the side, please."

"You got it, sweetie," she said, quickly jotting down my order. "And for you, Beck?"

"I'll just have a large Cobb salad—hold the gorgonzola, ranch on the side," she said. "Oh, and a side of curly fries."

"You two enjoy your break, and I'll be right back with your order," Tammy told us.

She headed toward the kitchen and handed Dante our order through the window before disappearing behind the doors. I used to think I would be working or cooking in this diner one day. I loved the hustle and bustle of the food world, but I didn't think I could be on my feet for that long each day. I also really enjoyed cooking at home, and I was always afraid my hobby wouldn't be as fun if I turned it into a career.

"So," Becky said and looked at me so intently I thought I might fall off my chair. "Back to Luke. When's the wedding? Your kids would be so beautiful."

"Becky!" I exclaimed. "You don't stop. I already told you, he came in for information about his properties. He knows one of my former clients and wants me to work on his resorts."

"Sure, but what else does he want to work on?"

My eyes widened and I swatted at her across the table. "What would my mother think hearing you talk to her baby girl this way?"

"She would be the one asking these questions," Becky countered.

I laughed. "You are absolutely right."

My mom was certainly one of a kind. Kind being the operative word. She would do anything for anyone and she always did. I could remember being a child and thinking how wonderful it would be to grow up and be just like her—loved by everyone and loving everyone. Wanting to see everyone succeed and selflessly helping each and every person on their own paths. My father used to say that was the one quality he both loved and disliked about her. Of course, it was something that made him fall in love with her, but he was so afraid she would burn out one day from doing too much. I didn't think she ever would. God put her on this earth to do exactly what she did—change the lives of everyone she met. I still aspired to be like that.

"But in all seriousness," I told her. "I'm not interested in getting involved with him or anyone right now."

"I know, Leah. I'm just teasing you."

We talked back and forth for a bit and before we knew it, Tammy was setting my food in front of me.

"Soup and sandwich for you," she said. "And your salad and fries, Becky."

"Thank you, Tammy," I said and took a small bite of my sandwich. "Oh, wow, this is delicious."

"I'll let Dante know. He's been working on a new remoulade."

"Sit with us, Tam," Becky said, sliding over to the chair next to her. "If you've got the time, that is."

"I'd love to," she said. "Let me go get myself some lunch, and I'll be right back."

Before we had a chance to blink, Tammy was coming back out of the kitchen with her food—soup and salad, a fantastic lunch choice.

"It was already made," she said with a laugh. "So, what's on the agenda for you two today?"

"I have to work late at the shop," Becky said. "I have so many boutonnières, corsages, and centerpieces to make for the prom."

"I just have a few potential clients I need to reach out to who will hopefully sign contracts this week," I said.

"Look at you," Tammy said. "Living out your dreams. I am so proud of you, Leah. And your mom would be so thrilled to know you're doing exactly what you were destined for."

"Thank you, Tammy. It's hard without her here, but I'm happy to be working in the same building she spent most of her time. It helps me feel closer to her."

"What about you, Tammy? Are you catering the prom this year or are they branching out?" Becky asked.

"I'll be catering. Dante is going to help me cook, and Caleb will help set up and serve. I'm so grateful for the extra set of hands this year," Tammy told us. "Last year was torture with all the food mishaps."

"Food mishaps?" I asked.

Full of Grace

"I'm surprised your dad didn't tell you," Tammy said. "There was a foreign exchange student who was staying with the O'Connors during her senior year. She had a severe corn allergy that the school was never made aware of. Well, I used corn oil in one of the dishes, and she was rushed to the hospital where, thankfully, they could help her. And after that, one of the underclassmen who was there with her date accidentally danced a little too hard, lost her balance, and landed smack-dab in the middle of the buffet. Poor Dante had to rush to the Kratz's to see if they had any desserts we could buy off them since the cupcakes, brownies, and cookies were smeared across the girl's dress."

"I'm so sorry," I said between laughs. "I know I shouldn't laugh, but this is the stuff that only happens in movies. That poor girl. I would have been mortified."

"She was a trouper—wiped off her dress and went right back onto that dance floor," Becky said. "I chaperoned so I witnessed the entire debacle, and it was just as funny as you can imagine."

Tammy's cell phone rang, interrupting us but also giving me time to eat some of my lunch.

"Hi, honey. Yes, I'll be home around five tonight," Tammy said and then paused. "I don't think we have any shrimp in the freezer. Spinach is in the fridge. Mm-hmm. Yes. Okay, that sounds wonderful, Caleb. I'll see you tonight, then. Love you."

"Tammy?" I asked when she hung up the phone. I was already regretting what hadn't even left my mouth. "What's Caleb doing back in Grace Valley? Doesn't he have a lot to do in Tennessee? And why has no one in this town mentioned anything? Everyone here is in everyone's business twenty-four seven."

The table grew quiet, and if I had blinked, I would have missed the quick glance Tammy and Becky shot each other. Tammy cleared her throat and wiped her mouth with a paper napkin.

"Oh, um, I think that's something you should ask him, dear," was all she replied before stabbing her fork into her salad.

I knew better than to pry, but something seemed off. I might not have asked about Caleb since I left for college, but it was really weird that he was up in Connecticut and not in Tennessee with his fiancée.

"Thank you for letting me crash your lunch, but I must get back into the kitchen and make sure we're all set for the dinner rush since I won't be here tonight," Tammy told us before rushing away from the table and our conversation.

Becky and I finished our lunch rather quickly and had some time to spare before we needed to submerge ourselves into our work yet again.

"I really hope the rain holds off tonight. My poor flowers are going to drown." Becky told me. "Oh! I forgot to tell you. Dooley's decided to reopen the horse training school. All of the horses have been transferred from the small barn to the big boarding barn, and the small barn will be turned into the office."

"That sounds incredible. I'm so happy for you both," I said. "You might luck out. I think it's only supposed to rain this weekend, but who knows anymore. We keep getting all these micro storms, and I have a feeling that one of them is going to cause some serious damage."

"Hush your mouth, girl. Don't talk like that," Becky said in a teasing yet maternal tone. "He's been so stressed out lately, and I think this school is exactly the thing he needs to bring him back to his happy and goofy self."

"Please tell him to let me know if he needs any help setting up the office. I imagine it's going to take a lot of work, given the current residents' odor," I teased.

"You are your mother's daughter. We would love some help this weekend. Jackie will be around as well, so we can probably get everything out of there so he can start reframing next week."

"This is so exciting. I don't know if he ever told you, but Dooley taught me how to ride when I was a little girl. I used to go to the farm every day after school for lessons," I told her. "Gosh, I haven't been on a horse in years. Maybe I'll see about taking one for a ride one of these days. I would love to get back into it."

"Absolutely! We can take a ride around the meadow if you want."

"I would love that."

"It's a date," Becky replied. "I have to head back to the shop, and you have to go call Mr. Sexy Pants."

"Becky, you are too much," I said, reaching for my wallet. "I've got lunch today. Maybe you should go home and shower to cool off before you start making those flower arrangements. Wouldn't want you to get too hot and bothered and prick yourself."

Becky winked and I opened my wallet to leave a tip on the table. I handed the young girl at the register my bill and some cash and headed back to my office.

7

CALEB

Leah. Everywhere I turned, there she was. They hadn't noticed me at first, and I'd watched as Leah folded her sweater and draped it across the crook of her arm. She never knew how to dress for the weather, and it was comforting to see that hadn't changed.

She'd looked beautiful in her simple blouse and jeans. Her hair had bounced across her back with every step she took, and it reminded me of walking behind her when we were younger. I'd missed her while we were apart, but I moved on. Now that she was back in my life—sort of—I was back to the same thoughts as a nervous middle school boy. I couldn't get her out of my head.

"Ladies," I'd said, holding the door for Becky and Leah.

I turned back toward the diner just as the door had closed behind her. From the looks of it, she hadn't turned back to look at me. I couldn't blame her. I hadn't exactly been truthful with her, and she had apparently moved on. Again.

"Hello, Mrs. Kratz," I said as I passed by the bakery.

"Hello, Caleb," she replied, sweeping the sidewalk in front of her door. "Beautiful day today!"

"Yes, it is," I said and smiled at her. "Enjoy it, Mrs. Kratz."

Full of Grace

She nodded and winked before turning back to her sweeping. It was moments like these that helped me remember why I came back. Aside from my mom, of course.

I'd always known it wouldn't work out with Brittany, even if I didn't want to admit it to myself at the time. But looking back, I could see the red flags were there. Things were great in the beginning, but they quickly started to deteriorate, and she was no longer the woman I was supposed to be with. She knew how to manipulate better than anyone I had known, and I'd fallen victim to her trap numerous times. But it honestly wasn't until I came back to Grace Valley for Lucia's funeral that I knew it was over between us.

Brittany had no place in a small town. She was the worst kind of woman—a wolf in sheep's clothing. There was no blending in, no one to impress. The people of Grace Valley cared about kindness and how to make the world a better place. They cared about waking up every day and helping their neighbor. Brittany wasn't that person and never would be. All she ever seemed to care about was her image, as much of a lie as it actually was. But the worst of it all, the hardest thing for me to come to terms with, was that she'd never be Leah.

Now it was time to man up. Enough was enough. I needed to tell her, at least for my own damn sanity.

If I had known she wasn't with that city boy at Christmas, I would have said something to her before she left, but I was stubborn and stupid and let my pride get in the way. The same way I had when she left for college. We could have made it work. I could have easily applied to any school in the city instead of pushing her away. Maybe we would have been married by now. Had a kid or two. Who knows? But it had to be better than this—a grown man making his mommy keep his secrets for him while he hid his feelings.

I knew what I had to do. I was going to win her back, and then

I could stop sulking over this crap. I crossed the street and walked through the parking lot to the school for my meeting with Bill Palmer. It was crazy that he offered me the position of school principal; even crazier that I accepted.

I pressed the buzzer on the door and waited to be let in. It made me sad that even in a quaint little town like this, the school needed to be locked at all times. But it was far better to be safe than sorry.

"Hi there, Caleb," Bill's secretary, Joan, said. "Come on in. He'll be with you in just a few minutes."

The familiar sights made me feel right at home, and for the first time, I became truly excited about my future. I had big shoes to fill, but I was ready to fill them. I followed her across the school's foyer and to the office, pausing outside of the guidance office.

I'd spent so many hours in that office with my guidance counselor, Mr. B. He was the kind of person most aspired to be—smart, kind, humorous. But above all, he genuinely loved his job and the students he worked with. Right before I graduated, we had our senior assembly, and he made a speech to the entire school. At the very end of his speech, he tossed oranges to the students who impacted his life the most. If I could have stopped a fruit from rotting, I would still have it.

One winter during a really bad snowstorm, and highly against my mother's wishes, I'd gone out to a neighboring town and slid down a road and got stuck in a snowbank. I pulled over and put my hazards on and waited, prayed, for someone else to be crazy enough to be out at the time. I had no cell service and couldn't call for help, so I just sat and waited. I wasn't waiting too long when I saw headlights behind me, and a pickup truck slowed down and opened their passenger side window. Wouldn't you know it was Mr. B there to save the day again. He had since passed, and I wasn't able to say my goodbyes to him, but I hope he would have been proud of the man I'd become.

I took a seat and waited for Bill.

"Caleb. Come on in," Bill said, extending his right hand to shake mine and nodding toward his office door. "Glad you could make it in today. I'm sorry for the short notice, but we have so much to do in preparation for my inauguration as the new mayor, and I didn't want to let this slide under the radar."

"Completely understood. Congratulations again. I know this is a big honor, and I'm happy to be a part of this new chapter of your life," I said. "How is Marina? I haven't seen her in a few days."

"She's doing well. Very busy with, well, everything in this town," he said with a laugh. "She just can't help herself. She's the textbook definition of a doer, and I couldn't be happier to be her husband."

"You were always such a sap, Bill," I teased.

"Yeah, well, we all should be," he said. "You'll see one day."

"I think I messed that one up," I said, rubbing my neck. "But I appreciate the kind words."

I had known Bill my entire life. His eldest daughter, Melanie, used to babysit me when my parents would go out for date nights with the Pattersons and the Butlers. Every time he would drop her off to watch me, he would bring over a batch of Marina's famous brownies and sit and talk with me until my parents left. If I was still awake when he came to pick up Melanie, he would sit and talk with me then, too. After my dad passed away, Bill and Marina would come over with their kids and have dinner with us so my Mom wasn't lonely. It was the smallest act of kindness, but that's who they were. I was proud to be standing in front of him as a grown man and still having these talks.

"Caleb, we aren't here for this type of chat, but if I may?" he started. "When you've found something, anything, that makes you want to be a better person, you follow through on it. Trust me when I tell you, nothing is easy. Nothing. But if it's important to you, you'll find a way to make it happen. And forgive me, but if I know you, and I think I do, this is about Leah, am I right?"

"Yes, sir," I said and looked down at my hands.

"Tell her the truth." He raised his eyebrows and nodded toward the desk, covered with papers. "Now, let's get this meeting started so we can enjoy the rest of our day."

He was right. And I valued his input greatly, just as I had my entire life. *I'll talk to her in the morning. I'll take her a coffee, and I can clear the air before she opens for the day.*

We spent most of the afternoon discussing the boring parts of what was to come from this new position. A lot of paperwork, relatively unruly kids, parents who just could not understand why their perfect children weren't succeeding, etc. But we also spoke about what an amazing opportunity it was for me to have the opportunity to enrich these students' lives. Being an educator had always been an extremely important thing to me. I knew I wanted to make a difference in people's lives, but I hadn't truly understood why or how I would do it. Being able to witness the growth of a child who was exceeding all expectations was thrilling. And now I'd get to watch an entire school grow.

"Now that we've gotten all that out of the way, what do you say we go grab a beer?" Bill suggested. "Marina has book club tonight so she won't be around, and I'd really like to try to catch the end of the ball game."

"I'm down," I agreed. "Pub?"

"I'll drive," he said.

The Pub was a tiny, hole-in-the-wall sports bar just over the line in Broad Brook, the next town over. It'd been owned by the same family since before I was born, but it had recently undergone a full renovation. Even though it was small, it lacked nothing but space. Flat-screen televisions, framed sports jerseys, and autographed pictures of every athlete who had visited lined the walls. Surprisingly, there were a lot who had traveled through over the years. Upstate Connecticut was New England country, and it was home to some of the wealthiest people who preferred to stay out of the spotlight.

"A pitcher of Coors Light," Bill said to the bartender as he slid a twenty-dollar bill across the bar. Looking directly at me, he said, "Don't you dare laugh at my beer of choice, boy."

I wasn't much of a beer drinker, so it didn't matter to me which one he chose. Also, I didn't know the difference anyway. I was a whiskey guy. Apparently, just like my father—Jameson neat. That was my go-to if the occasion arose.

The bartender placed the pitcher and two frosty beer mugs in front of us. "Can I get you anything to eat?"

"I'll have a cheeseburger, medium rare, Swiss cheese, mushrooms and onions, and a side of curly fries," I said.

"Chicken patty melt, extra mayo on the side, with regular fries," Bill said. "Thank you."

"Gimme about ten minutes and it'll be out for you," the bartender told us.

"Extra mayo?" I laughed. "That'll kill ya."

"Marina isn't here to yell at me, so I may as well eat what I want tonight," he said.

Our food came out quickly and we dove right in. I hadn't had a burger like this in a long time, and it was another check in the happy-to-be-home box. Brittany was a control freak who only allowed me to eat organic food that I had to prepare. She was always too worried about getting her nails dirty to help with any of the cooking. The day after we broke up, I think I ate an entire pig's worth of bacon.

I took another large bite of the burger, savoring every bit of it and not caring about the juices that were now dripping down my hands.

"Caleb," Bill said, interrupting my love affair with the world's best burger. "I know you're going to have a lot going on come September, but I thought I'd ask you this anyway. Joe is retiring this year, so we have an opening for head basketball coach. Normally, we would prefer someone other than the principal to be the basketball coach, but there is only one Caleb Patterson. We would be honored to have you head up our team. What do you say? Would you be interested at all in coaching? You can keep the assistants that Joe has now, or you can hire your own staff, completely up to you."

"I don't know, Bill. That's a lot of responsibility, and I want to make sure I'm not putting too much pressure on myself," I told him. "Of course, I would love to be a part of it, but I'd like to take some time to think about it. When are you looking to have that position filled?"

"As you know, the season won't start until December, but we'll need to have tryouts and practices, so I'd like an answer by the end of summer," he said.

"Okay, I can do that. Thanks a lot for thinking of me."

"Are you kidding? You hold all the boys' basketball records in the school. I'm surprised you didn't go pro," he said, looking at me with incredulous eyes. "These kids will lose their minds if they're coached by you."

"I wouldn't go that far, but I appreciate the kind words," I said.

"You were always so humble, even as a child. I'm happy to see that you're still the same Caleb we all know and love."

8

CALEB

ALL RIGHT, MAN. YOU'VE GOT THIS. IT'S JUST A CONVERSATION. You're not asking her to marry you.

Leah's office opened at eight a.m., and if I still knew her to be the same girl she'd always been, she would be opening those doors at seven-thirty. I had plenty of time to back out of this and let things play themselves out, but I didn't want to do that this time. I paced back and forth across my bedroom floor, waiting for a sign. I couldn't even tell you what for; I just knew I was panicking.

"Caleb?" I heard my mom call out. "Did you want a ride into town? I have some errands to run this afternoon, so I'm going to need the car today."

"I'm all set, Mom, thanks," I yelled back. "I'm hoping mine will be out of the shop this afternoon. Have a good day."

"You too," she said. "Bye, honey."

I heard the familiar smack as she kissed her hand three times and blew them up the stairs to me. I didn't need to see her do it to know it was happening. She'd been doing that my entire life, and I secretly hoped she'd never stop. I was never the type of guy to be embarrassed about sharing my feelings. From what I remembered of my dad, and what others had pieced together for me, he was the same way, and I cherished every single similarity between the two of us.

My mom had always been a badass—raising me on her own, choosing my happiness over remarrying. Sure, she'd dated over the years, but she was so happy just being with me and her friends that she never wanted anything too serious. I admired that about her. I asked her once if she would ever get remarried, and she told me she didn't feel the need to. She was still married to the love of her life, even if he was no longer with us. I could always empathize with that, but now more than ever. I knew deep down the love she shared with my dad was the same kind of love I shared with Leah.

That's why I knew I couldn't chicken out.

I put on my shoes and quickly raced down the stairs. I grabbed my house keys and phone off the kitchen island and took a final look at myself in the hall mirror. I hoped she wouldn't see the fear and borderline desperation smeared across my face. I locked the door behind me, looked up at the sky, and took a deep breath.

Feet, don't fail me now.

After living in Tennessee for so long, where it was already hot in the early morning, the crisp and cool air was a nice reprieve from feeling like I needed a shower the second I walked out of my house.

The neighbors' kids were already outside on their front lawn, setting up their T-ball game before school. I envied their ability to wake up early and play. When I was their age, I slept until the last possible second, when my mom would physically drag my ass out of bed. I loved my sleep; still do. But now, at least, I'm able to manage it better.

"Hi, Caleb!" one of the little boys called out to me as I passed their driveway. "You wanna play with us?"

"Aw, Tucker. I wish I could, little guy," I replied. "I've got to get into town early today."

"Okay," he said, his innocent eyes slowly moving from mine to the pavement beneath us.

Who was I to break a kid's heart? "Toss it over here. I'll pitch one to you before I go, and then what do you say we play catch this afternoon after school?"

"Really?" he squealed, throwing the ball over to me.

"Sure, kid," I said, tossing the ball back. "Just run along and make sure your mom is okay with it. Have a good day at school, boys."

Tucker and his older brother, Tommy, were six and eight years old. I remember their parents moving in right before Leah and I broke up. I had so many plans for the two of us, and watching this young couple start their lives in Grace Valley, a little baby in tow, made it seem all the more attainable. Until that fateful night that quite literally changed the entire course of my life.

I was determined to make it work this time. The way I felt for her now was far stronger than what I felt in high school, and although it had been many years since we were together, there was no denying she felt it too. I took a quick glance at my watch—seven fifteen a.m. I still had time, but I knew I should hustle. Luckily, there shouldn't be a line at the bakery, and I could get in and out quickly. Mrs. Kratz made Leah's favorite coffee, and if I knew Leah, she was craving caffeine right about now.

"Good morning, Caleb," Mrs. Kratz said, smiling at me from across the counter. "What can I get for you this morning?"

"Morning, Mrs. Kratz. Could I please have two of the usual?"

"Of course, dear," she said, turning around to the coffee machine to make the drinks.

I loved that she knew how I took my coffee, and I loved that it was the same way Leah took hers.

After a few minutes, she walked around the counter and handed me the coffees. "You have a wonderful day."

"You too, Mrs. Kratz."

I smiled and walked out the door. I turned to my left to head to the agency when I noticed the lights were still off. I decided to wait across the street in the gazebo on the green. It might weird her out if I was standing in front of her door, waiting. I sipped my coffee and went over the speech I'd written in my mind. Every time I went over the words, I started with a different version of the same sentence, but I had a feeling that as soon I saw her, I was going to jumble my words and look like a loser.

It was surprisingly quiet that morning. Although it was a small town, there were usually more people running about. I guess fate was on my side—the fewer people out, the less likely a fabricated story would be created on whatever they thought they saw. And that was something I was banking on.

I should have bet money on it, because at seven thirty on the dot, I saw her round the corner to her shop. I stood up quickly and brushed down my shirt, smoothing whatever wrinkles may have started to form while I was waiting. After picking up the coffees, I took a deep breath and started to walk across the street.

You've got this. Relax. Breathe. Here goes nothing.

My heart raced, and I could feel the sweat slowly trickling down the side of my face.

"Caleb?" she said when I reached the sidewalk. "What are you doing here?"

She opened the door and motioned for me to follow her. When she turned around, she had that familiar sparkle in her eyes, clouded over with confusion, and I knew this was going to be harder than I thought. I swallowed and continued to follow her inside. Our arms brushed against each other, causing every hair on my body to stand on end.

"Do you want to sit?" she asked, pointing to a table and chairs.

"Thanks," I said, handing her one of the cups. "This is for you."

She smiled and sat down across from me, taking a sip of the coffee. I could watch her savor the taste all day.

"This was very unexpected, Caleb. Thank you."

"Welcome," was all I could say as I sat there watching her and feeling like a creep.

"So, what's up?

It's now or never, man.

I cupped my hands around my coffee and paused for a moment before answering her. She knew me better than I knew myself so I needed to make sure I didn't fumble with this one.

"I've been wanting to talk to you for a while now," I started, but froze. "I'm really happy that you followed your dreams and opened this place."

What? Say something else.

"And ... I really miss you," I finally told her.

She stared at me, her jaw dropped, tears slowly filling her eyes. I waited for her to say something but she stood frozen. I cleared my throat and reached an arm across the table to hers.

The undeniable spark was evident for a fraction of a second before she flinched and pulled her hand back the second my fingertips grazed hers. "I'm sorry, I think you should go."

"You want me to leave?" I asked, instantly regretting the conversation.

Her eyes slowly filled with tears, and she stood up and walked to the door. "Yes, please go. I can't do this right now."

"I'm sorry, Leah."

She nodded, her head barely moving. "Thank you for the coffee."

I didn't want to hurt her more, so I did as she requested, stopping when I stepped onto the sidewalk. I wasn't sure what I was expecting to come of our conversation, but it wasn't that. I turned around in time to see her sit at her desk and place her head in her hands. Her body shook, and seeing her cry like that tore me in two. I walked toward the door to go back in and check on her but quickly decided against that and walked to the farm instead, leaving her to her tears and trying to comprehend what just happened.

THE SUN WAS BEATING DOWN by the time I got to the farm, and I was thankful I'd chosen a polo shirt instead of a button-down as I had originally planned. As I walked through the meadow, I thought of everything that had transpired on this land over the years. The happy memories, the sad ones, the devastating ones, the unforgettable ones. This was home, regardless of the turn of events.

"Hey, Caleb," Dooley called out from the open barn door. "What brings you here?"

"Just out for a walk and thought I'd swing by to say hi. Maybe take Darb out for a ride. See how things were going over here. Mom said you were thinking about turning the land back into a riding school."

Besides Leah and Matt, Darb was my best friend growing up and got me through the worst of times after my dad passed away. He was my secret keeper—easy considering he couldn't talk—and was the first to know that I loved Leah as more than a friend. Some could argue that he was my saving grace. I always tried to visit him as often as I could.

"You're damn right!" he said, his comical voice booming. "Things were getting stale, and I wanted to bring back some of the old, ya know? Plus, I want to have something nice to leave

Jackie one day. Of course she's got The Flower Pot, but I really want her to have more land and opportunity if she wants to use it. It's been in our family for almost a hundred years now. May as well keep it that way."

"What can I do to help?" I asked.

"Well, for starters, you can take off those damn loafers and burn them. Why the hell do you wear those things anyway?" he said with a laugh. "Here, put these on."

I laughed right along with him as I pulled on the work boots he'd stashed away in the barn.

"All right, funny guy. Where do you need me?" I asked.

"Well, I'm planning on turning this smaller barn into the office. It's fully wired for electrical, and the stalls can be revamped into smaller spaces. So, I guess maybe just start unloading the stalls and transferring everything to the big barn. If you think there's anything that needs thrown out, just toss it. I trust your judgment."

"Sounds good, man," I said and got to work.

By the time I'd finished clearing out the stalls, it was lunchtime. I didn't want to go to my mom's diner for fear of running into Leah again, so I opted to just go home. I had a lot of paperwork to read for the new school year, and I still needed to think about the coaching position. Being alone with my thoughts might not have been the best choice, but at least I'd be in my own house.

"Dooley, I'm gonna head home for lunch, but I'll swing back here in a bit and help you some more," I said.

"All right," he said. "Try changing your clothes before you come back, though."

9

LEAH

HE MISSED ME? WHAT KIND OF SICK JOKE WAS THAT? ONE YEAR in college, I went on a few dates with this guy and he ended things with me to start dating a former teen-beauty-pageant winner. He ended things abruptly and then made it a point to come to my dorm to tell me how beautiful I was, flirt with me, and then leave after telling me it was still over. All because his new girl and her group of friends thought it would be funny. I felt the same way that day as I did when Caleb told me he missed me.

"Good morning, sunshine," Luke said as he swung open the door and waltzed in with more coffee. I hadn't even heard the chime ding.

"Oh, hello," I said, carefully wiping the tears off my face and hoping he hadn't noticed. "I wasn't expecting you here so early. Our meeting isn't until this afternoon."

"I know," Luke said. "I just thought I'd brighten your morning with a little coffee."

"That is so kind of you."

I placed my hands on my desk and pulled myself up, welcoming his distraction. He handed me the coffee when I reached him, and I immediately took a large sip. I definitely needed caffeine.

Oh, this tastes awful. I smiled and put the cup down, disappointed that, out of spite, I had tossed the one Caleb brought me.

"Since you're already here, would you like to start working on your project?" I asked him.

"I have a breakfast meeting I must attend, but how about we discuss this over dinner?" His eyes grew more seductive with each word he spoke. "The owner of the bed and breakfast I'm staying at says there are a lot of nice restaurants in Litchfield."

"I'm sorry, Luke," I said, taking a step back. "But I only do business in the office."

"Okay, so then leave the business at the office and have dinner with me as a date instead."

Shit . . . I appreciated his efforts but Caleb or not, I was in no position to start something new. I never thought I would be the type to be married to my job, but at that moment, I was fully committed to it. And I was okay with that.

"Listen, Luke. I'm terribly sorry if I've given you the wrong impression, but I'm not dating right now," I explained.

"I see," he said. "Well, how about lunch at the local diner? It's close enough to the office that you could make an exception."

"Luke, I really appreciate your efforts, but that is too much like a date. I really can't."

"All right, listen. I'm going to need to eat again today and so are you. So how about I just bring lunch to you, and we can eat here and go over the numbers you've crunched for me. It's not a date. It's a business lunch, here in your office, where no one can get confused."

"Fine, Mr. Dalton. You've made your point," I said, shaking my head. "A business lunch will be fine."

"Excellent. Do you like sushi? I can grab some on the way."

"I love sushi," I told him. "That sounds wonderful."

"Great. Preference on rolls?"

"Surprise me."

"I need to be heading out," he said, glancing at this watch. "My meeting should be over at about eleven, so by the time I grab the food and get back, I could be here at noon."

"I'll see you then," I said, pausing as our eyes met.

The intensity of his stare burned, and it made me uncomfortable. Caleb's admission made me uncomfortable. What was happening?

I threw myself into my work to avoid thinking about any of the events that had occurred that morning and spent the next few hours working on my proposals for two of Luke's three resorts. They were both family-friendly but were lacking in quite a few areas, so I wanted to make sure they encompassed the true vision of the resort without compromising the fun that led families to vacation there. The third resort was an adults-only resort that catered to newlyweds. I found myself drawn to this one. The idea of getting away with the love of your life sounded more than appealing. And although my idea of love had changed over the course of the years, I still held out hope I would find the kind of love I once had with Caleb. Sure, we were only seventeen when we broke up, but I knew in my heart it was real. Even if it was confusing and messy right now.

I went to my favorite spot in my office and made myself a vanilla latte. There was no such thing as too much caffeine in my book, and considering the first two that were brought to me ended up in the trash, I needed something to get myself through the rest of this workday. As an office warming present, my dad bought me a dandy little machine that made cappuccinos and lattes at the push of a button. I just popped in the little capsule and pressed the top, and, boom, Espresso. There was even a little frother, so all I had to do was pour my milk in and, again, press a button. Let me

Full of Grace

tell you, this little contraption was going to save me thousands in coffee shop drinks.

I sat back down at my desk and got comfortable, sipping my latte and putting the final touches on the proposals for Luke. I had just put the packet together when I heard the chime of my door. It wasn't noon yet, and I wasn't ready for him. I took a deep breath and pushed my hair behind my ears, standing up to greet him. I was surprised to see Becky and Jackie walking through the door and not Luke.

"Hey, love! Want to grab an early lunch?" Becky asked, smiling at me.

"Um, you look weird," Jackie commented when she saw me, walking around her mother and sitting on the corner of my desk.

Her light-blue blouse complimented her navy capri pants and floral wedge heels. *Ah, to be a teenager again.* She reached across my desk to my candy bowl and unwrapped a chocolate truffle. She raised her eyebrows at me and popped it into her mouth.

"Mom tells me you've met someone," she says, covering her mouth with her hand as she chewed. "Gimme the tea."

"What does that even mean?" I asked.

"It means give the deets, the details, tell me who he is," she explained. "Inquiring minds want to know, Leah."

"I think you mean *you* want to know, Jackie," I said, a small laugh creeping up my throat. "I met a client I'm doing business with and that's it."

"I call bullshit," she said and laughed.

"Jackie, watch your mouth," Becky scolded. "If she doesn't want to tell you, she doesn't have to."

Jackie scoffed and started putzing around my office, fingering the brochures that were strategically laid out across the tables.

"Thank you, Becky," I said, relieved that the interrogation was over.

"Thank me for what? You might not have to tell her, but you

still need to tell me," she said and winked. "Are you going to see him again?"

"As a matter of fact, I am. He's coming to the office at noon for a business lunch. But, before you get your hopes up, it's strictly business," I said to her frowning face. "Now, get out before he gets here. I still have some work to do, and I don't need you two freaks in here when he arrives."

"Mm-hmm. I may only be a teenager, but I know nerves when I see them," Jackie commented. "And you, Leah Abernathy, have a crush on this man."

"When did you become so grown-up?" I asked her.

"I expect a full report by this evening. You have my number," Jackie said, tossing her hair over her shoulder and walking out the door.

Becky and I burst out laughing. She was so much like both of her parents, and I loved every bit of it. Jackie was like the little sister I never had but always wanted. She was far less annoying than she was when she was little, but she was still one of the funniest people I knew. I looked at my watch. Eleven forty-five.

"All right, Becky. You've got to go," I said, jokingly shooing her out of the office. "I'll stop by the shop this afternoon, okay?"

"Okay, love," she said, giving me a big hug. "Have fun on your lunch date, and don't do anything I wouldn't do."

"Oh my goodness, Becky," I said, rolling my eyes.

I went back to my desk to collect my work and set up the table where we could eat and talk about his resorts. I was so nervous, I worried the sweat from my palms was going to cause the ink on the papers to run. I needed to calm myself down, but I couldn't drink while I was working, and another cup of coffee would not help my anxiety. Just when I thought I was going to start hyperventilating, Luke walked through the door. I slowly lifted my head, my gaze meeting his, and he smiled so big I thought my soul was going to fly out of my body.

Full of Grace

He raised his arms, showing me two paper bags that I assumed were full of sushi. "I brought rainbow rolls, salmon rolls, spicy tuna rolls, kani salad, and dumplings. It's a lot but I didn't know what you liked."

A small giggle escaped my lips. "That's my exact order."

"Do you want me to grab drinks from the store next door?"

"I have water in the back. Unless you want something else?"

"Water sounds great, thanks."

I went to the small kitchen in the back of the office and took two bottles of water out of the fridge. I felt like I was practicing hypnobirthing with the way I was breathing my anxiety in and out. I rushed back out to the office to see him taking his suit jacket off and draping it over the back of one of the chairs. His biceps gasped for air inside his button-down.

I cleared my throat. "Here you go," I said, handing him a bottle. "I've been working on all three of your resorts, and I made a proposal for each location."

"You did all of that in one morning?" he asked.

"This is what I do. It's what I'm good at. I love to create new places and ideas and help bring the old up to speed," I told him. "Oh, I'm sorry. That sounded incredibly cocky of me."

"No, I like it," he said.

"Um, so I thought maybe we could start with the adults-only resort and then go over your other two after," I told him. "That way we can focus on the things that might still need to be added. Did you bring your paperwork?"

"Yes, I have it. And that sounds wonderful," he said, opening the bags of food and placing them all in the center of the table.

We continued to eat and discuss my plans for his resorts, and before I knew it, two hours had gone by. It surprised me how easy it was to talk to him.

"Leah, I know you said no many times already, but I would

really like it if you would join me for dinner tonight," he said as he began to pack up his briefcase.

"I'm sorry but my answer is still no," I told him, annoyed that he continued to push. "I have enjoyed your company over lunch, but I mean it when I say that I don't mix business with pleasure. I hope you understand."

"I respect that. You can't blame a man for trying, though," he said, his eyes growing increasingly more seductive.

I held my ground as he packed up the proposals and tucked them neatly into his bag. It was clear that he wasn't used to being turned down. He was beautiful, but my heart was somewhere else, even though I was too afraid to admit it to anyone else.

"I'll get the rest of the information over to you tonight, and then we can schedule another meeting for later next week if that works for you," he said, his flirtatious demeanor no longer visible.

I reached out to shake his hand, relieved that this was over and I could get back to my mountain of paperwork. "That sounds great, Luke. I look forward to hearing from you."

10

CALEB

"Hey, Dooley," I called across the meadow as I jogged toward the barn. "I'm back."

"You're just in time for a beer," he said, handing me a bottle. "I figured I'd take a quick break before we get back at it. There are also waters in the cooler if you want. Becky thought it would be best to keep me hydrated."

"You laugh, Dooley, but you've got yourself one hell of a woman."

"Don't I know it."

"You introduced her to us all at just the right time."

"What do you mean, son?"

"Well, you remember the day Dad died—it was such a great day. Leah and I were running around, so carefree. I remember watching my parents holding hands and sneaking kisses, and I thought it was gross at the time, but as I've gotten older, I've learned to appreciate the love they shared," I said. "Anyway, when you introduced us to Becky, I remember feeling so comfortable around her."

"Yeah, she's pretty special, that one," Dooley said, tipping his head back and taking a long swig of his beer.

"When the ambulance took my dad away, Lucia was comforting my mom, and you and Paul were comforting each other. I never thought of it as no one was worried about me and Leah, so please don't take this the wrong way, but Becky, she didn't skip a beat. She immediately came to me and Leah, wrapped her arms around us and made us feel safe," I told him. "I'll never forget that."

"Aw, man," he said, his eyes welling up with tears. "Now you've gone and made this old man cry."

I stretched my arm out to clink our beers together. "I hope they're happy tears."

"Always," he said. "You know, Caleb, when your dad died, your mom never asked me to stand up and help her out with you. I did it because I love you like you're my own son. I hope you know I'm here for you—for anything, anytime."

"I know, Dooley. I appreciate that," I said quietly. "Thank you for making my childhood feel as normal as possible."

Dooley cleared his throat and wiped his tears away. I respected his ability to respond so well to all of life's curveballs.

"Look at that old heap of junk over there," Dooley said, pointing to the pickup that had sat in that very spot for at least ten years.

"Don't you talk about my beautiful girl like that," I said and laughed. "That truck was present at some of the most important moments of my life."

"Yeah, well, I'll tell you what. I'll tow it up into the garage, and if you can get it up and running, it's yours."

"Get out."

"My dad would have wanted you to have it. You know this," he said. "It's definitely going to be a lot of work, but I know you can do it. When's the last time you worked on a car?"

"Besides oil changes and replacing random lights and fuses?"

I asked. "About ten years ago when I helped you fix your old Mustang."

Dooley laughed. "That thing was such a piece of shit. I was so happy when it finally died so I didn't have to spend any more money on parts I knew wouldn't fix it anyway."

"That thing was the money pit of cars," I said, kicking at the loose dirt in front of me.

"You're damn right," he replied. "Well, I'll have it towed then, and you can work on it here. I've got all the tools up in the garage."

"Thanks, Dooley," I said, reaching out to shake his hand.

"Is something on your mind, son?" he asked. "You don't seem as happy about this as I thought you'd be."

"Yeah, I've just got a lot on my mind. But the truck will be a welcome distraction," I said.

"What's on your mind?" Dooley asked again.

"It's Leah."

"Is everything okay with her?" His voice was charged with concern.

"Oh yeah, everything is fine," I assured him. "It's just that I can't stop thinking about her."

"I see. And have you told her this?"

"I went to her office earlier this morning to tell her. I congratulated her on the agency again and handed her a cup of coffee. Then I blurted out that I missed her and she asked me to leave."

"Well, son, missing someone is far different than having feelings for them. All I have to say is this: if you have feelings for her, you need to tell her, not only so she knows but also so you can move on if she doesn't feel the same way. You can't go through life walking around like a lost puppy and hoping she'll be able to read your mind and figure out what you want."

"If I had a dollar for every time someone told me that this week." I shook my head, embarrassed to be caught out again.

"It's true. You're letting this run your entire life, and for what? What does it bring you other than stress and confusion?" He looked at me, and I felt more like a child in that moment than the twenty-eight-year-old man that I was.

"Every time I try to tell her how I feel, something gets in the way." I stood up and paced back and forth.

"Your mom told me you haven't even told Leah that you and Brittany broke up," he said. "Caleb, what kind of shit is that?"

"Like I said—" I started.

"No," Dooley cut me off. "If I ever found out that someone was keeping things from Jackie, I'd lose my mind. You aren't being fair to her or to yourself. As much as I love ya, you're annoying me with this bullshit. You two need to figure your shit out."

I laughed. "You're right, Dooley."

Knowing he had said his piece, I nodded and got back to work. I couldn't stand to keep simmering over this Leah situation. I needed to keep busy, and I needed it to happen right away. I began to load the truck with all the junk I took out of the barn earlier so I could take it to the junkyard.

I looked over at the other truck and smiled. "Don't worry, girl. You're not going anywhere."

The sun was beating down on me, and it felt good on my sore shoulders. I hadn't been to a gym in months, and I hadn't worked out aside from running in probably the same amount of time. I still had Bill Palmer's coaching offer to mull over as well. The thought of adding more to my plate actually drove me harder. I loved being busy. I loved pushing myself to the limits. I loved being able to show the world what hard work and determination could get you.

And it was those thoughts that led me to answer my own question. I'd tell Bill yes when I saw him at the town meeting.

"Ready to call it a night, Caleb?" Dooley asked. "I've got to get cleaned up. I'm taking my ladies to dinner, and I can't go out smelling like piss and horse manure."

"Sure you can," I teased. "They already love you."

"You should try this fragrance when you talk to Leah," he rebutted.

"Okay, I see your point. You going to the town meeting tomorrow?"

"Nah, I have to meet with the financial advisor to run the numbers for the training school," he told me.

"See you this weekend for the game then?" I asked.

"You know it," he replied. "Tell your mom I said she better bring her famous monkey bread or else Becky will have a fit."

"I'll let her know."

11

CALEB

I COULD SMELL THE BLUEBERRY PANCAKES WAFTING UP THE stairs, and I peeled myself off my bed. You could always count on a stack of pancakes to wake me up and get me moving. I threw on a pair of sweats and went downstairs to see if my mom needed any help. Another trait I'd inherited from my father—and one I was thankful for.

"Hey, Mom," I said, kissing her on the cheek and snatching a pancake from the pile. "Need any help?"

"Hi, honey," she said and motioned to the french press. "Could you finish that up? The water is just about boiled on the stove. I'll have these done in just a few minutes. Oh, and can you grab the newspaper from the front porch? I haven't gotten out there yet."

"Of course."

I shoved the pancake into my mouth and poured the almost boiling water into the press. I let it steep while I went outside to retrieve the paper. In a town this small, the news was usually relatively boring. Someone's kid made the honor roll. The Kratz family came up with a new cookie flavor. A poll for what color lights should decorate the gazebo for the Christmas Festival. But this morning, the front-page news was printed in big, bold font. **Bill Palmer to be formally announced as Mayor of Grace Valley. Principal successor to be announced at town meeting this Saturday.**

I dropped the paper on the island and grabbed the milk from the fridge. "Coffee's ready, Mom. You want me to pour you a mug or bring the carafe to the table?"

"Table is fine. Thank you, sweetheart," she said, placing the last pancake on the plate and bringing it over.

I sat across the table from my mom and took note of how, even with everything that life had thrown at her, she was the epitome of strength and beauty.

"Are you ready for the meeting?" she asked.

"Yes and no. I don't know how many people already know about me taking over Bill's position, so that will be interesting. But also, I just never understand these things. Standing on a stage and making a speech in front of the town is the last thing I want to do," I said.

"Caleb, honey. You're going to be the principal of an entire school. Standing up on a stage and making a speech is a big part of what you're going to be doing for the rest of your career, so you better get used to it now."

We finished our breakfast, and I cleaned up the kitchen while my mom got ready. I brushed my teeth and threw on some Dockers and a short-sleeve polo shirt and grabbed my loafers. I laughed when I looked at them. When had I become a loafers kind of dude? Maybe I'd head over to the shoe store later and get a different pair of shoes. *What kind of shoes does a principal wear anyway? Probably loafers.*

My mom tossed the keys to me when I got downstairs and said, "You drive."

"All right," I said. "Let's do this."

"I'm proud of you, Caleb," she said. "And I know your father would be too. He's with you every step of the way, and I know he is looking down on you and smiling at every barrier you continue to break through."

I smiled and nodded, silently thanking her for her supportive words. I knew she didn't need me to say anything in response. I was lucky to have her, and I was more than grateful she agreed to have me move back in after the Brittany fiasco. I turned onto the main strip and looked for a spot along the side of the green. It looked as though every single resident of Grace Valley had shown up for the meeting. I couldn't remember the last time I saw more than fifty people at one of these things. I parked the car, and we made our way across the street to the meeting house. The building had been there for hundreds of years and was only used for the changing of the mayor. Grace Valley had always been a small town, but over the years, the citizens had grown in numbers and the room was becoming tighter and tighter.

"Good morning, Tammy, Caleb," Bill said, shaking both of our hands. "Quite the turnout."

"I was just thinking the same thing," I agreed.

"Are you ready?" he asked me.

I nodded in agreement and followed him to the stage.

"So, there will be a small speech, and then they'll announce me as the new mayor, effective today. I'll make my speech and then announce my successor for principal. At that point, you'll come up and make a speech, and then we can all be on our merry way. Sound good?"

"Sounds good to me," I said. "Thank you again for choosing me to follow in your footsteps."

"I wouldn't have it any other way," Bill said.

He walked confidently up to the podium, his speech in his left hand and his right hand in his pocket. He nodded his head a few times at the crowd before pulling his reading glasses out of his blazer pocket. He cleared his throat while unfolding his speech, and I held my breath.

"Good morning, Grace Valley," he started. "It is with extreme pleasure that I formally accept the role of mayor of this beautiful town we all love. As you know, I grew up here and raised all my beautiful children here. I plan on remaining here until the good Lord tells me it's time. Let's all hope that isn't for many, many more years to come."

The small crowd laughed lightly, and I eased up a bit. Bill continued his speech for what seemed like hours, and then it was my turn.

"Before I wrap this up, I would like to call someone up here with me," he said, looking down to where I was standing and nodding me over. "Caleb, would you mind joining me?"

As I made my way to the podium, I noticed Leah standing close to the back with Paul. I hadn't noticed her earlier and honestly didn't think she would even be here. I couldn't remember the last time I had attended one of these myself, and they definitely weren't her cup of tea anyway. I smiled and shook Bill's hand, standing tall on the left of him. I couldn't believe this was about to happen, but I was damn proud of how my future looked from here.

"Now, as you all know, I'm leaving Grace Valley School," he said. "Just in case you all forgot why we're here so early."

Laughter, again, filled the room. A comedian and a mayor—only in Grace Valley.

"I would like to announce my successor, Caleb Patterson," he said. "Everyone, please give Caleb a round of applause."

I smiled and looked toward the crowd. The already small room seemed even smaller in that moment, and I could see Leah's face drop and her head swivel to look at her father.

She took in a deep breath, pursed her lips together and turned around and left. That would have been the perfect time for me to follow her and talk to her, but of course, I was stuck on this stage about to make a speech that would change the course of my life and begin a brand-new chapter for all the children of Grace Valley. I managed to make it through the speech without insulting anyone or making myself look like an asshole, and the very second the meeting was over, I got off the stage to go talk to Paul. I knew it was too late to look for Leah, as she was long gone by now. But I needed to straighten out what I could. I wasn't about to let this stew for weeks like everything else.

"Paul," I said as I stopped in front of him. "Is everything okay with Leah? I saw her leave."

"She'll get over it," Paul said. "She needs to learn that sometimes people can't just spill the beans when it's not their story to tell."

"I see," I said. "For such a nosy town, there seems to be an awful lot of secrets here lately."

It was true that the members of this town generally knew everyone else's business, but one of the things I loved the most was the level of loyalty the citizens exhibited. There was a difference between gossiping and holding someone's trust and half the time that's in your favor. This time was not.

"Funny you should mention that," he said, almost looking through me. "Now that she knows you're back for good, are you ever going to tell her you're no longer engaged? Or did you want her to find that out in some random way too?"

Ouch.

"Paul, every time I've tried to tell her, something or someone gets in the way. I don't even know if she's dating anyone, and if she is, whether it's serious or not. I'm not the type of man to break anything up. I love her but I want her to be happy, even if that's not with me." My head was spinning, and I was turning into a lovesick puppy.

"Well, son, that's a very admirable thing to say, but I don't think you'll ever get to know how she feels if you don't tell her," he explained. "I also think it should be her decision—not yours—of what she chooses to do in her romantic life."

"You're right. I just don't want to get hurt again."

"And that's understandable, Caleb, but you're a grown man and getting hurt is a part of life. You'll never know unless you try. You already know this. So, either you tell her the truth about Brittany and your feelings, or you let it go and let her go. It's your choice, but you need to make it soon."

I nodded and shook his hand. "I hear ya."

I loved Leah, but a part of me knew I didn't know her anymore. Communicating with someone you don't know takes time, and while I knew the old her in and out, the new grown-up version would take some getting used to. I just hoped I would be able to find the right words before it was too late.

I needed some air, so I walked across the street to the green and sat in the gazebo. It was one of my favorite places to think, and it helped that it was directly opposite her office.

"Why didn't you tell me you were back?" Leah's soft voice snuck around the side of the gazebo.

This was my chance to come clean and make things right. I couldn't hold out on her any longer. It wasn't fair to either of us.

"I tried to catch you before you left at Christmas, but I didn't make it to the station in time," I admitted. "And then I tried again in your office the other day."

"That *was* you at the station," she said, raising a hand to cover her mouth.

"You saw me?"

"I thought I did. But then I wondered if I was seeing things," she told me, taking a seat on the bench across from me. "Why were you there?"

"Leah, I'm just going to come out and say this before I lose my nerve. I can't stop thinking about you."

"What about Brittany?"

"It's over," I told her. "We ended things the night of the festival."

"What? Why didn't you tell me?"

"I thought you were in a relationship with that guy, Josh. Your dad told me that you weren't, and that's when I went to the station."

"Oh my God," she said, standing up.

Her hands shot up, covering her face. She began pacing, and for a second, I thought she was going to leave. I watched her take a deep breath, place her hands on her thighs, and slowly lower herself back onto the bench.

She's staying?

She licked her lips and opened her mouth as if to say something, but quickly shut it.

"Leah—"

"No," she snapped. "You don't get to talk right now."

"Hey, that's not fair," I said, standing up.

I towered over her, and while I didn't want to appear threatening, this wasn't all my fault. She followed suit and stood up, glaring at me, and opened her mouth to say something, but I didn't give her the opportunity.

"I understand that you're upset, but to be quite honest, I don't owe you anything," I spewed. "We're not together. You made that perfectly clear. So, I'm sorry that you're hurt and that you didn't find out sooner, but that's no reason to hate on me."

Surprisingly, I could still read Leah like a book, and there was once a time where one could say I almost knew her better than she knew herself. It was all coming back as natural as it used to be, and judging from knowing her then and seeing the expression forming on her face, things could go one of two ways.

She sucked in a deep breath and paused for a moment before releasing it. Her bottom lip jutted out before it was sucked back into her mouth as if it were protecting the words that threatened to spill off her tongue.

"I want to be so mad at you right now."

Her face contorted back to an expression I knew all too well: regret.

"But, you're right," she continued. "You don't owe me anything. I did this to us. I'm so sorry. I have to go."

I stood frozen, my brain and my mouth at war with each other, and I couldn't speak. By the time I realized what had just happened, she was almost out of sight. I didn't want to be left tending to my wounds yet again, so this time, I ran after her.

"Leah, stop," I called, panting when I finally reached her. "This ends now. You can't run away every time something bothers you. It isn't fair to either of us. You may not feel the same way I do, but at least respect me enough to stay."

I stared at her back, not knowing what move she would make next. But I knew she felt something—that I was sure of. What she felt was going to have to wait.

She slowly turned to face me and had tears streaming down her face. "You're right, again. And I do want to talk to you about this, Caleb. Right now, I just need some time. It's a lot for me to take in, and I want to be in the right frame of mind. You understand that, don't you?"

I reached a hand out to hold hers, letting her take the lead of whether or not she wanted to hold mine back. She did. I nodded.

"I do. I really do. Take all the time you need," I told her.

She dropped my hand and looked up at me. Her caramel-brown eyes looked so intently into mine, I was afraid I would fall apart right there. Placing her hands on my shoulders, she reached up on her tiptoes and gave me the lightest kiss on my cheek.

"Thank you," she said before spinning on her heels and walking away, leaving me grinning like a clown.

12

LEAH

"Ugh, where is my phone?" I yelled to no one but myself.

When I finally found it, I punched my password in and frantically searched for Sara's contact information.

"Hey, girl," Sara answered, sporting a huge smile that quickly faded when she saw my face on the other side of our FaceTime call. "What's going on?"

"Caleb is back in town," I blurted out.

"Yeah, I know. You've already told me this."

"No, I mean like forever."

"What do you mean forever? Is this a bad thing?" she asked. "Oh shit! You're gonna be neighbors with that bitch, Brittany!"

"Nope," I said, pacing across my bedroom floor. "They broke up."

"Back up and tell me what's going on."

I filled her in on what happened at the meeting and the conversation Caleb and I had after.

"Okay, so let me get this straight," she said in an authoritative voice. "Your ex-boyfriend is the new principal and basketball coach. His fiancée is no longer his fiancée, and she's not moving to Grace Valley. Your business is booming. And you're absofreakinglutely still in love with Caleb."

"Yes, exactly," I said. "Wait, what? No, I am not in love with him."

"I call bullshit, Leah. You are totally still head over heels for him. And guess what? He probably is about you too."

I sat in silence for a minute, taking everything in. Could she be right? Was I still in love with him? The more I thought about it, the more I realized I had never really stopped loving him. Maybe I paused a bit over the years, but I definitely didn't stop.

"I mean, I love him. I've always loved him, and I'll probably love him for the rest of my life. But I don't even know him anymore. I can't talk to him like I used to without sounding like an asshole. I couldn't possibly still be in love with him."

Sitting on the edge of my bed, I started to cry. I was so overwhelmed with everything. I tried to not let it consume me, but I was so confused with everything that I had been hearing and seeing. I came back home for a fresh start ,but I never once expected him to be there, too. And knowing he was staying and I was staying made it so hard to not want to jump right back to where we were when we were kids.

"Do you want me to come there? I don't have a busy weekend. I can move a few things around and hop on the train in an hour," she offered.

Yes, I wanted her there, but I knew it wouldn't change anything. And I knew that when she said she could move a few things around, they were more than just nail or hair appointments.

"You're the best, but no," I said. "I don't want you to have to do that. Let's definitely plan for you and Aiden to visit soon, though."

"That sounds great," she said, and I could feel her warmth through the phone. "Now, go take a hot bath, have a glass of wine, and relax. Put some of that lavender oil I sent you in the bath too. It'll help you relax."

"What would I do without you?" I asked.

"Love you, girl," she said, and we hung up the phone.

A bath and wine were exactly what I needed. I turned the water on to heat up and went downstairs to get a stemless wine glass and a bottle of wine.

Where did I put those oils?

I hadn't used them since she sent them. I finally found them on the top shelf of the linen closet. I poured myself a glass and placed it on the bath tray that sat across the clawfoot tub. There really was no other way to soak.

Once the water was hot enough, I put a few drops of the lavender oil in and got into the tub. I closed my eyes and breathed in deeply through my nose and then out of my mouth. I took a long sip of wine and sunk down into the tub until my shoulders were fully submerged underwater. I didn't plan on getting out until the water was cold.

It was late by the time I finally exited the bathroom. I wasn't in the mood to talk to my dad, so I pulled on my comfiest pajamas, grabbed the remote, and snuggled up in bed. I was still so confused that I didn't even care that my wet hair was making a puddle on my pillow. I wanted to disappear for a while and come back with all of the answers. Life didn't work that way, but damn, I wish it did.

Caleb had been right, though; he didn't owe me anything. And who was I to expect him to?

Nothing on the television was remotely interesting, so I let myself fall into the memories I had stashed away for years. I lay in bed, staring at the ceiling and remembering all of the good times we'd shared when we were kids.

"Leah, phone's for you," my mom called up to my room.

I wasn't expecting anyone to call. "Hello?"

"Oh, um, hi, Leah. It's Caleb," a shaky voice came out of the other end.

"Oh, hey, Caleb. What's up?"

"Hi, is this a bad time?" he asked.

The tone of his voice splattered goosebumps across my arms, and I wasn't expecting that at all.

"No, not at all," I said. *"Just working on my algebra homework. Mrs. Flynn gave us so much, and I don't want to be working on it all weekend. How are you?"*

"I'm good. Just got home from taking Darb out for a ride," he said. *"Um, the reason I'm calling is because I was wondering if you were busy tomorrow?"*

"I was just planning on going into town and maybe helping my dad out at his store, but nothing is set in stone," I replied. *"Why?"*

"Do you want to meet me at mini golf tomorrow?" he asked. *I could hear his voice shake, and it took all I could not to comment on that.*

"Sure," I agreed, confused as to why he sounded so nervous. *We were best friends and we always hung out, so it was weird to hear him like that.*

"Great," he said. *"Is eleven okay for you?"*

"Yeah, I'll just have to see if my mom can drop be off, but I'm sure it'll be fine," I said. *"I'll see you there."*

I hung up the phone and went back to my algebra homework. Mini golf, huh?

"Hey!" I exclaimed, giggling. *"You cheated!"*

"I did no such thing." He smiled, his pearly whites glistening in the sun.

How had I never noticed his piercing blue eyes before? He

looked so good, and I wasn't sure what to make of my new feelings for him. They came out of nowhere and they scared me.

"Oh, don't you dare smile at me like that. You cheated and you know it," I said, playfully swatting at him. "Go get your ball; you're done with this hole."

He laughed and went to retrieve his ball. "Yes, boss."

I rolled my eyes and followed him to the next hole. I was determined to beat him, especially now that I knew he was a cheater.

"Are you rolling your eyes at me?" he asked, reaching across the small green and pulling me to his chest. I fit perfectly in his arms.

My heart began to pound, and I was afraid he would feel it against his. I looked up at him and everything between us felt so natural, but it was also so unexpected.

"No," I said, swallowing deeply, my eyes darting from his eyes to his lips. "I was just thinking of how I'm going to win the next hole."

He loosened his grip and grabbed his putter. "Oh, not a chance in hell that's happening!"

"You wanna get some ice cream?" he asked after we finished the game.

"Sure, but you get to pay since I won," I teased him.

"That's fair," he said and ordered two vanilla cones.

The kid at the counter handed us our cones, and we made our way over to a picnic table in the shade. We sat on the same side of the bench facing each other. Part of me felt like I had my entire life with him and another part felt like I was a completely different person.

"What are you thinking about?" Caleb asked, breaking me from my thoughts.

"Just how much fun today has been," I said, smiling at him. I could feel my cheeks begin to burn and it wasn't from the sun.

Caleb opened his mouth to say something, but instead, he scooted closer to me and placed a gentle hand on my cheek. Pulling my head up, he lowered his and his lips connected with mine, sending lightning bolts from my head to my toes and causing me to drop my cone onto the ground.

He pulled back quickly and jumped up off the bench. "I'm so sorry!"

I reached out and grabbed his hand before he tried to pick up the cone. "Don't be."

And that was the beginning of the new version of Caleb and Leah—a couple I never thought would break up. But now look at the mess we were in. I knew in that moment that it was up to me to fix things, and if I wanted to make it work, I needed to make the first move. I picked up my phone and called Caleb, feeling a bit defeated when I got his voicemail. I wanted to hang up and go to bed, but I knew I needed to leave a message.

"Hi, Caleb. It's me, Leah. I'm ready to talk. Meet me at The Putt-Putt Hut on Saturday at noon. See you then."

13

LEAH

IMMERSING MYSELF IN MY WORK ALWAYS KEPT MY MIND OFF things I had no business dwelling on, so I was grateful when Cameron called me to discuss a few new business strategies he had learned. I carefully took notes, making sure I didn't miss anything he said. He had so many years in this business, and any help or advice he offered, I made sure I didn't miss.

"Great. Thanks so much, Cameron," I said, my fingers lingering over the speakerphone button. "I really appreciate it."

"It's nothing, Leah." Cameron's tone was always so genuine. "I like being able to send clients your way. You've got a way with these local vacation resorts, and I want to see you succeed."

"Next time I'm in the city, we need to get lunch," I told him. "On me!"

"That sounds wonderful," he said. "Talk soon."

I couldn't believe I was still at the office at seven p.m., but I had been slammed with work all day and hadn't even had a chance to eat dinner, let alone go home. I checked my email one last time and decided that everything could wait until morning. I was exhausted, and all I wanted to do was get out of here and eat a quick dinner and soak in the tub. My back was on fire from sitting at my desk all day, and my head felt like it was about to pop off. I really needed to think about hiring an assistant.

My business was growing in ways I had only imagined, and I didn't anticipate it slowing down anytime soon. With the work I'd done for John, I'd been able to acquire over twenty new clients, which was relatively unheard of. But since most people were traveling across the country more and abroad less, more and more resorts were being purchased and reworked. It was a win for all of us. But no one would end up having anything if I didn't get some help and some sleep.

I packed up my stuff, locked the door, and started to walk home. The grocery store was long closed, and I took my phone out of my pocket to call my dad.

"Hi, pumpkin."

"Hi, Dad. I'll be home in about fifteen minutes," I told him. "What do you feel like having for dinner tonight?"

"I made chicken cacciatore and gnocchi," he told me. "It's just about done now, so I'll get the table ready."

"Aw, Dad! Thank you," I said appreciatively. "It was my turn to cook tonight, though."

"I peeked into your office earlier and saw you with your nose to the grindstone and figured I'd do it tonight," he told me. "Besides, I had a long day, and I needed something to keep me busy."

"Everything all right?" I asked.

"Yeah, just got a couple of wrong shipments, and one of the deliveries had to be returned because of potential contamination. A kid threw up in aisle seven and someone almost tripped in it. The credit card machines were all down for an hour, and nobody carries cash or checks on them anymore. Everything is fine now but, whew, what a day!"

"Oh man, that does sound like quite the eventful day," I said, happy I had been hunched over a desk staring at a computer screen and not dealing with someone getting sick all over my floor. "I'll see you in a bit."

I loved living so close to my job because the walk home was such a great way to decompress. Although, I still hadn't heard from Caleb, so I wasn't sure if he had gotten my message the night before. Or maybe he did and just wasn't interested in talking anymore. As if he could read my mind, my phone dinged and his name flashed across my screen. Text message.

Caleb: Got your voicemail. I'll be there at noon. :)

I walked the rest of the way home with a goofy smile and an anxiety-ridden brain. I was happily confused without a damn clue what to do about it.

When I walked through the front door, the aroma of the peppers and onions on the chicken tickled my nose, and my mouth immediately watered. I was so glad I grew up in a house where everyone loved food and loved to prepare amazing meals. My dad always made his sauce and gnocchi from scratch. My mom taught him that when they were dating, and he'd been doing it that way ever since. It was a great tradition to pass down to my own children one day. I was just sad she was never going to meet them.

My adorable father handed me a plate full of food, and I quickly sat down at the table ready to devour every last bit of it. I waited for him to sit, and as soon as he did, I dug my fork into the gnocchi.

"Oh my goodness, Dad," I said with a mouthful of food. "I think this is your best gnocchi yet."

"You say that every time I make it," he said with a laugh. "But thank you. I think I might try a different kind next time. Maybe sweet potato or butternut squash with a creamy sage sauce."

"That sounds amazing."

"I don't understand how you're so tiny when you eat so much

Full of Grace

damn food all the time."

"I don't know either, but I'm not going to question it," I replied, shoving more food in my mouth.

"Mmm, this is pretty good," he said, admiring his work. "You have a lot of work to do if you're going to top this tomorrow."

"Oh no, tomorrow is your night to cook," I teased.

I grabbed a roll and dipped it into the sauce on my plate. I didn't want the meal to end. We finished the rest of it in silence, enjoying the food, and went out to the front porch with glasses of wine. It was a beautiful night. The calm before the impending storm. I sat on the porch swing, and my dad half-sat on the railing, his right leg holding the majority of his weight.

"So, how is work going, pumpkin?" he asked.

"To say it's great would be the understatement of the year," I told him. "I'm so busy that I don't know where I'm going to find the time to get all the work done, but I'm so overjoyed."

"That's great!"

"It really is. I never thought this would be my reality."

"I'm so proud of you," he told me. "Are you working on anything new or the same few resorts?"

"The same resorts for now. The new ones are mostly on the back burner until the fall. I do have quite a few bed and breakfasts who have reached out as well, so I'm trying to figure out how to fit them in before the summer is over. I was just thinking that I need to hire an assistant. I'm taking on too much at once and am all alone. I don't want to end up getting burnt out before I even hit the six-month mark."

"I agree," he said. "Running your own business is tough. It makes sense to have a partner or an assistant. You should reach out to some of the local colleges and see if they have any students who are looking for summer internships. It's a bit late in the year, and there might only be a few students who are still available, but it's good to see. And who knows, maybe you can sign them on for bigger roles once they graduate."

"That's a really great idea, Dad," I said. "I'll make a list and start calling around tomorrow. I think there's also a local Facebook page where I can post an ad looking for help. I'll see what I can find out."

A strong gust of wind blew across the porch, and I shivered. It had gotten very chilly outside once the sun went down. I wrapped my arms around my body and rubbed up and down on my arms to warm up. Just as I was starting to feel a little bit better, another gust tore through, knocking both of the rocking chairs over and breaking one of the arms.

"We should probably head inside," my dad said. "I think this is going to be a bad one."

"I don't know about you, Dad, but I am over these storms. It feels like when one ends, another is lurking in the shadows waiting to pounce at any given moment."

"This is New England, pumpkin," he said, holding the door open for me. "Anything goes and no weather pattern is strange."

"Do you remember when I was in the Girl Scouts, and we went on that camping trip in April? It was unusually warm, so Mom packed all springtime clothing for me, but then it snowed."

"Oh, yes, I remember," he said and smiled. "You melted your brand-new sneakers trying to warm up by the fire."

I remembered that day like it was yesterday. We were hiking in the woods, trying to earn some badge, and we were all in jeans, T-shirts, and sneakers and it started to snow. We laughed it off and hiked out further until the sun hid behind a cloud and the snow started to come down harder. It went from warm to freezing in what seemed like a matter of seconds. We all decided we still wanted to stay, so we bundled up in our tents and went to sleep for the night. When we woke up the next morning, there was a foot of snow, and it had been so cold that the one faucet the campground had was frozen. We had to melt snow in pots on the fire to boil water.

"You were always such a trouper," my dad said. "You're so much like your mother, you know. She would have stayed at that campground too."

"How did you know that was what I was thinking about?" I asked him.

"Father's intuition," he said, winking. "We know all. Didn't you know that?"

"Sometimes, I miss those days. The innocence and wonder. The ability to not have many responsibilities but feel like such a grown up," I said. "Now look—I'm a grown-up with a million responsibilities and no time to relax."

"It's worth it, though. You'll see. You're making a name for yourself, and you're creating a future that will not only be financially secure but also one that you absolutely love. Not everyone gets to do that."

"I know," I said.

I took a long sip of my wine and was placing it on the coffee table when we heard a loud pop and a crackle, and then lights out.

"Uh-oh," my dad said. "Sounds like a transformer blew. I'd better get the lanterns because we're going to be out of power for a while."

"Wonderful," I said. "This is never-ending."

He came back about ten minutes later with all the lanterns and handed me two. "Keep one in your bedroom, and use the other one to walk around the house if you need to do anything," he said.

"Thanks, Dad," I replied, already knowing how power outages work but not wanting to insult him. "I'm gonna take a bath while I can still get hot water."

"Okay," he said.

I needed to soak in a tub so badly I probably would have resorted to boiling pots of water on the gas stove and filling the tub that way if I had to. I was just about to start the tub when my dad called up to me.

"Leah, get down here right now!" he yelled. "We have to go."

I grabbed the lantern and ran back down the stairs.

"What's going on?" I asked, out of breath.

My dad held his hand up to me and put his phone on speaker. "We're on our way. Is there anyone else you need us to call?"

"No, Becky is on the phone with Tammy right now, and Jackie is talking to Melanie Palmer," Dooley's voice came out of the speaker.

"We're leaving now," my dad said. "Don't worry."

He hung up the phone and looked at me, panic frozen in his eyes.

"The Butler's farm is on fire," he said.

14

CALEB

I WAS GETTING TIRED OF ALL THE STORMS AND THE SHITTY POWER lines in Grace Valley. It seemed like every time the wind blew, the power went out. Gas was expensive to keep filing and running those generators, not to mention the energy it took to keep going back outside to make sure it was still chained to the side of the house and no one had tried to run off with it before I could lock it back up in the garage for the night.

I wanted to take a shower, and luckily, I knew there would be a bit of hot water since we had a large tankless water heater installed a few years back. I rinsed off quickly in case my mom wanted to take one and wrapped a towel around my waist. I eyed my reflection in the mirror, the faint glow of the lantern illuminating my now slender frame. *God, I need to get back into the gym.*

I was no longer cut in all the places I used to be. My arms looked weak and my once lean body was now lanky. I felt like crap. I vowed to myself to stop being lazy and start a new workout regimen in the morning. There was a great gym in the next town over, and if I got there early enough, I might be able to book a few visits with the trainer. Anything to get back into shape.

I picked up the lantern and went back into my room to change and get ready for bed. If I had enough battery life on my cell phone, I could probably watch a show or two before I fell asleep. There was a bowl of soup and a plate with a grilled cheese sitting on my desk with a note. *"You shouldn't go to bed hungry. Love, Mom."*

Gotta love having a gas stove in the middle of a power outage. I was so thankful for food that I didn't even get dressed. I sat at the desk eating in my towel and stopped feeling sorry for myself. The power outage felt symbolic of my life. There would always be dark times, but it was what I chose to do when the light seeped through that mattered.

I finished eating and pulled my pajama pants on. I walked my dishes downstairs and saw my mother sitting alone in the dark at the kitchen table. That wasn't a sight I was used to seeing. My mom was a strong woman, or maybe she was strong because of the things that had happened to her. But it was very unlike her to be sitting alone in the dark like that, and it made me worry.

"You okay, Mom?" I asked her.

"I was just thinking about your father," she told me. "It hasn't been easy without him, but I am just so proud of you. I know I say it often but it's true."

She smiled softly at me as she held my hands. She used to do that when I was a little boy, and she wanted to remind me of how loved I was. I never needed reminding, though. She showed me daily and I loved her for it.

"Caleb, you have grown into such a wonderful man," she said. "You have accomplished so much, and I am honored to be a part of it all. I've enjoyed watching you become who are, and I can't wait to see what the world still has in store for you. Your father would feel the same way."

"I hope so."

Missing out on so much with my dad was hard, but I was thankful I was able to remember so much from the years I had with him. I felt him all around me everywhere I went. Some people say that heaven and the afterlife are myths, but I knew my dad, and I knew when he was around. I also knew I wouldn't have been able to get through some of the more challenging parts of my life without him. He was there, and I didn't care who believed me.

"I know so," she countered. "You picked up everything and moved to Tennessee to care for your ill grandmother when no one else wanted to. You earned two degrees and are on your way to earning your third. You are the new principal of an entire school, and you aren't even thirty yet! I'd say those are accolades that anyone would be proud of."

"Thanks, Mom. And thank you for letting me come back home and stay here with you."

"I wouldn't have it any other way, honey," she said, kissing my hands. "It's been fun having you back, and I hope you'll stay here as long as you need to."

I smiled and kissed her hands back. "I'm going to head up to bed if you don't mind. I'm exhausted."

"Of course," she said. "I'll probably be heading to bed soon myself."

"I only did a quick rinse, so there should be plenty of hot water left for you if you need."

"Thank you, sweetheart. Good night."

It was still pretty early, but I could barely keep my eyes open. I brushed my teeth and hopped into bed, turning my phone on to try to watch a little something before I passed out.

"Caleb," I heard my mom's voice yelling up the stairs, pulling me from my slumber.

I rubbed my eyes while I adjusted to the light that was pouring into my bedroom from my mother flinging my door open. I knew something had to be seriously wrong because she wasn't the type to enter unannounced, and certainly not like that.

"Caleb, get up! We have to leave right now," she said, grabbing my jeans that were hanging on the desk chair and flinging them across the room at me.

"Geez, Mom," I said, pulling them off my head and jumping out of bed. "What's going on?"

My mother looked like a maniac. Clothes were flying from every direction. T-shirts, basketball shorts, socks, flip flops, and sneakers. I drew the line when a pair of boxers whipped me across the face, stinging my cheek.

"Mom!" I exclaimed, finally breaking her out of her psychosis. "What is going on?"

Her chest rose and fell with a quickness, and I reached over and gently placed her hands in mine. "Mom, breathe," I said softly.

She took one long, deep breath and cleared her throat. "Becky just called me. The barn is on fire, and we need to get over there and help put it out."

I threw on my jeans, a T-shirt, and my old running shoes and flew down the stairs. I grabbed the keys and ran out the front door, leaving it open for my mom and calling out behind me for her to just leave it unlocked. Grace Valley was a safe town, and at that point, nothing mattered but saving the farm.

I remembered nothing about the drive over there. I couldn't even tell you who was there, where I parked, or if I actually even drove. All I remember was running down the meadow to Dooley and racing into that barn to save Darb, the only horse that remained inside.

The second I entered the barn, the smoke began to burn my eyes, making it difficult for me to see. I'd been in there thousands of times before, but with all the smoke, I couldn't figure out where I was going. I was panicking while trying to remain calm, an unlikely feat for anyone. I felt around for the stall doors, and I heard the wood blazing behind me, popping and crackling. I kept running throughout the barn, dodging pieces of the roof that were burning and falling to the ground and hoping that would find Darb.

I could hear muffled yelling from outside—people calling my name—but I wasn't leaving that barn without Darb. He saved my life, and now it was time to repay the favor. Something dropped from the roof and landed on my shoe, immediately catching my pants on fire. I smacked at it until it stopped burning and put my hands above my head, afraid of whatever else might fall. The smell of my entire life burning to the ground was gut-wrenching, but I wasn't about to turn back now.

"Darb," I cried out, praying with everything I had inside me that he would make some noise, indicating where he was.

I waved my hands in front of my face, hoping to remove some of the smoke and create a path clear enough for me to see. It only seemed to make things worse. I kept tripping over random objects in my way, and I was beginning to lose hope. *We're both going to die in here.* Someone—or something—must have been looking out for us both, because just when I was ready to throw in the towel, I heard him whinny to my left.

I flung myself into his door, landing in a pile at the foot of it. I reached my hands up along the side of his stall, trying to regain my balance. I finally found the metal latch but kept fumbling with it. It was burning my hands, and no matter how hard I tried, I couldn't get it to open. I knew his stall inside and out, and I raced around to the other side to grab the broom I kept propped up to clean his stall when I came to visit. I flipped the broom over and tried to use the handle to shimmy the latch, but it was too big to fit into the tiny space. I was almost out of ideas when it hit me.

Darb, I really hope you're at the back of this stall right now.

I attempted to kick the door, but I was failing with every shot I took. I rushed backward, took a deep breath, and with all of my might, raced into the door shoulder first, falling to the ground with it. Darb's tail brushed along the side of my face as he ran by me, and hopefully, out of the barn. I rushed back up to my feet and tried to follow him, but the smoke was crushing my lungs. I crawled as far as I could before I attempted to get up again. It was dark outside, but I could see the lights on the fire trucks, and I ran to the door, tripping over my feet.

Just as I was almost there, I heard a loud crack, and then I was knocked out.

15

LEAH

I HAD NEVER SEEN MY DAD DRIVE SO FAST. HE FOLLOWED THE rules, never going above or below the speed limit. He stopped at every stop sign for the full three seconds you're supposed to and always let someone go in front of him, even if he needed to be somewhere. Tonight, he was someone else. There were only three stoplights in all of Grace Valley, and he blew through every single one of them. I held onto my *Oh, Jesus! handle,* and I swear my life flashed before my eyes.

"Dad, you have to slow down," I said through clenched teeth. "Getting into an accident is not going to help the situation."

"It's fine, Leah," he said, clutching the steering wheel so tightly his knuckles were as white as chalk. "I need to help Dooley."

We were quickly approaching the fifth stop sign he would inevitably fly right past when I yelled, "Dad, stop!"

He slammed on his breaks as the sirens blared and the fire truck passed us in the opposite direction. "What the hell? Where are they going?" he shouted.

"Probably away from you and your irresponsible driving," I muttered.

"Now is not the time, Leah," he scolded.

We got to the farm in four minutes, though it was a ten-minute drive on a good day. The smaller barn in the meadow was the one up in flames.

Jackie and Becky hugged each other and cried while Bill, Marina, and Melanie Palmer tried to hose down the barn as best they could. Dooley paced back and forth, yelling and holding his head. We parked and raced over to them just as we saw Tammy running toward the barn and Dooley grabbing her, pulling her away from the flames. I couldn't hear what he was saying, but as soon as Tammy saw me, she shoved Dooley away and fell into my arms.

"Tammy, what the hell is going on?"

"Caleb's in the barn," she told me through broken breaths.

"What?" I immediately began to panic. "Why is he in there?"

"Darb is in there," Becky said, coming from around Tammy and gently pulling her into her arms. "Dooley tied him up after a ride this afternoon and hadn't gotten around to transferring him to the other barn."

"Oh my gosh! Darb!" I said, adrenaline pumping through my veins. "I'm going in there."

"No, you're not," Tammy said, her voice soothing and positive. "Caleb will be out in a minute. Hopefully, the firefighters will be here by then."

"We saw them on the way here," I told her. "They were going the other way. They're not coming."

Just then the horse ran out of the barn and into the meadow. But where was Caleb? It had been at least five minutes at this point, and I was preparing myself for the worst. A loud crack pierced the air, and the back of the barn crashed to the ground, the front of it barely hanging on. Through all the smoke, I could faintly see Caleb limping out of the barn. He was coughing, and before anyone could reach him to help him walk out, the last

Full of Grace

beam dropped, slamming Caleb to the ground. Dooley, Bill, and my dad rushed to him and tried desperately to get him out from under the burning beam, but it was too heavy.

They didn't ease up, determined to save him. But just as I was about to lose hope, the fire truck blared through the meadow and began to spray the barn. It took three additional firefighters to get the beam off Caleb. No doubt broken, but he was still breathing. I feared the smoke would do too much damage to his lungs, and I found myself sitting in the meadow crying and praying.

Why had I walked away from him in the gazebo? He was right; he didn't owe me anything. I was so quick to judge him for not telling me about her sooner, but not once did I tell him how I felt about him. I kicked him out of my office, and then I walked away from him, again, just like I had the summer we broke up.

An ambulance quickly made its way next to the fire truck, and I was so afraid that history was about to repeat itself. The same meadow and the same group of people.

I couldn't watch as Tammy hopped into the back of the ambulance and went with Caleb to the hospital. I didn't want to imagine her saying goodbye to her husband and her child in the same place, twenty years apart. The rest of us stayed and stared at the barn, hoping that everything was going to be all right. By the time the firefighters had it put out, the entire thing had burned to the ground.

I looked over at Dooley, and he was crying in my dad's arms. I couldn't imagine the pain he was in right now. His family's legacy, gone. And the guilt he must be feeling over Caleb . . . I just sat there, alone, not knowing who to go to or what to say. I felt as though tragedy was following us again. It was more than I could take, and I broke down in the middle of the field.

Someone gently touched me on my shoulder, and I looked up to see Becky's grief-stricken face.

"We can rebuild it," she said. "New life can come from this. We mustn't cry."

I looked at her, wondering how she could be so positive in the middle of this nightmare. But I got it. The barn could be rebuilt. A horse's life was saved.

The horse was alive, but was Caleb?

I didn't want to think that God would play such a cruel trick on us all and take him too. Tammy had lost everything. Caleb and the diner were all she had left, and I couldn't bear the thought of her losing him.

I stood up slowly, brushing ash off my sweats, and I leaned in so I could hug Becky. Being in her arms calmed me and allowed me to see things more clearly. I prayed Caleb was all right. I prayed for Dooley and his family; for the horses and the students that rode them. I prayed for anyone and anything that I could in that moment. And I prayed for myself. I prayed for the strength to lift this family back up and provide them with some sort of comfort. We all had a long road ahead of us, but together, we would be able to rebuild.

Becky and I walked back over to the group, and I stood next to my dad. He put his arm around my shoulder and rested his chin on my head. We stayed like that for a while before everyone started to head home. They vowed to meet back up in the morning to assess the damage in the daylight, but I couldn't go home. I wanted—no, I needed to see Caleb.

When my dad and I arrived at the hospital, Tammy was pacing the waiting room, her eyes puffy. She looked defeated. She tilted her head to the side, and her lip began to quiver at the sight of us.

"Oh, Tammy," I said, rushing toward her and enveloping her in my arms.

We stood there for a few moments, me holding her, and her holding onto the hope that her only child would be okay. It felt like hours before someone finally came out to talk with us. By that time, we were all impatiently waiting and exhausted. The doctor called Tammy over to him, and he spoke to her in a hushed voice that we were unable to hear. I watched as her shoulders slumped, and she began to cry, the doctor gently reaching out a hand to her shoulder. Tammy stood up, nodded, and walked toward us while the doctor disappeared through the double doors back to where he came from.

"He's going to be fine," she cried out, collapsing into a chair next to where my dad and I were sitting. "My baby is going to be fine."

"Oh, thank God," my dad said, walking around the chairs and rubbing Tammy's shoulders. "What do you need? What can we do?"

"Go home and get some rest," she ordered. "I'm going to wait here until he wakes up."

"Do you need any food? Clothes? Anything you need, I'll go get for you," I told her.

She looked up at me and half smiled. "I'm okay, Leah. But thank you."

I glanced to my father, who nodded toward the door, and we gathered our things to leave. As I approached the exit, I took a peek back toward Tammy just in time to see her sink into the chair and close her eyes. I hoped she would get some rest, too.

16

CALEB

"Where am I?" I asked, my eyes darting around the room in confusion.

Someone reached over and gently squeezed my hand, rubbing their thumb softly across my knuckles. I tried to turn my head to see who it was, but the pain was unbearable.

"No, no," my mom's gentle voice said in a whisper. "You stay put. I'm here with you."

"Mom?" I asked. "Where am I? Why can't I move?"

"Caleb, do you remember the fire at the Butlers' farm?" she asked.

I tried to nod, but my head felt like it was going to explode. "Yes," I answered.

"You must have been trying to run back out of the barn when a beam fell and landed on you, honey," she said. "But you're okay. You're in the hospital, and everyone here is taking wonderful care of you."

I looked up and down my body—as much as I could see without moving my head—and my arms were covered in bandages. I felt as if I'd been run over by a tractor-trailer and left for dead. My arms were in a level of pain I'd never felt before,

Full of Grace

and I was afraid to see what was under all the gauze. I couldn't move the rest of my body.

"Mom," I choked out. "Am I paralyzed?"

I tried to look at her, to see her face and examine her expression. I was afraid to try, but I did. And thank God they moved. I was still afraid of what her answer was going to be.

"Oh, Caleb," she said softly, rubbing my hand again. "You're going to be just fine. You suffered a minor concussion, and you have some burns, but you're not paralyzed. The doctor will explain everything to you when he comes back in."

"Burns?" I asked. "Wait, is everyone else okay? Darb? Did he get out?"

"Well, you didn't run into a burning building for that baby to not be okay, now did you?"

Relief flooded my veins. Those horses meant everything to Dooley, and without them, his training facility wouldn't be able to operate. The doctor and nurses came in.

"Good morning, Caleb." The doctor flipped open the manila folder containing my patient chart. "I'm Dr. Miller. Glad to see you're awake."

"Barely," I tried to joke.

"I'll bet," he said. "These are your two nurses for the day—Brandon and Jess. They'll be checking in on you throughout the day. If you need anything, just press your call button, and they'll be right in."

"Hi, Caleb," one of the nurses said. "I'd ask how you're doing, but I think we all know the answer to that already."

I know that voice.

"Jess?" I asked, squinting. They must have taken out my contacts because everything was a bit blurry.

Leah and I had hung out with Jess and her boyfriend, Matt, all through high school. Unfortunately, they broke up about a year after we had due to their college distance. I always knew she would end up in a career that helped others.

"I came in this morning a few hours after you arrived, but you were sleeping," she told me. "You're looking a little bit better, if that helps."

From the blurry looks on everyone's faces, I probably didn't want to look in a mirror anytime soon. I wasn't a self-absorbed man by any means, but I always tried my best to make sure I looked and felt good. I took decent care of myself, ate right, tried to work out, and ran occasionally. I'd even tried yoga to clear my mind after I broke up with Brittany. It turned out leaving her was all the clarity I needed.

"Caleb," Dr. Miller said. "I just want to run a few more tests, and then you'll be able to rest."

"Great," I said. "Um, am I able to walk?"

The doctor laughed lightly. "You should be fine, but we will wheel you out of here regardless."

"Oh, that won't be necessary," a voice came from the door. "I'll just throw him over my shoulder and carry him out. Throw him in the bed of the pickup like the old days."

"Matt," I said. "What the hell are you doing here?"

Jess raised her left hand and wiggled her ring finger.

"Wait, you two are engaged? I didn't even know you were dating again," I said.

"Well, now you know," Jess teased. "We started back up after you left for Tennessee, so it's been quite a while now."

"Wow, sorry, guys," I said, slightly embarrassed for not fully keeping in touch. "I had no idea. Congratulations!"

"Thanks, man," Matt said, wrapping an arm around Jess's waist.

"Excuse me," Dr. Miller said, directing his gaze to Matt. "She's on the clock."

"Oh, right. Sorry about that," he said with a smirk. "Just

wanted to drop off some food for her for lunch. I knew Caleb was here, so I wanted to say hi."

My mom just shook her head and looked back toward the doctor. "I assume my boy will be on bed rest once he's discharged?" she asked.

"Yes," Dr. Miller said. "However, that won't be for a few more days."

"Days?" I sat up quickly in the bed and winced in pain.

"Just take it easy, Caleb," he said. "I'd like you to really focus on taking care of yourself. Your burns are second-degree and should heal easily. You won't even know they were ever there. However, I want you to stay for observation because of the concussion and swelling in your brain."

"Yes, sir," I said. *This ought to be fun.*

Jess smiled and walked over to the right side of my bed. "I just need to check your vitals."

It was nice to see her in her professional element. She checked my temperature, my blood pressure, and my pulse and then put some clip thing on my finger that was supposed to check my breathing.

"All right," she said. "Everything looks great. I will pass along this information to the doctor and let you get back to resting. I hope to never see you in this hospital again, Caleb Patterson."

"You and me both." I laughed.

"I'll be back in about an hour or so to check on you again."

"Thanks, Jess," my mom said. An exhausted smile crossed her face, but it seemed forced.

"It was nice seeing you, Tammy," Jess said and walked out of my room.

"Mind if I stop by your house when you get out of here?" Matt asked me. "Keep you company for a bit."

"That sounds great," I answered, rolling over in bed as I tried to get comfortable.

As nice as this little high school reunion was, I was ready to be alone and back to my resting. My body was shot, my ego shattered, and I really just wanted to ask my mom more details about the accident. The last thing I remembered was unlatching the gate to the horse stall and then waking up here.

"Mom, what happened to the barn? Is everyone else all right?"

"Let's not talk about that now, dear," she said. "Let's just focus on you getting some rest and getting out of here so I can feed you some real food."

I didn't like that answer. It left me feeling like something horrible had happened, and I wasn't the only one who was hurt. I knew she was trying to protect me, but I wasn't a little boy anymore.

"Mom, tell me what happened," I urged.

"The barn is gone, honey," she whispered. "Burned to the ground."

I stared at her, waiting for her to continue. "What about Dooley? Is he okay?"

"Yes. Everyone that was there is fine," she finally answered me. "No one else went into the barn, and the fire department came and tried to extinguish the fire. Unfortunately, the barn was so old that it just didn't make it."

"I need to get out of here," I demanded. "I need to get over to Dooley's and see what I can do to help. I'm handy. I can frame it out and help rebuild it. Get me out of here!"

I could barely move without my body feeling like it was going to fall apart. My mom seemed to know that because she sat there as calm as can be, just stroking my hand.

"We'll go back to the meadow when you're able to go out again, dear," she said. "I promise."

Full of Grace

I sighed loudly. I didn't like not being able to offer any help, and I sure as hell didn't like the thought of being confined to my own home as a grown-ass man. I guessed it was better than being stuck in the hospital room, but what the hell was I going to do alone for two weeks?

"How long was I sleeping for?" I asked my mom.

"About fourteen hours I would say." Her lower lip started to quiver and she leaned forward, resting her head in her hands. "I knew you would be all right, but I wasn't sure about the severity of your burns until about an hour ago."

"You haven't been here alone since last night, have you?" I asked, eyeing her in last night's clothing.

"I've been here the whole time," she answered. "What kind of question is that, Caleb? Do you think I would be anywhere other than by your side?"

I smiled. "Wouldn't expect anything less."

"Dooley and Becky came very early this morning. They were so worried about you, and even though I told them you were fine, they wouldn't take my word for it. I think Paul is going to stop by again later," she told me.

"How does Paul know about what happened?" I asked her.

"They were there too," she told me.

"They?"

"Paul and Leah," she said matter-of-factly. "They were here with me last night, too. They stayed until the doctor told us you were going to be okay."

"Oh." I was so fixated on Darb that I hadn't noticed anyone else at the meadow.

Oh no! I was supposed to meet Leah for mini golf and to talk.

17

LEAH

I WAS AFRAID I WOULDN'T BE ABLE TO GET ANY SLEEP BECAUSE my mind was racing. But I took a hot bath when I got home and climbed into bed anyway. As I curled into a ball, wrapped my comforter around me, and closed my eyes, the tears began to fall unapologetically, and I fell into a deep slumber.

I woke up to the sun beating down on me and the birds chirping. I lay in bed for a while, looking at my ceiling and reliving the night before. One minute we were having a nice glass of wine on the porch, and the next minute I was watching Caleb get rushed to the hospital in an ambulance.

"Knock, knock," my dad said quietly. His tapping barely made a noise on the door.

"Morning," I said with a forced smile.

"You hungry? I made blueberry pancakes."

"Not really, but I'll come down anyway. Let me throw some sweats on."

He quietly closed the door, and I rolled back over, flinging the comforter over my head. I wanted to stay like that all day, but that wouldn't help anything. *Ugh!* I sat up in bed and looked around the room before I finally got up. My clothes were strewn across my bedroom floor, and I sighed while I picked them up and threw them in the hamper. I never left anything on the floor, but I could barely see through my tears the night before, so I had just left them there.

I caught a glimpse of myself in the mirror as I walked by my dresser, placing my jeans in the hamper. My eyes were puffy and bloodshot. I didn't think I had been crying that long or hard, but I looked like a mess. My throat burned from all the smoke, and the lingering smell clung to every part of me. I opened my window to let some fresh air in and found a clean pair of sweats. I grabbed my hamper and headed downstairs to the laundry room. If I could get some laundry done, I would at least feel somewhat productive.

"Coffee is ready and piping hot," my dad said, poking his head into the mudroom.

"Thanks, Dad," I said. "Let me just throw this load into the wash, and I'll be right in."

It was barely eight a.m., and I already felt like I'd been up for hours. The weight of the world hung on my shoulders, bringing me further and further down. I needed caffeine to, hopefully, feel somewhat normal again. Dad had the food and the French press in the middle of the table, an empty plate in front of him, and an empty mug at my spot along with a bottle of Bailey's.

"It's too early for liquid lunch, so how about beverage breakfast?" he asked, nodding at the Bailey's.

A shot of Bailey's in a hot cup of coffee was one of the world's greatest treats. I discovered it when I was studying for finals in college, and it became a tradition at the end of every semester. It held just enough kick to curb my anxiety without making me feel like I partied all night. I took a big sip and let the Irish cream burn going down my throat. *You're right, Dad. Definitely makes things easier.*

"So, um, have you heard from Dooley?"

"Yes, he called me earlier this morning. The barn is gone. We're going to help him rebuild and give him the business he's dreamed of. It's the least we can do," he said, not looking up from his pancakes.

"I'll help. I can do a lot of work from home, so I'll head over there as soon as he's ready for some help."

He finally looked up at me. "He would love that."

He stabbed at his pancake again and paused, looking from his pancake to his empty mug, his eyes finally resting on the bottle of Bailey's. "Hand me that, would you?"

Smiling, I slid the bottle across the table. "Just a little."

"I have nowhere to be today," he said, pretending to pour a heavy amount into his cup.

I swallowed another large sip of my coffee and chewed on my bottom lip.

"Something you want to say, pumpkin?" he asked, reading me like an open book.

Embarrassed, I stuck my fork into the stack of pancakes and put one on my plate. *Maybe if I start eating, he'll stop asking me questions.*

"I take it that's a yes," he said, reaching out to hold my hand.

I quickly pulled my hand out from under his and placed it under my leg. "I'm fine."

"Leah, you can talk to me about anything, you know," he said. "It's okay."

I looked up at him, tears carefully teetering on the edge of my eyelids, ready to spill over any second.

"Have you talked to Tammy?" I managed to get out.

He gently placed his fork on the edge of his plate and crossed his hands. His expression was hard to decipher, and I wasn't prepared for what was going to come out of his mouth, good or bad. I couldn't hold my tears in anymore, and they slid down my cheeks, dripping onto my pancakes.

"Don't cry, pumpkin," he said. "Tammy called a bit after I got off the phone with Dooley. Caleb is still going to be okay. He has some burns on his arms and back, but they won't cause any serious scarring and should go away soon. He has a concussion and will have a pretty bad headache for a while. And surprisingly, there was no damage to his lungs from the smoke. He's gonna be fine. He must have had a few guardian angels looking after him."

I let out the breath I didn't realize I was holding and burst into tears. "Are you going to see him?"

"Tammy said they'll allow visitors this afternoon after the doctors perform a few more tests on him."

"A few more tests?" I questioned. "But I thought he was fine."

"Just as a precaution. They probably just want to double-check and rule everything out. Don't worry, pumpkin."

"I want to see him now." I wiped my mouth with the back of my hand, kissed my dad on the cheek, and headed for the door.

"Um, Leah? Forgetting something?" he called out to me.

"Oh yeah, keys! Thanks, Dad."

"No, pumpkin. You're in a pajama top and slippers. You might want to change."

"Oops," I said, biting my lower lip.

I ran upstairs and changed and was out of the door in a matter of minutes. The drive to the hospital was quiet. I wanted to think about what I would say when I got there. Even though my dad said Caleb was going to be fine, I couldn't help but think of the worst. I parked in one-hour visitation, assuming that this would be a quick visit, and went straight to his floor after checking in.

"Hey, Jess," I called out when I saw her walking toward me. "I didn't know you were working today."

"Yeah," she said, giving me a big hug. "I took an extra shift. Gotta save for the wedding."

I had been friends with Jess since the third grade when she moved to Grace Valley from the Midwest. We sat next to each other in science class and became fast friends. We were near inseparable when she started dating one of Caleb's best friends, Matt, in high school. The stories I could tell you about our friendship. Numerous sleepovers, Girl Scouts, proms, driver's ed—the list goes on. We reconnected when I moved back to Grace Valley, and it was nice to have her friendship back. I only wished we hadn't lost touch for so long after high school.

"I'm late for my rounds," she told me. "I'll see you later?"

"Call me," I suggested. "Maybe we can grab coffee soon."

She smiled and headed down the hallway in the opposite direction of where I was going. A part of me wished she was going to see Caleb as well because I hated being in a hospital. The smells. The sounds. The people. I had a really hard time seeing anyone in pain. I'd almost turned around and gone back home six times, but I knew in my heart that the right thing to do was check in on Caleb. I *wanted* to check on him. I needed to know he was okay, and I needed to see it with my own two eyes. There was too much history between us to potentially watch him almost die and then not visit him.

My heart raced so hard that I thought it might jump out of my chest.

"You gonna knock or just stand there all day, missy?"

I smiled softly at the old man who was sitting in a chair across the hall. He was bundled up in sweatpants, a brown turtleneck, and an oversized blue-and-brown cardigan. It always amazed me at how cold they kept hospitals. A nurse rounded the corner and took hold of the handles on the man's wheelchair.

"Come on now, Ed," she told him. "Let that young lady be."

I smiled at them and internally thanked him for boosting my morale.

I raised my hand and gently knocked.

Full of Grace

"Is it okay if I come in?" I asked.

I almost passed out when I saw Caleb lying in that hospital bed. I screamed and broke down on the inside, but I tried my hardest to maintain my composure on the outside. I couldn't understand how he could still look so damn handsome all wrapped up in bandages. I smiled at Tammy before she let herself out, giving us some space.

"I'm sorry," I said. "I should have called first. Do you want me to leave?"

Caleb sat up slowly in his bed, readjusting his position a few times before he answered.

"No, please stay."

My heart skipped several beats. I closed my eyes and sat down. I couldn't look at him. I didn't *want* to look at him. I'd loved this man my entire life and because we were both too stubborn to admit our true feelings, we still weren't together.

A single tear trickled down my cheek before landing just above my lips. I wanted to wipe it away, but another part of me wanted to keep the memory of this conversation on me for as long as possible. My brain and my heart were working against each other, and I didn't know what to say or do. I wanted to curl up beside him and go back to how we once were—connected, together—but we weren't kids anymore. We were adults with separate lives, and we had people who depended on us.

"Caleb," was all I could say.

"I am so sorry, Leah," he said, a tear rolled down his cheek this time.

Before I knew what I was doing, I was sitting next to him, our hands clasped together.

"No, I am," I rebutted. "It was so selfish of me to treat you that way. I had no right to be upset about your personal life."

"Water under the bridge."

He squeezed my hands gently and leaned his head on his

pillow. He looked exhausted, and I didn't want to keep him from his rest. I watched his eyelids slowly droop and his chest rise and fall in a relaxed rhythm. I kissed his hands and gently placed them on his stomach.

"Sweet dreams, Caleb," I whispered.

18

LEAH

The windows were rolled down, my hair whipped in the wind, and I was singing at the top of my lungs. And then the song changed. I couldn't tell you the name of it, but when that man started singing about the love of his life leaving him high and dry, I pulled over on the side of that highway and cried my eyes out. *Are you sending me signs again, Mom? Because if you are, please stop.* I knew if my mother were here right now, she would have me at his doorstep before he even got back from the hospital. She was a true pioneer of fate, and she would have told me off in the sweetest way possible.

But she wasn't here. And if she were, honestly, I probably wouldn't be in this mess. I probably would still be dating Josh and living in the city. My mother gave me so much when she was alive, but I couldn't begin to tell you how much she had given me after she left this earth. I flicked my hazards on, unbuckled my seat belt, and leaned backward in my seat. I stayed like that for a while and finally opened my eyes. Looking at the sky out of the sunroof, tears gently slid down my cheeks, pooling in my collarbone.

"What do I do, Mom?" I said to the sky, hoping she would hear me all the way up there and guide me somehow.

I picked at the skin on my thumb until it bled. *No man wants to hold a bloody mess of a hand, Leah.* But I couldn't stop picking. Somehow the tiny pings of pain from the skin leaving my fingers helped me forget some of the pain I felt over my encounter with Caleb. I knew he was the one, but I just couldn't bring myself to fall back into that only to get hurt again.

I leaned over and grabbed a handful of napkins out of my glove compartment and doused them with water from the bottle in my center console. I wiped my face and all remnants of desperation and got back onto the highway. Now was no time to be sulking.

Twenty minutes later, I was home and in my safe space. The crunching of the gravel in my driveway always made me smile. My dad pulled in seconds after me, and I could smell the aroma from the Chinese food from the driver's seat of my car.

I couldn't wait to curl up on the couch and have dinner. Eating in the den was never allowed growing up, so it was always a treat when Dad and I did.

"Food should be consumed at a table," my mother would always say. *"In a kitchen or dining room, not at a coffee table or those TV tray things you two always try to convince me to buy."*

I laughed to myself as I emptied the bags of food onto the coffee table and handed my dad his order.

"Thinking about how we're going to get in trouble for eating in here?" he asked me and chuckled.

I smiled back at him. "You know she's watching."

"I hope she is."

His eyes darted toward the bag of knitting needles and yarn that my mom kept next to the loveseat. I hadn't realized he left it there. I watched as he kept his focus on the bag and wondered how often he did that. I didn't know if he noticed me watching or

Full of Grace

if he realized what he was doing, but he quickly grabbed the remote and tossed it my way.

"Please be kind to me, Leah," he teased, knowing the likelihood of me picking another chick flick was relatively high.

"I was actually thinking about *The Breakfast Club*," I told him. "Does that meet your approval, Father?"

He tossed a balled-up napkin at me and threw his head back in laughter. "Yes," he replied, nodding his head.

I logged into my digital video account and scrolled until I found the movie. I hadn't seen it in ages, but it was a classic, and I couldn't wait to take it all in again. The ending, when Bender fist pumps the air, gets me every time. When I was younger, I swore I would marry him one day. And one time in NYC, when I was out to dinner with Sara and her parents, the actor who played him walked by us in the restaurant. I kid you not, I almost fell out of my chair. He looked back at me and smiled while I turned beet red and tried desperately not to crawl under the table.

My phone buzzed on the corner of the coffee table and fell to the floor.

"Here you go, pumpkin," my dad said after he reached down and retrieved my phone for me.

I didn't bother to look at the phone right away. I wanted to enjoy my night with my dad; whomever it was would have to wait. The movie ended, and I hoped to watch another with him.

"Another movie, Dad?" I asked, my eyes dancing like they did when I was a little girl and wanted chocolate that my mom said I couldn't have.

I always knew how to charm my dad into doing what I wanted, although I never really tried because we were pretty similar. Tonight, though, I just wanted to enjoy his company, so if I had to pull out all the stops, I would.

"Sure," he said, and my heart danced just like my eyes had

seconds before. "I'll grab a bottle of wine. Would you like popcorn, or are you full from dinner?"

"Wine and popcorn both sound great," I answered. "How about another eighties movie? *Sixteen Candles*?"

"Molly Ringwald fan tonight, eh?" he teased. "Works for me."

I was definitely born in the wrong decade. I knew it, my parents knew it, everyone around me knew it. I had been referred to as an "old soul" for as long as I could remember. When I was younger, I hated it because I didn't understand what it meant. But the older I got, the more I appreciated being a little bit different. I valued things on a different level, even when I was being an immature, spoiled pain in the ass. I could admit when I was wrong. Well, now I could. Before . . . not so much.

By the time I'd gotten the movie up and running on the TV, my dad was back with the popcorn and wine. I grabbed a blanket and a small bowl full of popcorn and snuggled up while my dad poured us some wine. He laughed as he sat on the love seat, propping his feet up on the matching ottoman that my mom forced him to buy because she refused to allow him to own a leather recliner like he wanted. *Such a weird request, Mom.*

"I still don't understand how it's June and you're curled up under a blanket like there's a blizzard coming," he said.

"I will never not have a blanket. In fact, I want to be buried with one. Preferably, also dressed in my comfiest sweats. I think I'll put that in my will."

"You are too much, Leah," he said, shaking his head. "Press play."

I fell asleep on the couch less than thirty minutes into the movie, and I woke up on the couch a few hours later. My dad must have covered me with the blanket because of the way it was draped around me. I was too tired and mentally drained to move, so I slept there the rest of the night. One perk about sleeping on the couch in this house was the pleasant aroma of freshly brewed coffee early in the morning.

I laid there for a few minutes before I got up and went into the kitchen. Dad wasn't there, so I poured myself a cup of coffee and went outside to sit on the swing. It was still pretty early, and the mornings were always so peaceful. Sitting on that swing and listening to the birds chirping, alone with my thoughts, brought me back to Caleb. I missed him. I wondered how he was holding up in the hospital, but I didn't want to call him and risk waking him. We fit well together and being with him made me realize how much of life I missed when I lived in the city.

A small pond sat at the back of our property just at the neighbor's line, where we used to swim in the summer while growing up. Two ducks floated across the water with their flock of babies in tow. I watched as what I assumed to be the mother duck kept carefully floating around to make sure all her babies were still following. Every so often, the other duck would gently waddle over to her and nudge her beak as if to say, "I love you. You're a great mother." It was a beautiful sight.

As I got up to refill my mug, I noticed a box on the porch by the front door. It must have been delivered after we came home yesterday because I didn't remember seeing it there last night. I didn't remember ordering anything, but these days, all it took was one click, and everything you could possibly need showed up on your doorstep. I placed my mug on the railing and sat back down on the swing to open the box. Inside was a smaller box with a journal and a beautiful pen. The note read, *"Just a little something to jot down all your dreams and wishes. This is only the beginning, my sweet friend. Love you always, Sara."*

Sara was the most thoughtful person I'd ever known. She always went above and beyond to make her loved ones feel special in the simplest of ways. I headed into the den to grab my phone to call her.

"Hey, girl!" Sara's voice shot through the phone as she answered on the first ring. "You're up early. Everything okay?"

I loved how easy it was for her to read me. I wasn't an early riser unless I had to be somewhere, and even then, it was tough for me to get out of my coziness. I liked my bed.

"I've been up for about an hour now," I told her. "Passed out on the couch last night after watching eighties movies with my dad."

"Oh, that sounds like fun," she said. "I miss your dad. How's he doing?"

"He's great. Some days I can see he's really missing Mom, but I think he's happy having me back home with him. Fills a void, you know?"

"Yeah, I can see that. I'm happy you're both doing well. How's work? I'm sorry I haven't been able to talk much. Work has been crazy busy lately."

"You don't have to apologize to me. I know how this game works, believe me. I've been up to my eyeballs in paperwork, but I wouldn't have it any other way."

"Yay! So everything is going well then?"

"I'm so busy and so happy. I couldn't have dreamed up a better work environment," I told her. "I've thanked Cameron about a thousand times at this point. I really don't know how to fully thank him for everything he's done for me. And I can't figure out just how I'm even worthy of such love and support."

"Oh no, something is wrong. I know you, Leah Abernathy, and you are not a self-deprecating person unless something isn't right. What gives?"

"I don't know what you're talking about," I said, smiling because she was right, but I wasn't ready to own up to anything.

"Mm-hmm," Sara responded. "Why'd you really call, Leah?"

I looked down at the box and remembered why—the journal. Maybe I could sidetrack this conversation with the journal talk, and then I wouldn't have to come to terms with the fact that I am petrified to fall in love again. *Yeah, right. She'll see right through it.*

"I just wanted to thank you for the beautiful journal," I said. "It must have been delivered yesterday, but I didn't notice it until this morning when I came out to the porch to have my coffee."

"You are very welcome, my dear," Sara said. "I know you prefer to write all of your thoughts on your laptop or the notes section of your iPhone, but I saw the cover of this and thought you might like to have something to actually put pen to paper with."

"It was a very pleasant surprise," I told her. "I love it and I'll definitely use it. Who knows? Maybe I'll start jotting down all your crazy antics and write a book about you."

"Very funny. You could start traveling the world and writing about your experiences. Travel agent turned traveler turned novelist. Your books would sell like hotcakes!"

"You're a mess," I said and laughed. "I barely even travel out of town, let alone the state or country. Dad and I were thinking about going to Italy in August to see my grandparents, but we haven't set anything up yet. I definitely think it's a possibility, though."

"Do it! And maybe I'll fly out for a day or two, and we can do some girlfriend sightseeing. I absolutely love Italy."

Sara was a world traveler. She grew up visiting all the top vacation spots at every school holiday or break. The stories she would tell me about her childhood were paralleled to celebrity children, but I was never jealous when she spoke. She never bragged or made anyone feel inferior. She genuinely just had a love for travel and couldn't help but tell you all about a place if it were ever brought up. I loved her for it, and I always looked forward to hearing about the next stop on her journey across the globe.

"I think we should plan this trip today. You've got me totally excited now!"

"Good," she said. "Now tell me what's really on your mind because I know it's not the damn journal. Is everything okay?"

"Yes, everything is okay," I told her, then let out a big sigh. "Caleb is in the hospital. He got hit by a beam trying to save a horse from a burning barn."

"Oh my goodness!" Her voice raised with each word. "Is he okay? Oh shit, Leah, I'm so sorry. Do you want me to come there? I think I can make the next train if I leave right now."

"It's barely eight a.m., and you sound like you're on speed. How much coffee did you have already? He's okay. He has a concussion and some second-degree burning on his arms. He'll be out of there sometime this week."

My phone started ringing in my hand, and I could see Sara was Facetiming me through our call. I smiled as I pressed the green button to answer.

"I can't imagine how scared you must have been," she said, her eyebrows drawing together. Something must have clicked in her brain because then her mouth opened and her eyes widened.

"Wait a minute," she said, wagging a finger at her phone camera. "Have you been spending time with Caleb?"

I bit my lower lip. "No, but we made plans to go mini golfing. That was derailed by the fire, though."

"Ahh!" she screamed. "This is fantastic! The plans, not the fire, clearly. I am definitely coming to see you soon because I need all of the details. You should do something for him. Like, bring the mini golf to him or something."

"How would that even be possible, Sara? Besides, he's going to need all the rest he can yet. He took a pretty bad hit."

She chewed on the tip of her finger and nodded, fully

immersed in the conversation. One could venture to say that she may have been more excited about the news than I was.

"I don't want to get ahead of myself, but I get butterflies whenever I'm around him. I know we haven't been together in years, but I see a future with him."

"I'm so excited for you, Leah," she said. "Does he feel the same way? Of course he does! Who am I kidding?"

"I just want to talk with him, and then we can see where things go."

"Live it up, girl!"

"All right, Sara," I said. "I should go shower and get ready for the day. I'll text you later."

"Bye, love," she said.

I had no idea what was going on with me and Caleb, but I was gonna roll with it. I opened up my new journal and began to write. It was scary yet oddly satisfying to put my inner thoughts to paper, and I hoped it was the beginning of something new and exciting. At the very least, it would be the world's best love letter.

19

LEAH

"Good morning, pumpkin," I heard my dad call from the kitchen doorway. "You're up bright and early today."

I smiled at him. "Are you heading to the farm? Mind if I hitch a ride?"

"No, not today," he told me. "Dooley has to meet with the insurance appraisers again, and then he'll let us know when we can lend a hand. I think I'm just going to head into town, though. You're welcome to join me."

"Oh yeah?" I asked. "What are you planning on doing?"

"I don't really know yet. I just felt like getting out and enjoying the fresh air. I might swing by the bakery for coffee and a donut. I do need to stop at the butcher for some steaks. Do you have dinner plans?"

I lived for little moments like these and how happy my dad was to include me in all of his plans. Sure, we were father and daughter, but the older I got, the more we became friends. Lately, I'd wished that my mother was still here because I knew once I had outgrown my stubborn phase, the three of us would have been thick as thieves once more. I missed her with every fiber of my being.

"I don't have plans," I told him. "I just figured I would go to the farm and take it from there, but I would love to join you in town. Do you have any interest in checking out that new bookstore on Main? I heard they were planning on doing monthly readings from local authors."

If I hadn't ended up in travel, I might have become an author. It was always a dream of mine to create something from nothing, and I loved to write. I'd never once mentioned my love of writing to Sara, yet she'd concocted this whole travel writer turned novelist idea for me. Maybe I'd start to write down everything that happened last year, and I'd see where that took me.

"Dad?" I asked when he didn't respond. "Everything okay over there?"

"Oh, yes," he said, shaking his head and looking up at me. "I'm sorry about that. I just zoned out for a bit there."

"You seem to be 'zoning out a bit' quite often, Dad," I said, worry spreading across my face. "Are you sure you're all right?"

"I'm fine, Leah," he said sternly, causing me to take a step back. "I've just had a lot on my mind lately, that's all. Would you like some breakfast, or did you want to grab something from Mrs. Kratz?"

If I'd learned anything over the years, it was knowing when to keep my mouth shut. My father wasn't the type to withhold information from me—aside from Caleb being back in town for good, but that was a whole other issue. I kept that little moment in the back of my mind and prepared to keep an eye on him. I'd have to have a discussion with him about going to the doctor.

"The bakery sounds great, Dad," I said, trying to smile and act like I wasn't becoming his keeper over morning coffee.

He nodded and walked out of the kitchen and down the hall without uttering another word. He paused when he reached his bedroom door, and his head slightly turned like he wanted to say something. But instead, he disappeared into the room. Something was wrong, and I was going to get to the bottom of it.

An hour had passed before my dad finally came out of his room. I was starving at this point, but if something was bothering him, I didn't want to make him feel any worse.

"You ready to head out?" I asked.

"Sure, pumpkin," he said, grabbing his house keys. "Let me just lock up, and we can be on our way. Did you feed Gnocchi by any chance?"

I nodded and walked outside. It was a gorgeous morning. The sun bounced brightly off the pond, reflecting in all the right places. I wished I had been up for the sunrise because I could only imagine the beauty it possessed at that hour. The O'Connors' canoe was wobbling back and forth gently in the water every time a small gust of wind blew. I couldn't believe that old piece of junk hadn't sunk by then. It was falling apart when I left for college, and it was in far worse shape now.

"That piece of junk is still around?" I asked my dad.

He started to laugh, and I was glad to see his spirits rise. "I keep telling them to get a new one, but they just keep plugging up the old holes. One day they're going to be fishing out there, and they'll sink right to the bottom! I sure hope they know how to swim."

Our walk to town was peaceful. We didn't talk much, but not because we didn't want to. The morning was so serene that we just wanted to take it all in. I'd become so accustomed to quick, loud, and busy morning walks to the office or the gym or brunch, that I'd forgotten towns and spaces like this existed. Even in Central Park during its quietest of hours, there was always someone around. But there was no hustle and bustle in Grace Valley, and I was thankful for that.

We got to town around nine, and I almost ran through the doors of the bakery. I was so grateful that Mr. Kratz had convinced Mrs. Kratz to put breakfast food on the menu. The diner was almost always packed through lunch, so it was nice to have another small place to grab a bite. Especially when I'd been up for hours and only had coffee corroding my stomach.

"Leah, my darling," Mrs. Kratz said, winking from the other side of the counter. "What a pleasant surprise. Paul, you as well."

"Good morning, Mrs. Kratz," we said in unison, and all three of us laughed.

"What can I get for you two this morning?" she asked us.

"I'll have a sausage, egg, and cheese on a Portuguese roll with a coffee, please," I told her. "With some room for milk too, please."

She nodded without writing a thing down. "And for you, Paul?"

"Hmm, you know, I think I'll have the same," he said. "Could you throw in an order of Mr. Kratz's hash browns?"

"Oh, good call, Dad. That sounds amazing," I said. "Me too, please!"

I don't know what Mr. Kratz did to those hash browns, but they were the best I'd ever had. And I had a lot. They were golden and crispy on the outside, but soft and chewy on the inside. Just a hint of spice and never too salty. They were right up there with a freshly baked bagel and a fresh-out-of-the-oven chocolate chip cookie. Mrs. Kratz handed us our coffees, and we went over to the milk and sugar bar to finish making them. I made my way over to our regular booth, and our food was already waiting for us. *Man, I love this place.*

"I really hope she never retires or closes this place down," I told my dad.

"Well, that's a wonderful thought, pumpkin," he said, unwrapping his sandwich. "But she is going to have to retire eventually."

"I know," I said. "Let's just hope that isn't for another decade or two."

I took a big bite of my sandwich and burned the roof of my mouth with the cheese. I was so hungry that I didn't even care; I just kept on eating. My dad stared at me in disbelief as he had only taken a few bites of his food, and I was already done.

"Worked up an appetite this morning?" he teased.

I smiled and grabbed some hash browns, putting them on my plate and dousing them with ketchup. I was contemplating ordering another sandwich, and then I saw Dooley walk in. I waved him over to us, and he came and sat next to me, tousling my hair.

"Oh, come on," I called out. "I'm twenty-seven years old, Dooley."

"Always a kid in my eyes," he said, his eyes sparkling with mischief.

"Glad to see you're back to your old self," I said, going back to my plate of hash browns.

"Paul, you mind swinging by the farm later this afternoon?" Dooley asked. "I'd like an outside party to be present when the appraiser comes. I don't think I can do this alone, man."

I'd never seen Dooley like this. Not even when his father passed when I was in high school. He was a walking disaster. His clothes were all wrinkled, and he was wearing two different shoes. I didn't mention anything because I knew he was already under an obscene amount of stress, but I was concerned for him. To him, losing the barn must have felt like losing a child, an extension of himself. The way he always spoke about the farm was uplifting and powerful. Right now, he just appeared to be confused and defeated.

"Of course," my dad replied. "You don't mind, do you, Leah?" he asked me with questioning eyes, as if I would ever mind him helping his friend.

"I'll go with you," I said. "That way I can start pulling some stuff together for when you're ready to rebuild."

Tears pooled in Dooley's eyes, and I gently reached over and placed my hand on top of his. I didn't need to say anything. He and I both knew just how important a simple gesture like that could be.

A short while after my mom had passed, Dooley stopped by to check in on us, but Dad had gone off to run some errands. I was sitting on the porch swing in the middle of a snowstorm, crying. Dooley sat next to me, pulled the fleece blanket up over my arms, and just stayed with me. He didn't talk, didn't question what I was doing out in the cold, or even try to get me to go back inside where it was warmer. He was hurting too. He had lost his friend, and the quiet comforted us both.

Now, he nodded and carefully removed his hand from under mine, as if he were afraid it would shatter against the table if he moved too quickly. He nodded his head up and down and rubbed his hand on his thighs before standing up.

"All right then," he said, unable to make eye contact. "I guess I'll see you two later. Around three-thirty, please."

"See you then, Dooley," my dad said as Dooley quickly made his way out of the bakery empty-handed.

THREE-THIRTY CAME a lot quicker than I had expected, and before I knew it, Dad was driving down the gravel road that led to the back entrance of the meadow. The sight of the destroyed barn took my breath away. It was burned to the ground with the exception of a few spots where the framing seemed to be holding on for dear life. Half-melted saddles lay in a pile along where the side wall used to be, and there were giant piles of roofing begging to be carried out.

I'd spent the majority of my life in that barn, and I couldn't contain my sorrow when I walked up to it that afternoon. I dropped to my knees and sobbed into my hands, not caring who saw me. I wasn't sure if it was from all the stress from the amount of work I threw myself into, or the fact that I just kept losing important people and places in my life. There was no coming back from this; not in the literal sense. Everything about this barn was gone except for the memories. And, shit, those might as well have just died along with the barn.

I wasn't sure how I had turned Dooley's loss into my own, but I knew I wasn't the only one affected by that devastation when my dad came and sat down next to me, pulling me in close to him.

"Let it out, baby girl," he said and kissed the top of my head. "This was a part of all of us."

I sat there for a few minutes until I heard the sound of a car engine slowly pulling up next to us. The appraiser had arrived, and she didn't look like someone who truly cared about what was lost. She wore a pantsuit and a no-nonsense expression that was more annoying than threatening. She was there to assess the damage and hopefully give Dooley the news he so desperately needed to hear, which was that he'd receive the insurance money so he could rebuild his livelihood.

She nodded a hello and roughly threw her hand in Dooley's direction.

"Good afternoon," she said boldly. "Mr. Butler, I presume?"

"You can call me Dooley," he replied.

"Mr. Butler, I'm here to assess the property damage from your unfortunate conflagration. I'll be with you in a few moments," she declared.

Once she was out of sight, we all turned and looked at each other.

"Conflagration?" Dooley said, dumbfounded. "Shit, just say fire. No need for formalities and SAT words. My goodness."

I couldn't help but laugh, and as soon as I did, she turned and looked me dead in the eye. I turned to look at my father and wait for her to finish her appraisal. The entire ordeal was over in less than twenty minutes.

"Thank you for your time, Mr. Butler," she said. "I can see that the damage to your structure is immense. You have been approved for the full amount requested, and you should receive the money in your account in five to seven business days. I'll send a messenger with the paperwork on Monday morning, and you can begin to rebuild then if you so choose."

I wasn't sure if that was how it usually worked, but it seemed easy enough and relatively painless. Dooley could start cleaning out at least, and with the town's help, maybe the process of rebuilding could start this week. She left quickly, and Dooley did his typical, goofy, happy dance.

"Oh man," my dad said with a laugh. "All right, shall we get out of here and start grilling some steaks?"

"Definitely," I said. My stomach had started growling an hour ago, and I wasn't sure I was up for waiting for another meal twice in one day.

20

CALEB

"Ugh," I groaned. "Get me out of here. I'm gonna turn gray laid up in this place."

I'd been in the hospital for five days at that point, and I was ready to get out and get my life back—even if that meant I was restricted to the inside of my house. I just couldn't stand being around all the beeps and bells and sick people any longer. I was ready to rip the literal, and metaphorical, Band-Aid off and head for the hills.

"Caleb, you'll be fine," my mom said, rolling her eyes. "And it's 'going to,' not gonna. I would expect far more from a principal."

I stared at her, not caring enough to respond in that moment. She wasn't the one wrapped in bandages.

"Okay, Mr. Patterson," the doctor said, walking to the end of my bed, clipboard in hand. "You are free to go. I just need you to please fill out the discharge papers the nurse will bring in momentarily, and you're all set."

"Great," I said, wanting to get out of bed but realizing I only had on a hospital gown. "Mom, could you please hand me my clothes?"

Full of Grace

"Oh," she said. "I have to run home and get you some new ones. Your clothes from the fire are in the washing machine. It should only take me about thirty minutes."

"It's fine, Mom. Thank you for taking them home to wash," I said. "I'll just go home in these. I don't care who sees my ass anymore."

I hope I'm wearing underwear.

The doctor chuckled and placed her hand on my knee. "You have time. Discharge papers won't be in here for about twenty minutes or so, and then they'll need to be processed. Hang tight. You'll be home before you know it."

She smiled and nodded before exiting the room. My mom placed a quick kiss atop my head and rushed out of the room to retrieve my clothing. It was easier being in here knowing that I would be gone within the hour. I was starving at that point and just wanted to be in my shorts in my own house. As I lay there daydreaming of leaving, the doctor walked back in.

"One more thing," she said, an apologetic but serious look on her face. "Per Dr. Miller's orders, you need to rest for a week. With your concussion, it's best to limit screen time, but I understand that's tough for some people to do. It's best if you stay put at your house. Understood?"

"Yes, ma'am," I said, sucking at my teeth.

As soon as she left, I started making a mental list of everything I needed to get done for work that could be done from home. Luckily, there was a lot of paperwork and planning that I had yet to start, so that would keep me plenty busy. *Maybe Dooley can tow the truck over to my house, and I could work on it in the garage. That's technically not outside, and it's also not using a screen. I'll have to call him. Where is my cell phone?*

As soon as I started thinking about that truck, I was in far better spirits. I loved that old beat-up piece of junk, and I was honored that Dooley thought I was worthy of fixing it up and keeping it. Growing up, I would always help him in the garage. He was so talented and could fix anything, and if he didn't know how, he would teach himself. They saved tons of money doing the house projects themselves.

After he passed, I continued to learn as much about fixing cars and home repairs as I could, and I've been able to fill his shoes and help my mom with things around the house. I actually made her TV stand and coffee table in the family room one year as a Christmas present. She'd wanted more of a farmhouse look, and I made it happen. Before going to Tennessee, I had contemplated making furniture for a living. But my mom reminded me that sometimes the things you did for fun could backfire when you were no longer enjoying the process. I still thought it might be a nice little side job one day.

I missed him. I missed him every single day, but for some reason, I missed him more that day. Maybe because my accident was in the very same place that he took his last breath. The last breath that he used to tell me he loved me. Not my mom. Not his friends. *Me*. It was something I cherished every day since, and I'd long ago learned to not feel guilty about. My father had done a great job of not only telling but also showing how deeply he cared for, loved, and respected me and my mom. I was lucky to have a mother who did the same. And I knew I would be the same kind of father and husband someday.

I looked out the window at my wonderful view of the parking garage and watched a little girl skipping alongside her father. Her pigtails bobbed with every step, and I could almost hear her giggle from the giant smile spread across her tiny face. It reminded me a bit of Paul and Leah when she was younger, and that thought alone made me happy.

"Okay, I'm back," my mother said breathlessly from the door. "I grabbed your basketball shorts, a T-shirt, boxers, socks, and your sneakers. I was going to get sweats because of the burns, but

I figured we would only be outside for a couple of seconds before we got into the car."

She handed me the stack of clothing and went to leave.

"Where are you going?"

"Just giving you a bit of privacy."

"Mom, I need a little help getting out of the bed."

"Oh, I see," she said. "Okay, honey, grab on to my hands."

I towered over her and weighed a considerable amount more than she did, and I was concerned I was going to hurt her. But I knew she was tougher than she looked. I was Bambi on ice trying to stand up. My legs were Jell-O, and I was almost completely out of breath before standing upright. I looked down and was thankful that I at least had boxers on.

"Mom," I said, looking at her in embarrassment. "I hate to ask you this but…"

"Yes, honey," she said, anticipating my question the way she always had. "I will help you get dressed. Here, why don't you sit on this chair? It will be easier for you to get your clothes on."

Having my mother dress me at twenty-seven years old was never something I thought would happen. I would have much rather had one of the nurses come back in and dress me rather than my mother. Before I could finish my inner monologue of complaining, which had rivaled any soap operas level of overdramatic whining, my mom was done and we were ready to head out.

"Thanks." I wrapped my arm around her shoulders lovingly, but also as a crutch so I didn't fall.

"Anytime," she said, stretching up to kiss my cheek. "But let's hope it doesn't happen again."

"Mom, do you mind swinging by the deli so I can grab a grinder on our way home?"

I was famished, and a deli sandwich always hit the spot. I also knew that if I was going to be stuck at home for a week, I could at least take a little detour and see the outside world. I wasn't an overly social man; I kept mostly to myself. But when I was forced to stay away from everyone, that was hard for me.

"Sure," she agreed. "But I'm going in, not you."

I smiled and nodded in agreement, knowing better than to put up a fight. And honestly, I didn't think I would physically be able to walk anywhere. My hands and forearms were sore, but my legs felt like they'd been run over.

About fifteen minutes later, we pulled into the deli's parking lot. We weren't in Grace Valley, so I estimated we would be home in another forty-five minutes or so. My mom was in and out of the deli quickly.

"Mom, what the hell did you buy?" I asked her, my eyes widening as I tried to hide my laughter.

"What? It's just a few bags of snacks for you," she said, smiling and placing them in the back seat.

"Three bags of snacks? How long am I supposed to be holed up for? Months? Years?"

"Well, I ordered a few sandwiches just in case. Got some pasta salad, macaroni salad, and fruit salad. Some chips and dip and a few bottles of ginger ale, since the doctor said your meds might make you nauseous."

"Geez, Mom. You realize I'm only one person, right?"

"Yes, you ungrateful brat," she teased, tousling my hair. "I'll be home for dinner and thought I would barbecue some chicken. We can eat the salads with that."

I would much rather have too much food than not enough, but this was going a bit overboard, even for my mother.

"Do you mind if I eat in the car?" I asked her, knowing damn well she would say no.

Surprisingly, she agreed. *She must feel bad for me.*

I ate my sandwich in silence, enjoying the drive and company. Time flew by, and soon we were back home, unloading the food. The boys next door were playing in their yard, and they smiled and waved when we got out of the car. That would have been the perfect time to toss the ball around with them, but that wasn't a possibility. I looked over at the garage and remembered I needed to call Dooley about the truck.

"Hey, Mom?" I asked. "Do you know what happened to my cell phone?"

"You left it at home when we went to the farm, dear," she told me. "I put it on the charger when I came home for your clothes."

I would be lost without her.

21

CALEB

I WALKED RIGHT INTO THE HOUSE AND DIRECTLY UPSTAIRS. I needed to shower badly, but I was afraid to get my arms wet and opted for a bath. I never took baths. When was the last time you saw a six-foot-three man in a regular-sized bathtub soaking it all up? Exactly. I ran the water as hot as I could handle and stripped down. I lowered myself into the tub, careful to not let my arms fall into the water. I was lucky and had only suffered minor burns on my forearms, but I didn't want to chance anything. I sat and soaked in the tub until the water turned cold. I needed to feel the water cleanse my soul as well as my body.

Redressing was a chore in itself and took quite a while. By the time I was finished with everything and made my way downstairs, it was nearing dinnertime. I found my phone on the charger and dialed Dooley's number. He picked up on the first ring, and his voice boomed through the phone as if he hadn't had a huge catastrophe just hit his family.

"Caleb, my man," he exclaimed. "Glad to hear your voice. How are you holding up?"

"Sup?" I said, running my fingers through my desperate-for-a-trim hair. "I'm okay. Really sore, but I'll be fine."

"I talked to your mom earlier," he told me. "I wanted to stop by the hospital, but she said you were sleeping and would be coming home today. Are you home now?"

"Yes, I'm home," I said. "I have to stay inside for a week. Doctor's orders. Sucks, but what can you do?"

"What can we do for you?" he asked, like he didn't already have enough on his plate. "I'm sure your mom has you covered with food, but we can drop off anything you need. I can stop by with some beers when you're ready for company."

"Thanks, Dooley," I said. "I appreciate that. Hey, um, did Darb get out of the barn?"

"He did," Dooley said, his voice softening. "You saved his life. I'm forever grateful."

I slowly sat down on one of the kitchen chairs, my elbow landing on the table while resting my head in the palm of my hand. Hearing that Darb was going to be fine made this entire quarantine completely worth it. The barn could be rebuilt. My body was still intact, albeit badly bruised and extremely sore. But if anything had happened to Darb, I don't know if I would have been able to forgive myself. He was irreplaceable, and we all knew it. He was a part of me.

"Oh, thank God," I said, a tear rolling down my cheek.

I'd always been a sensitive, in-tune-with-my-feelings kind of guy, but ever since I returned to Grace Valley, my emotions seemed more intense. To be honest, I wasn't sure if I liked this version of me or not. I assumed it was something I was going to have to get used to, and it certainly didn't bother any of the people who surrounded me, but it was still a bit off for Caleb Patterson. Perhaps this was a part of my new beginning.

"Not even a scratch on him," Dooley told me. "He was lucky you threw yourself in there for him."

"I'd do anything for that horse," I said. "Anything."

"I know," he said softly. "Hey, listen, I know you're itching to get over here, but we won't be able to start working on anything for a few more days. You're welcome to come by after your sentence is up."

"Funny," I said. "Warden Tammy is cracking the whip, and we all know not to mess with her."

"I'm going to call her that from now on," he said with a laugh. "That's a good one."

"Hey, Dooley," I said. "Do you think you could tow the truck over to my house for me? I'm not supposed to be outside, but I could work on it in my garage."

"Yeah, I think I can make that happen," he said. "You good with waiting a couple of days for it? I have some things to do with the barn first."

"Of course," I said, grateful he was willing to put in the work to get it here. "That'll give me some time to rest."

"All right, man," Dooley said. "You take care, and I'll see you in a few days. Call us if you need anything."

"Thanks," I said. I hung up the phone, my eyes searching the kitchen for my meds.

I was getting a killer headache, and my body was throbbing all over. These two weeks were not going to be relaxing at all. I stood up and hit my head on the kitchen chandelier. *Who moved the table?* My hand quickly rose to rub the egg forming on the left side of my head, and my eyes landed on the paper bag from the pharmacy. I reached for the bag and a bottle of water and swallowed my pills. I could have rested on the couch, but my bed was calling my name.

"Hi, honey," my mom said, quietly closing the door behind her and dropping her keys in the bowl by the door. "You almost ready for dinner?"

"I just took my meds, and I think I'm going to lie down in my room for a bit," I told her. "I'm not feeling too hot right now."

"Okay," she said and kissed my forehead. "I'll come check on you in a bit and bring you some food if you're awake. Are you sure you don't want to try to eat anything now?"

"I'm all right," I told her. "Thank you."

She smiled and nodded, understanding that my body couldn't handle much at the moment and rest was the best thing for me. My pills said I shouldn't take them on an empty stomach, but my appetite had all but diminished. I felt like I might be sick if I ate anything. I walked up the stairs to my room slowly, holding onto the railing and hoping I didn't fall backward. I didn't know what was going on with me, but as soon as I got to my room and closed the door, I collapsed into my bed and didn't wake up until morning.

I didn't get out of bed right away. I was afraid the second I moved, I'd be in excruciating pain again, and I didn't feel like dealing with that. When I finally started to move, I did so slowly until I realized my body wasn't as sore and stiff as it felt last night. I rubbed my eyes and noticed my door had been cracked open a bit—Mom had been here. I desperately needed food and coffee, and I hoped my mom was home so I could make up some of the time I missed when I blew her off for dinner the night before.

Before I could stand, there was a light knock on the door, and the pleasant aroma of a freshly brewed cup of coffee filled my room. My mother's voice soon followed.

"Rise and shine, sleepyhead," she said, opening the door further. "Oh, you're already awake, dear. Here, I made you some coffee."

She smiled as she handed me the mug and then took a few steps back. She was never the crowding type, and I appreciated that about her.

"Thanks, Mom," I said and took a big sip. "You mind if I take this downstairs? I'm starving."

She nodded her hear toward the door, and I followed her

downstairs. You would have thought she was feeding an army with the amount of food scattered across the kitchen table. Scrambled eggs, sausage, bacon, pancakes and waffles, oatmeal, toast, and a fruit salad.

"Mom." I shook my head. "You're insane."

She threw her head back and laughed so hard tears started to form in her eyes. I hadn't seen her this free in years, and the infectious sound caused me to follow suit. Pretty soon, we were both laughing and crying and clutching our stomachs. Talk about working up an appetite.

"When my boy needs food, I make sure he has it all," she said, tousling my hair like I was a child.

I grabbed a piece of toast and shoved it into my mouth before I started piling the food onto my plate. This wasn't the norm, but if she kept feeding me like this, I was going to need to do two-a-days at the gym or else I'd be rolling into work come fall. I ate like my life depended on it, but it's true what they say—a good meal feeds your stomach and your soul.

I cleaned the kitchen after we ate so my mom could get some things done around the house. I never minded helping out when I was a kid. I'd watched my dad pick up his fair share of the responsibilities, and I was taught to always pitch in regardless if it was my mess or not. However, it felt different this time. I was the man of the house then, but now, I was actually a man. It was my duty and no longer my chore.

"Okay, sweetie," my mom said, walking out of her bedroom and twisting her hair up into a bun. "I have to run a few errands in town, but I'll be back in a few hours. There's plenty of food in the fridge if you get hungry, although I don't know how that could be possible."

"All right," I said. "I'll be here doing nothing."

"You better not do anything, Caleb," she said, her eyes like lasers shooting into me. "The doctor said you needed to rest."

"Yes, Mother," I said, smiling sweetly. "I know."

She kissed me goodbye, and as soon as the door closed, she opened it up again to check on me. I was still standing in the same spot and just laughed, turned, and walked away. I had no idea what I was going to do for the next week. *Please bring that damn truck, Dooley.* I walked around the house hoping something would come to me soon. I was already bored, and it had barely been a day. Somehow, I found myself in the guest room, staring at the unbelievable number of bins.

Hmm . . . I wonder what old jewels I could find in here.

The first few boxes were just old movies and CDs—nothing crazy, and quite honestly, kind of boring. The next box I opened was filled to the brim with my old Playstation and an insane number of games. *Oh, jackpot! Definitely setting this up.* I played the shit out of those games when I was younger. I don't know how they even survived all those years. High school sports memorabilia, some of my childhood photo albums, and a bunch of crap that I hadn't ever seen before but I assumed was to be donated filled more of the bins I went through.

Finally, my eyes landed on a bin that was shoved all the way to the back. I opened it and peered inside. A picture of my dad's beaming face looked back at me, and I swiftly plucked it from the pile. He was standing alone, leaning against the weeping willow at the meadow. I had never seen it before. He looked younger than I remembered, so I wondered if it was taken before I was born. He had his right hand in his pocket and his left leg propped up against a bucket that was full of apples.

I noticed he wasn't wearing a wedding ring. *Did Mom take this picture?* I kept digging to see what else was in there and found his old denim jacket. I pulled it out and put it on; it fit perfectly. I wondered if my mom would be okay with me having it or if it would make her uneasy. It had been almost twenty years since he passed, but I knew it was still painful for her. I put my hands in the jacket pockets and pulled out another old picture. It was of me and my dad during summer. It was folded in half, and on the back, in his scratchy handwriting, read—me and my boy. I rubbed my thumb back and forth across our faces. I looked so much like him.

It wasn't fair that he was taken from us so early. We weren't ready. I wasn't ready. I needed my dad, and my mom needed her husband. This town needed their Brad Patterson. He was a staple. I would never be able to fill his shoes, but I could say I spent every day of my life trying my hardest to make him proud.

I packed everything back up—minus the jacket—and stood in the room imagining what my life would have been like had he not passed. I probably never would have gone to Tennessee—or college, for that matter. I certainly wouldn't be the principal of Grace Valley School. Maybe I would still be living at home. All I knew was that my life had turned out pretty great, and I really believed I had him to thank for that. I knew he was looking down on me and guiding me in the right direction.

I grabbed the bin with my Playstation and went to my room to set it up.

22

LEAH

It was the kind of day where I just wanted to lay out on a hammock for hours with a good book. And I would have done just that had it not been for the obscene amount of work I had to catch up on. I couldn't believe all the clients that had referred my services to others. Abernathy Travel & Leisure was booming, and I was exhausted but loving every minute of it. I was going to have to either hire someone or only take on a select number of clients per month.

I walked outside and sat on the swing, soaking up as much sun as I could before I headed to the office at noon. I really wished I could have just set up shop on the porch, but I knew I wouldn't get anything done beyond relaxing. I leaned my head back against the swing and closed my eyes, listening to the birds chirping and leaves crashing into each other as the breeze swept through.

I opened one eye and looked over to the door when I heard the heavy footsteps.

"What's up, Dad?" I asked.

"I'm heading into town in thirty," he told me. "Would you like a lift and some lunch before you go to work?"

"Yeah," I said. "That sounds great. Thank you."

He winked and went back inside.

I closed my eyes again and sunk deeper into the swing. If I had thirty minutes before my dad was leaving, I was going to enjoy the sun on my face for at least twenty of them. I'd made a promise to myself when I moved back to Grace Valley to stop and smell the roses. My life in New York City was a fly-by-the-seat-of-my-pants type of lifestyle, and I knew I needed to slow down if I wanted to truly enjoy all that life had to offer me. While that didn't look the same for everyone, and I definitely loved every second I spent there, but I knew in my heart that it was only temporary.

"You ready to go, pumpkin?" my dad asked.

I opened my eyes and stared at the fan slowly blowing down on me from the ceiling of the porch. The whirring, white noise was such a soothing sound. No wonder babies loved it so much. I was far too relaxed in that moment to do anything, but I knew I had to move if I was going to accomplish anything. I grabbed my things from the mudroom and met my dad in the car. His infectious smile glowed in the reflection the sun made on the windshield.

Today is going to be a good day.

We drove in silence, and it was nice to just sit with someone who didn't expect me to fill all the empty space with words. Just the comfort of not being alone was incredible. We pulled into town, and it was nice and quiet.

"Bakery or diner?" my dad asked.

"Diner, for sure," I replied.

I was craving cheese and gravy fries, and even though I didn't need them, I was getting them! They reminded me of my childhood when we would stop by after church during the winter when it was too cold to picnic in the meadow. I would almost always get the fries with a grilled cheese and tomato sandwich. There was something about the nostalgia that got to me since being home. I craved the memories of the past and made it a point to bring them into my future. The smallest things became mountains I needed to move in order to create the life I deserved. *And here I am getting sentimental over fries and gravy. I need a hobby, but I'm too damn busy.*

"Sounds good to me," he said. "Want to park around back and walk? It'll be easier when you're done at the office later."

"That's fine," I answered. "With the amount of food I'm about to consume, it's probably best I get a tiny bit of exercise in."

We both laughed knowing damn well that the few hundred feet we would walk to the diner wouldn't even come close to excusing my appetite for the day. We parked and walked around the building, taking in the fresh air and praying the skies were done opening for at least a few days. We'd had enough rain to last a lifetime, and after the fire at the barn, I knew this town didn't need any more damage. Dad held the door open for me when we reached the diner, and Dante nodded at us before heading back inside the kitchen. We made our way over to our usual table and waited for someone to come take our order.

"Well, hello, you two," Tammy's cheerful voice greeted us.

"Hi, Tammy," my dad replied. "I thought you were off today."

"Hi," I said and smiled.

"I am," she answered. "Well, I was. I just stopped in to get something from the office, and Dante said the server for today never showed up. His wife was here helping out before, but she had to get the kids back home so they could nap. I'll just stay until the rush is over and our afternoon girl comes in."

"I'm sorry," I said. "You should have called me. I would have come in to help out."

Tammy was always going above and beyond for everyone, but lately, she was just having the worst luck. It didn't seem to matter how intense her vetting process was; all these college girls were just in it for some quick tips and were as lazy as they come.

"Oh, please," she said, gently placing her hand on mine. "You have enough to do. I don't mind. After all, it is my place."

She winked and looked toward my dad.

"Now, what can I get you two?" she asked.

"Burger, medium, and fries, please," my dad said. "Oh, and a chocolate milkshake."

"Living on the edge," I teased him.

"What can I get for you, sweet Leah?" she asked, smiling down at me.

I looked up at her and smiled like I did when I was a kid. "Cheese and gravy fries and a grilled cheese and tomato."

I closed my eyes, so ready to stuff my face with one of the most comforting things I could imagine eating in that moment. My dad and Tammy both started laughing, causing me to open my eyes and lose my precious daydream.

"What?" I asked, already anticipating the teasing I was about to endure.

"Nothing," they said simultaneously.

It was nice to have a genuine moment instead of suffering from one of the many intense events we've all been a part of lately. Tammy winked and nodded toward the kitchen.

"Your food will be out shortly," she told us, wiping under her eyes and disappearing into the back.

Now's my chance.

"Dad? What's been going on with you?" I asked. I looked him dead in the eyes.

"What do you mean?"

"I've just been having a feeling that something is off. Are you okay?"

"I'm sorry to worry you, Leah. It's just about six months since your mother passed, and I've been feeling it pretty hard the last few days," he confessed. "I promise you there is no cause for concern."

I didn't like the fact that he was hurting, but this was all still no new and was to be expected. I reached across the table and held his hand. We sat in silence for a moment, until he presented me with a smile to let me know he was going to be alright. I imagined we still had a long road ahead of us, but we could conquer anything as long as we had each other.

Tammy brought out our meals and we dove into them, not lifting our heads until we had eaten every piece of food on our plates. It was nice to have a quiet meal that wasn't alone.

"That was delicious," my dad said, wiping his mouth with the white paper napkin before neatly folding it up and placing it next to his plate. "I don't know how Dante makes diner food taste like that."

"I know," I said before drinking the last of my water and standing up. "He has to have some secret to that gravy. I've tried to make it, but it never tastes like his."

My dad threw a ten-dollar bill onto the table for a tip and went to the front to pay the check.

"I'll get this one, Dad," I said, reaching inside my bag for my wallet.

"You will do no such thing." He leaned over to kiss my head. "You can cook dinner and we'll call it even."

"Deal."

"Meet me in my office when you're done, and we can head home together," he said as we reached the front door to the agency.

"Sounds good, dad." I unlocked the door and heading straight to the coffee machine.

Vanilla lattes had become a part of my daily routine, and I was not complaining about it. I loved being able to make them myself and enjoy one hot or cold, depending on my mood. They got me through so many deadlines and stressful projects. I wish I'd been able to have them in high school, but they were far too fancy for me back then. Who knew they were so easy to make?

The bell chimed on the front door, and I looked up to see Gene, the town mailman, walk through carrying a package.

"Hi, Gene," I said, looking over my shoulder to him. "Would you like a coffee?"

"Oh, no thanks, Leah," he said, placing the box on the round table next to the door. "I've got a busy day of deliveries. People have been shipping things like crazy."

"Well, I'll be here all day if you need a little pick-me-up," I said, smiling at him as he walked back toward the door.

"Thanks. Have a nice day."

"You too," I replied and walked over to the table.

I placed my mug on a coaster with a picture of Tuscany on it and looked at the box. Ezekiel Wine & Spirits. I'd never heard of that place before and had no clue who could have sent me something. I got a letter opener from my desk drawer and sliced open the tape holding the center of the box shut. Inside was another box, this one made of Styrofoam, with an envelope sitting nicely on top. I picked up the pale blue envelope and opened it.

Leah,

I wish I was able to spend more time with you. Share this bottle of wine with your dad over dinner tonight. I know you said this one always reminds you two of your mother. Miss you.

Love you my girl,

Sara

PS. I'm having sushi delivered to your house at six, so I really hope you're home ;)

I reached into the box and pulled out the bottle of wine, slowly sitting down and letting the tears roll down my face. I told her about that wine during one of my meltdowns over my mom, and I couldn't believe she remembered it. Who was I kidding? Of course she remembered.

I reached into my back pocket and grabbed my phone to text her a thank you.

23

CALEB

I SPENT AN EXORBITANT AMOUNT OF TIME PLAYING OLD SCHOOL video games, and I needed to get out of the house. But I wasn't allowed to go anywhere. *Two weeks of this shit?* At that point, I had exhausted most of my outlets, so I resorted to eating, again. I definitely wasn't going to get back into shape the way I was going, but I honestly didn't care. The grinders were delicious, and it was nice to be able to open the fridge and grab whatever I wanted. Minimal effort with cooking—or anything, really—was a win in my book. *When did I become so lazy?*

I grabbed the grinder from the fridge and a plate from the cabinet and sat down to eat. Through the window, I could see the boys next door playing catch outside. With the number of children that preferred to be holed up in their houses watching TV and playing on their cell phones, it was nice to see these two always playing outside. Even in the dead of winter, you could look out the window and see them building snowmen or digging igloos out of the snow the plow had shoved against their mailbox. When I was younger, my dad and I would spend hours outside building anything and everything with the snow. One year, we built an entire snow wall made out of snow bricks. It took three days to do it and was worth every last second.

I wanted to be a dad like that one day, if I ever had the chance. The kind of man who would stop everything to go outside and play with his kids, regardless of the amount of catch-up he'd have to play later. I don't ever remember a time when I had to compete with anything for my father's attention; he always put family first. That's one of the things I would always remember about him.

I could hear my phone buzzing from the table in the hallway and had forgotten that I left it charging in there. It stopped after one long buzz, indicating a probable text message, so I finished eating before I got up to retrieve it. I figured it would just be my mom checking in or Dooley letting me know he was ready to get the truck to me.

I shuffled over to the phone, and the moment I saw who the text was from, I almost threw it back down onto the table. *Why the hell is Brittany texting me?* I was not in the mood for her. Truthfully, I hadn't been in the mood for her since she left last Christmas, and I hadn't spoken to her since. This was the third or fourth text from her in the past month. I wanted to swipe left across the screen and delete the message without opening it, but the nice guy in me wanted to make sure everything was okay.

Brittany: Hello, handsome. Just wanted to let you know that I found some of your old clothes while cleaning out my closet. You should come down to visit me and get them.

Caleb: I'm all set, thanks. You can toss them or donate them.

Brittany: I'd be better if you just came home.

Caleb: I am home. Glad to see you haven't changed. Take care now.

Brittany: You know how to reach me when you come to your senses. xoxo

There was absolutely no reason for her to be calling and texting me, and I didn't care enough to give her the time of day anymore. After I deleted her message, I decided I needed to call Dooley to see about the truck.

"Hey, man," Dooley said when he picked up. "What's going on?"

I felt bad complaining when he'd already been through so much, but damn, I was suffering in this house alone.

"Dude, I'm so bored," I said. "I don't know how people are able to just stay inside their houses all day long. I mean, I'd be fine if I was able to at least go outside and sit in the sun, but doctor's orders . . ."

"It'll go by quickly, Caleb," he said reassuringly. "I just hitched up the truck, so I'll head on over to your place in a bit. I've got to swing by the flower shop on my way. You need anything from town?"

"I'm good, thanks," I answered, relieved that I was going to finally have something to do.

"No problem. I'll see you in about an hour or so."

"Sounds good." I hung up the phone and headed upstairs to change.

I straightened up the house a bit in case my mom came home while I was in the garage. I didn't want her to have to do any more work than she'd already been doing. Just to be on the safe side, I threw on a pair of jeans, a thin long-sleeve shirt, and a baseball cap. I knew there wouldn't be much, if any, sunlight entering the garage, but it couldn't hurt. Luckily, it was a cool day, so I would be okay. The hour flew by, and before I knew it, Dooley was pulling into the driveway, the old hunk of junk clanking away behind him.

Oh man, I can't wait to get my hands on you.

I could have cried I was so happy to see that truck. The perfect shade of blue had only slightly faded, and I made a mental note to take it to the body shop for a full paint job once I had it up and running again. I couldn't help but think of this accident as a blessing in disguise. I definitely wouldn't have found the free time to work on this truck if I hadn't been injured. I would have poured all my energy into my new principal position and the future basketball team. But there I was, injured and full of hope.

"Here she is, man," Dooley said, tossing the keys my way.

I caught them one-handed and just stopped and stared at them for a moment. I couldn't believe that after all these years, this beautiful heap of metal was mine. I had wished for this truck since the moment I laid my eyes on it, and it had become a reality that I never imagined was possible.

"I'd say take her for a spin, but she doesn't start," Dooley said, shrugging his shoulders.

"Yet," I replied. "I will be cruising through town in no time."

"I'm sure you will." He smiled.

"How much work do you think needs to be done?"

"Honestly, I'm not sure," he said, shaking his head. "It's been sitting in that same part for years. It could need a lot or a very little. I really couldn't tell you."

"Well, I'm game for whatever blows my way with this one," I said, motioning to the garage with my head. "Can you help me roll her in there?"

"Of course," Dooley said, walking back to the truck and popping her into neutral. "I'm glad you decided to make her your project. It would be a shame to let this one go."

"Nah, man," I said, getting nostalgic. "This one has far too many memories to let go of."

Dooley smiled and shook his head in agreement. We both knew that was a loaded statement, but neither of us carried on about it.

"I've got to head out," Dooley told me. "I have a ton to do, and I need to call the carnival company to let them know about the fire and see if they want to set up this year's carnival in the lower meadow instead."

I had forgotten all about the Fourth of July Carnival that Grace Valley had every year. You would think with the number of activities and festivals this place hosted, it would be on the forefront of my mind, but it seemed I couldn't remember shit anymore.

"All right, man," I said, reaching my hand out to shake his. "I'll be able to help out at the farm in a week or so. Please, let me know if there is anything I can do for you from here. Phone calls, ordering, anything. I'm here for you."

Dooley cast a wide, toothy smile. "Will do."

I stood in the doorway of the garage and watched as Dooley and the trailer rattled their way down the street. When he turned the corner, I looked over at the truck with excitement that could only parallel Christmas morning. I couldn't wait to pop open that hood and see what type of hell awaited me. I was prepared for just about anything, but I really didn't want to be shelling out thousands of dollars. I took a deep breath and opened the hood, then jumped, slamming my body into the tool bench behind me.

"What the hell?" I yelled out as a small field mouse scurried across the engine and out the garage door.

This is not the type of hell I was referring to.

At quick glance, I could already tell I was in it for the long haul. Corrosion covered most of the engine, the timing belt had snapped and was dragging under the engine, and the battery was missing. I wondered who would have taken it out. I sent a quick text to the autobody shop to see if he was able to deliver me some parts. I knew he had a love of vintage cars and trucks and sometimes carried hard-to-find parts. I lucked out, and he had everything I needed in the shop.

I closed the hood and started taking inventory of the tools I would need to make this happen. My mom took immaculate care of my father's belongings, and even though they all belonged to me now, she made sure to keep them in the same great condition he did all those years ago. I was grateful to him for teaching me how to work on cars at such a young age. I was grateful for Dooley and his dad for teaching me what my dad wasn't able to. And I was grateful to my mother for allowing me the freedom to bounce from place to place to continue to learn these skills that were so very important to my dad.

I grabbed a towel and started to pull away at whatever I could remove from the engine. I figured a quick oil change would be a good place to start, so I grabbed my jack, lifted the front end and secured the jack stands, careful not to rub my body along the garage floor. Last thing I needed was another trip to the emergency room. Finally, I slid the tray under the tank and unscrewed the bolt. Slowly, the oil started to drip, but I had a feeling it had been in there too long. Just when I was about to lose hope, it started draining properly. *Thank God.*

I spent the remainder of the afternoon fixing what I could with the supplies I had at the house. It felt good to be able to use my hands again and not be cooped up inside. The boys from next door stopped by to say hello and asked if they could help. My teacher hat was once again securely fastened to my head, and I began to teach them the ins and outs of automotive mechanics. Before we knew it, it was dinnertime.

"Can we come back over tomorrow and help?" Tucker asked. Wonder and excitement filled eyes, and I knew that feeling all too well.

"Absolutely," I said. "Why don't you swing by after breakfast, and we can get an early start on it?"

"Thanks, Caleb!" They exclaimed, high-fiving each other before running home.

My mom pulled into the driveway as they were running across the front lawn, and almost immediately, I reverted back to a little boy afraid he was about to get yelled at for not picking up his toys. I was pleasantly surprised when she walked into the garage with a soft smile painted across her face.

"Wow," she said, almost breathlessly. "I haven't seen this beauty outside of the meadow in I couldn't tell you how long."

Her hand glided gently down the side of the truck, coming to a stop at the top of the hood. Her reaction to seeing it sitting in the garage matched mine, and I knew I made the right choice.

24

CALEB
TWO WEEKS LATER

"Can you drive?" my mom asks me in the middle of drying the breakfast dishes. "I'm reading this really good book on my tablet, and I don't want to miss anything."

Leave it to her to read a book in the car on the way to rebuild a farm. We are a family of readers, although I hadn't read anything since I'd been back in Grace Valley. I couldn't remember a time when someone in this house wasn't reading something, but the farm was only ten minutes away.

"Sure, Mom," I replied. A small chuckle escaped from my mouth, and she snapped her head back to me.

"Don't you laugh at me," she said sternly, even though I saw that glimmer in her eye that always meant she was teasing.

"I'm not," I said and laughed out loud this time.

"Oh, I hope you get kids just like you. Teasing your own mother." She flicked soapy water across the room at my face.

Over the last year or so, more specifically the last six months, I'd definitely started seeing things on a deeper level. Losing my dad as a child was horrific, but losing Lucia last year tore us all apart. It caused us all to relive what happened nearly twenty years ago, and the wounds that we desperately tried to close had ripped open once more.

"I miss them," I said softly, sitting down in the middle of the kitchen floor.

"Who, dear?" she asked, placing her towel on the counter and joining me on the floor.

"Dad and Lucia," I said. "Being home after all these years is weird, but being home without either of them is something I never dreamed of."

I'd been feeling off since I came back to Grace Valley, and even though it was where I was supposed to be, I couldn't put my finger on it all until that moment.

"Mom, I know this is going to sound crazy, but I guess a part of me always hoped it was just a dream. That one day I would wake up and Dad would be here, and we would be living life like we always had," I admitted.

She took in a deep breath and looked up at me. She tilted her head to the side and opened her mouth to say something, then quickly shut it. Shifting positions and now sitting directly in front of me, she took my hands in hers and gently rubbed her thumbs across the backs of my hands.

"Caleb, I would be lying if I said I didn't want that same thing every single day," she finally said, her eyes tearing up. "What I would give for just one more day with your father. Watching you grow up to be the kind of man he was has filled me with so much joy, but having him witness your growth would bring that joy to another level."

She reached up and wiped a tear off her cheek with the back of her hand. "The first two years after your dad passed, I would sit in my bed for hours at night and cry. I prayed more than I had ever prayed. I was angry. I didn't understand how one minute our life was perfect—we were all together and so happy—and then the next, he was gone, and we were alone and heartbroken. Eventually, I came to terms with the fact that this nightmare was real and that he wasn't coming back. I stopped feeling sorry for myself, and I focused more on the diner and on you. He must have been looking down on us, because look at us now!"

I looked around the kitchen and then back at her.

"Oh, stop," she said. "Not in the literal sense."

I stood up and reached out my hand for her to hold while she stood up. "Let's head out. I want to help, and it's already been two weeks."

I ended up driving, but she didn't read her book. Instead, she just stared out the window for the entire drive. It was peaceful, and I had a feeling our talk had sent her head into a tailspin. It wasn't my intention to shake things up like that. Quite the opposite. I needed to get it off my chest, and I thought she was probably feeling the same way. We pulled up to the meadow, and there were already a handful of cars parked in the makeshift gravel lot. I quickly parked, and we made our way to the barn. Or what was left of it.

The sky was the clearest shade of blue, not a cloud in sight. The birds were chirping, the ducks were waddling along in neat little rows in the pond, and the weeping willow tree gently swayed in the breeze, a vast contrast to the sight in front of us. To the left of the barn was a giant pile of what I could only assume was what was left from the fire. To the right was new wood and supplies to rebuild. It was a literal view of *out with the old and in with the new*. There was the familiar Grace Valley hospitality where each member of the community was assisting someone else in some capacity. Paul and Dooley were carrying the wood and placing it in the existing pile. Becky and Jackie were tending to the horses a little farther up at the other barn. Mr. and Mrs. Kratz, bless them, were setting up a little water and snack station.

"I'm going to go see if I can help the Kratzes, dear," my mom said and headed toward them.

And then my eyes settled upon the lone body standing in the middle of the doorway of the burned-down barn. Leah. I watched her closely as I walked through the meadow. She stood almost frozen in her spot, her arms dangling at her side as she stared blankly at the barn. It was like watching a robot as she pulled the sleeves of the shirt wrapped around her waist and tilted her head. I couldn't tell what she was looking at, and I was afraid if I moved any closer, she would see me, and I didn't want to creep her out. *Because standing behind her and watching her every movement wasn't creepy enough?*

Her hands shot up around her mouth, and I watched as her shoulders started to move up and down. She was crying, but I knew she had already seen the barn, so I was genuinely confused by her sudden surge of emotions. She wiped away her tears, smoothed her T-shirt, and crouched down, reaching across the ground to the only beam left from the barn. She carefully removed a small piece of fabric stuck on a nail, and my right hand immediately crossed my body and rubbed my forearm.

That's the beam that hit me.

I sat down in the meadow and rested my arms on my knees. My head quickly followed suit and landed in the palms of my hands. I'd let her go, but watching her suffer at the thought of what I could only assume was a worse fate than the minor injuries I'd sustained was killing me. I didn't need to be inside her head to know what she was thinking right now. That's the power of soul mates.

She stood back up, folded the piece of cloth, and stuck it into her back pocket while glancing carefully over her shoulder. *Point proven, Leah.* I grabbed my phone and pretended to be texting in case she noticed me sitting on the hill. I didn't want to ruin her moment. I could see her spot me, but it would have been hard for her to tell if I was looking at her or my phone through my sunglasses. Once she was headed in the opposite direction, I got up to see where I was needed.

"Hey, guys," I said when I finally caught up with Dooley and Paul. "What can I do?" I clapped my hands and rubbed them together. I was in no way responsible for the burning of the barn, but for some reason, I felt as though it were my job to rebuild it. A subconscious need to be who my father was, or to repay Dooley for helping me become the man I am now. It felt good to help, to be a part of something bigger, to be able to create something lasting and meaningful with my bare hands.

"Why don't you help us bring the rest of this wood down?" Dooley said, pointing to the wagon and the remaining pile of wood. "If we can get this framed up today, the entire job could be done within a week or so."

"All right. Sounds good," I said, my phone pinging in my pocket.

"You need to get that?" Paul asked.

"Nah, it's okay." I looked down at my phone and immediately canceled the call. "I'm sure they'll call back if it's important."

Brittany. Again. I wouldn't let her take up space in my head.

I wheeled the wagon down the hill, passing Leah along the way. She looked over to me and gave me a quick, awkward smile before rushing over to Jackie. I noticed her glance back toward me for a split second and then disappear behind the fence. She was obviously and actively avoiding me, and it couldn't have been cuter. Sure, we had that mini-conversation at the hospital, but I fell asleep before we really got anywhere. We definitely weren't back to how we used to be, and things were still up in the air, at least in my mind.

The morning flew by, and we'd made significant progress. If we kept it up, the barn would be ready for business by the end of the summer. I didn't have to report to work until the end of

August, so I was able to give one hundred percent of my time to the Butlers and this entire farm.

"Thanks a lot for the help," Dooley said, slapping me on the back. "Much appreciated."

My phone buzzed in my pocket, and I was thankful that I had turned it to vibrate because I wasn't in the mood for an interrogation. I didn't know what Brittany wanted, but I did know I wanted nothing to do with it. I needed her to just leave me alone, but I'd never dealt with anything like this before. Not with a friend or a crazy ex, and even though I'd always known there was something off about her, I didn't think she was this level of psycho.

I could see the wheels spinning in Dooley's head, wanting to ask questions, but I was saved by Jackie calling down to us, asking if we wanted to barbecue for dinner.

"I'll grab the salads," my mom called back to her. "Caleb, come with me to the diner to get everything, please."

"Sure thing, Mom," I agreed. "Does anyone need anything while we're out? Want me grab some beers or other drinks?"

"Caleb, get all the drinks from my store," Paul said. "I'll call and let Mike know you're on the way. I'll have him bring everything right out to the car so you don't have go in. Do you mind swinging by the butcher shop too?"

"Not at all," I said.

"Excellent," Dooley said, coming around the side of Paul. "I'll call in the order now. Thanks again."

"Mom, you want me to drive?" I asked her as we walked to her car.

"Thanks," she said and smiled, reaching into her bag and pulling out her tablet.

I was happy to see her in a better mood after our solemn morning.

25

LEAH

"So, you've just been building a barn and working?" Sara asked me after she surprised me at the office.

I was elated to have her there. I hadn't realized just how much I was missing her until she wasn't physically accessible every day. And I was so stressed out because I'd put so much of my free time into helping out at the barn that I hadn't been focusing enough at work, and I was struggling again. I hired an assistant for the summer, but she wasn't starting for another week, and I was already elbow deep in work.

"Yeah, it's been hectic, to say the least," I responded, wiping my brow with the back of my hand.

"You poor thing." She scooped me into one of her signature hugs.

Again, something that I hadn't realized I was missing.

"You must be exhausted. I'd offer to take you out to dinner before I catch the train back to the city, but it sounds like you might need a night at home to relax. Can I at least send dinner over for you and your dad?"

My best friend, ladies and gentlemen. She was the sweetest person, and I felt so lucky to have her in my life.

"You're the best," I said, squeezing her back tightly. "That sounds great."

"That's what friends are for."

"Just let me know what you guys would like, and I'll order it for you," she said, releasing me and taking a seat at the round table by the door. "Now, what can I do to help you?"

"Oh, Sara, you don't need to help me with anything. I'll get it all done," I stammered, wanting her visit to be about her and not her doing menial work at my office.

"Why not? I'm here and I'm available. Let me help you."

"How about we just have a coffee together, and then maybe you can help me with some of the filing?" I figured filing couldn't hurt, and I had a ton of it.

"Perfect," she agreed. "Why don't you sit, and I'll make us the coffees?"

"Nice try," I said, tilting my head at her. "I'll make them. You go get comfy."

It had been a few days since I'd seen Caleb at the farm. I'd thought that with time away from him, I wouldn't have still had those feelings, but there I was, overthinking him and everything else in my life once again. It wasn't just puppy love, after all. The more time we spent together getting reacquainted as friends, the more I was falling for him all over again. I wasn't about to run away this time, but I wasn't sure he was fully thinking the same thing. I reached my hand into my back pocket and pulled out the torn fabric that was once a part of his shirt. I rubbed it between my fingers and gently placed it to my lips. Closing my eyes, I kissed the fabric and shoved it back into my pocket. As crazy as it sounded, keeping it with me felt as though I had a piece of Caleb with me, and until I knew what was going on with us, it was going to stay right there.

Within two minutes, I had made both coffees, frothed the milk, and brought them over to the table. Sara was patiently waiting and reading the local paper, and every so often, she'd glance outside to the green across the street.

"This is such a cute little town," she said, putting the paper down to take a sip of her latte. "This is delicious."

"I love it here," I said, looking out to the gazebo and watching some kids play tag.

Just then, Caleb crossed the street and reached out to grab a kite that was about to get stuck in the tree. He looked back toward my office nonchalantly. If I hadn't been looking, I wouldn't have known he was even there, but I was, and I'm pretty sure he saw me. I watched as he handed a little girl her kite and continued on his jog.

"I can definitely understand why you chose to leave the city and come back here," she teased.

"Chinese," I said to her, and she looked back at me like I was crazy.

"What?" she asked. "Are you okay?"

"For dinner," I said, wiping some of the froth from my top lip. "I meant that my dad and I would like Chinese for dinner tonight."

"Oh," she said and chuckled. "Trying to ignore the fact that Prince Charming was just outside casually stealing a glance in your direction? Okay, Leah."

"Stop," I said, tossing my napkin at her. "Finish your coffee and get to filing."

Sara shook her head and smiled. Did I mention how happy I was to have her there?

"Are you sure you've got that Leah?" my dad asked as I filled another wheelbarrow with debris.

"I'm sure," I said, stubborn as ever.

I'd finally made a dent in my work and was feeling less stressed, but the thought of having all this crap in the meadow was driving me crazy. The Fourth of July Carnival was coming in just a few days, and I hadn't been to one since the summer before I left for college. It was the best event we had in Grace Valley, only second to the Christmas Festival, and I wanted it to be perfect. Not like I actually had a hand in setting anything up. They had carnival workers who did that. I just loved my town and wanted anyone who came to enjoy it to love it just the same.

I wobbled my way over to the dumpster that Dooley rented and started tossing the debris inside before turning back around to fill it up again. I could see Caleb parking his car, and I rushed to get back to the pile so I wouldn't bump into him. I was avoiding him for no reason other than I wasn't sure what to say. I started throwing anything and everything I could get my hands on into the wheelbarrow, determined to get back up to the dumpster before he got to the barn.

I overestimated my strength, or balance, or both and silently prayed I'd make it to the top before the whole thing toppled over. My wish wasn't granted, and down I went, wheelbarrow tumbling after.

"Leah," I heard him call out. "Leah, are you okay?"

Ah, shit! So much for that.

"Here, take my hand," he offered. "I'll help you pick this stuff up."

"Oh, uh, thanks," I said, accepting his hand and pulling myself up.

I looked up at him, and it was as if the stars had aligned and I was instantly pulled from my previous lapse of judgement. Caleb's touch sent shockwaves throughout my entire body, the intensity hitting me at my core. I couldn't speak, so I just stood there and stared at him.

"Are you all right?" he asked, looking at me nervously.

Full of Grace

"I'm fine, thanks," I managed to get out of my mouth. "I can get the rest of this myself."

"With all due respect, Leah," he said softly. "I think I'd better wheel this up for you. I'll dump it and bring it back down, and then maybe you can fill it a bit less next time?"

"Okay, thank you," I said, our hands still connected.

To be perfectly honest, I wasn't agreeing because I was afraid I would tip over again. I was agreeing solely on the fact that I needed to be near him in that moment. I needed to be near him forever.

"All set," Caleb said as he dumped the last of the contents into the dumpster for me. "We'll get this back down the hill for you, and you should be good."

"Thank you, Caleb," I said, following him back down the hill.

"See ya," he said as he put down the wheelbarrow and walked over to help Dooley.

"See ya," I repeated quietly, my heart still racing.

I watched him walk away and immediately regretted not saying more to him. I couldn't continue this back and forth of waiting to see who would make the next move. But I was so scared to be open and honest with him.

"Hey," a soft voice said from behind me, "let me help you."

Becky placed a gentle hand on my arm and guided me back over to the pile of debris. I thought I was in the clear, but apparently, she had seen what had just gone down. And while I didn't know just how long she had been watching, judging from her demeanor, it was long enough. I wasn't ready to admit to anyone here what had been going on between me and Caleb—if anything was even going on. Maybe in his mind we were just hanging out as friends, but I was determined to make it work this time. It was my turn to fight for this relationship and I wasn't letting anything get in the way.

Too late.

I looked at her and burst into tears. All these emotions were too much for me, and I didn't know what to do about anything anymore. The last thing I wanted to do was feel sorry for myself, especially in the middle of a meadow with half a dozen other people, but I couldn't help it. It was as if someone had unzipped a rain cloud and every emotion I'd felt over the past six months came flooding out.

"Shh," she said, wiping the tears from my eyes and motioning for Jackie to come over. "It's okay. Let's calm you down, and we can work through all of this."

"What's going on?" Jackie asked breathlessly.

"Just a little roller coaster of emotions," she told her. "Can you help Leah with the rest of this stuff and then meet me over by the willow tree?"

"Yes, of course," Jackie said. "You all right, Leah?"

"Yes, thanks," I told her.

We finished quickly and met Becky at the tree. She was sitting under it with a large blanket and a picnic basket.

"What's all this?" I asked her.

"Just a little ladies' lunch," she told us. "Looked like you might need some girl talk."

She held out a bottle of champagne in one hand and some pink lemonade in the other. *Did she have bottles of this stashed somewhere?* The signature drink for the women who spent time in this meadow. It seemed silly, but that drink made me feel closer to my mother. I could imagine what that conversation would have looked like had she been sitting there with us.

"Now, Leah," Becky said, looking at me sternly but delivering everything with love. "I won't tell you what to do, because this is not my life to live, but what I will say is this—the first person you think of every morning, the last person you think of every night, and the one who consumes your mind the most during your waking hours is not a coincidence. Your heart chooses who to love, and you can't fight that, no matter how hard you try. Sure, you could find happiness with someone else, but at the end of the day, you'll never be truly happy or fulfilled if you choose to look the other way. So, make sure you don't burn any bridges because second chances don't come around that often."

"She's right, you know," Jackie said as I sipped my mimosa.

I smiled and looked over to Jackie. "Your mother is a saint," I said.

"Oh, stop it!" Becky exclaimed, waving a hand and pretending not to agree.

"You think Dad will have this place ready in time for the carnival?" Jackie asked.

"I sure hope so," I said. "I've been dreaming of this since the Christmas Festival."

"I'm sure he'll have it cleaned up in time, but the barn will definitely not be finished before that," she told us. "We'll have them set up in the lower meadow and park on the other side of the farm. It'll be fine."

I could hardly contain my excitement, and I was happy to see that Jackie was as giddy as I was. I didn't care how old I got. I would always be excited for that carnival and a ride on the Ferris wheel.

26

CALEB

THE AMOUNT OF PROGRESS THAT WE'D MADE ON THE BARN WAS tremendous. Of course, there was still a lot to do, but banding together was what this town was known for and it showed. I made it to the meadow earlier that morning and spent quite a bit of time admiring everything it had come to be. A family farm that had been around for decades had become the meeting place for so many people, and I was blessed to be able to call it a part of my home.

I had originally planned on getting there early to do some work on the barn so Dooley wouldn't have to put so much on his plate again, but when I saw Darb hanging out at the stables, I decided to take him for a ride instead.

"Come on, ol' boy," I said, lifting his chin and placing a kiss on his muzzle. "Let's get you out for a bit today."

Since the fire, there hadn't been any riders at the farm. It had all but destroyed Dooley's business. Luckily, there were still a few loyals who continued to board. I wished I could take them all out, but that morning was all about Darb. I went into the tack room to find his blanket and gear and saddled up. I hadn't ridden

Full of Grace

a horse in a while, but I trusted Darb and I knew that the feeling was mutual.

"You ready?" I asked him, and he trotted slowly around in the grass.

I put one foot in the stirrup and hopped on. We started off slowly, making our way around the field. Once we broke free and were headed toward the lower meadow, we picked up speed. I watched in amazement as the wind blew through Darb's long mane while he began to gallop. I had felt like I was truly home for a few weeks at that point, but being with Darb in the meadow solidified every decision I recently made. It didn't matter if I was with Leah or not. All that mattered was that I was here, and I was home.

I came around the bend to see Dooley walking toward the barn, so I brought Darb back up to the stables.

"You're out here early," Dooley said, waving to me as I walked down to the barn.

"Morning," I said, stripping off my long sleeves, ready to get to work. "Where do you need me to start today?"

"You know, kid," he said. "If I didn't know any better, I'd say that your father inhabited your body. You two are so alike it amazes me. You're both the first one on a job and the last to leave. It doesn't matter how busy you could be, you'd both just make it happen."

"Thanks, Dooley," I said. "Sometimes I forget what he was like, and it's nice to hear that."

My phone started ringing and one quick glance sent me into a tailspin. I groaned loudly, silenced the ringer, and shoved my phone back into my pocket.

"Let's get started," I said, a low growl in my throat.

"Who was that?" Dooley asked. "Is everything okay?"

"It was nobody," I said gruffly. "Don't worry about it."

Dooley put his tools down and looked directly at me. "Listen, kid," he said. "If you're in some kind of trouble, you better let me know."

"It's nothing," I said, shuffling my feet and hoping for a way out of this conversation. "I swear."

I wasn't lying. It was Brittany again, and to me, she was absolutely nothing. I'd made it perfectly clear to her that we were over, and I wasn't about to let her back into my life and wreak havoc on everything and everyone that I loved. I had fallen into her trap before, and this time, I was prepared. I'd always known she was a bit crazy, but now she was bordering on harassment, and it was getting annoying.

"Okay," he replied, shaking his head. "Let's try to get that back wall up today. The electrician is coming on Monday, so I'd like to have it ready for him."

We worked in silence for the first two hours that I was there. My phone continued to ring, I continued to send it to voicemail, and Dooley continued to stare at me. By lunchtime, the back wall was up, Paul had arrived, and Becky had dropped off food from my mother. I was relieved for the break from building and the interrogation. I had turned my phone to silent, so there would be no telling who or what was going on.

"Hey," Paul said, mid-bite, pointing across the field.

The carnival workers had begun to arrive to set up for the carnival. This town had been through so much and the carnival was just the thing to pull us all out of the funk. The East Coast Carnival Co. had been setting up in Grace Valley for the past twenty-five years, and I hadn't missed a single one. Even when I was in Tennessee, I made sure to always be home for the Fourth of July. Disclaimer: It was also my mother's birthday, so technically, I was actually home for her. But it was a perk to have the carnival too.

When I was about eleven or twelve, I started a tradition of trying to win my mother a teddy bear every summer. I think she probably had about ten of them in her bedroom on the dresser. She once told me a story about how my father proposed to her with a teddy bear, and as a young boy, I just wanted to make her smile again. We were happy and able to move on from his death, but it wasn't the same. At times, we both struggled emotionally.

At the ring toss booth, you could either win a goldfish or a teddy bear. All of the kids wanted the fish, but I needed that bear. I looked at the guy and handed him my tickets and tossed the rings. I missed every single bottle. I handed him two more tickets and continued to miss. After an hour of trying, I had exhausted all my efforts and was completely out of tickets. I was crushed until Leah came over to me and handed the man all her tickets.

"Here," she said, her smile as bright as the sun. "You can have my tickets."

I'm pretty sure I fell in love with her that day.

"Looks like you get an extra turn, kid," the man said, handing me the rings. "I'll throw in an extra ring for you this time."

I took a deep breath and tossed the first ring. Missed. Tossed the second ring. Missed. I was embarrassed and only had two rings left. We were now both out of tickets, so we couldn't even go on any of the rides.

"It's just a ring, Caleb," Leah told me, putting her hand on top of mine. "You've got this."

It was hard to say how a feeling so strong could appear in the body of a preteen, but I knew from that moment on that she was it for me. I looked up at her and tossed that ring over the bottles blindly. The sound of the ring clinking and bouncing off the bottles was like music to my ears, and as luck would have it, that ring landed securely around the golden bottle. I had won my mother the bear.

"Yay!" Leah cheered, wrapping her arms around me in a bear hug. "Your mother is going to love it!"

I smiled at her, lucky to have her as my best friend. "Thank you, Leah."

"Anytime." She smiled, pulling two more tickets from the back pocket of her jean shorts. "Come on, let's go ride the Ferris wheel before the fireworks start."

"Why are you smiling like that?" Dooley asked, his balled-up napkin hitting me square between the eyes.

"What the hell, man?" I yelled, jumping. "There's tuna on that."

Paul and Dooley rolled on the ground laughing like they were kids. Two grown men in their fifties acting like children. They were exactly what I hoped to be when I was their age. The ability to find humor in anything was a trait I hoped I would carry through my adulthood, and it was nice to see that it wasn't a lost cause.

"Well, you've been acting fishy all day, Caleb," he said, his pun oozing out of his mouth.

"Funny, Dooley," I said, throwing it back at him and watching it roll down the hill.

"You better pick that up before it blows away," he scolded. "This isn't a dump."

"What do you mean he's been acting fishy?" Paul chimed in. "Something going on, son?"

Damnit, Dooley. Why can't you keep your big mouth shut? An inquisition is the last thing I need right now.

"No, nothing is going on," I said, going to fetch the napkin that was indeed blowing away.

"Don't listen to him, Paul," Dooley said. "He's been getting calls and messages all day and getting grumpier with each one. I know he's into something, and he just isn't telling me."

"It's nothing," I called, racing back up the hill with the napkin just in time to see Paul pick up my phone that must have fallen out of my pocket.

Shit!

"Give me that," I demanded, ripping my phone out of his hand and shoving it deep into my pocket.

"Caleb," Paul said, his eyes widening like he had seen who was calling, "are you kidding me?"

"It's not what you think," I said, running my hands through my hair.

How was I going to get out of that one? I had spent weeks —*months*—sulking over his daughter, professing and confessing my love for her, and now he sees that I'm communicating with my ex-fiancée? I'd dug myself into some holes over the years, but that one took the cake.

"So, then what is it?" he asked.

"What is what?" Dooley asked. "I'm confused. Somebody fill me in here."

"Our boy Caleb is back with Brittany," Paul said, shooting daggers my way.

"What?" Dooley questioned, his eyes about to pop out of his head.

"What?! No!" I exclaimed. "I'm not even talking to her at all. I don't know what these calls are all about."

"Caleb, son, your phone has fourteen missed calls and fifty-four text messages—all from Brittany," Paul said. "That seems like you're talking to me."

"I dunno, Paul," Dooley piped up. "That sounds more like she's doing the talking and he's doing the ignoring."

"Exactly!" I yelled out. "I don't know how to get her to stop. It's been going on for weeks now, and I just keep sending her to voicemail."

"And you don't want to find out what she has to say?" Paul asked.

"No," I answered. "We broke up over six months ago, and I

haven't spoken to her since. There is absolutely nothing that she would need to talk to me about."

As if she were sitting there with us listening to the entire conversation, my phone lit up in my pocket. Both Dooley and Paul looked at me with inquisitive eyes. I pulled my phone out, and for the first time in weeks, I read the text.

"It says, 'Caleb, if you don't call me back, I will keep calling until you pick up,'" I told them.

"So, she's definitely acting like a Psycho Sally," Dooley said and laughed. "You gotta nip this in the bud quick, kid."

Before I could put the phone back into my pocket, she was calling again. This time, I answered.

"Hello?" I said.

"Caleb! Finally," she said in a shrill voice. "I miss you. How are you?"

"What do you want, Brittany?" I asked, annoyance clear in my tone.

"I miss you. I want you to move back to Tennessee so we can get back to our lives together."

I took a deep breath and licked my lips. I wasn't a jerk, but I had been looking forward to this moment for a while now.

"Brittany, if you don't stop calling me, I'm going to call the police. We're over, and I don't ever want to hear from you again."

I hung up and went to throw my phone across the meadow and into the pond, when Paul grabbed my arm.

"I would not do that if I were you," he said. "Shit's expensive."

27

LEAH

I OPENED THE DOOR TO GET THE NEWSPAPER FOR MY DAD WHEN I heard, "Surprise!" I jumped backward, almost knocking myself over.

"Oh my gosh, Sara," I exclaimed, wrapping my arms around her. "What are you doing here?"

"She woke me up at the crack of dawn to surprise you," Aiden said as he made his way up the stairs.

He looked like he was about to topple over trying to carry all their bags in one fell swoop.

"It's true," she agreed. "I missed you, and I wanted to come and see what all the carnival hoopla was about."

"You were just here," I laughed, loving how she always knew when I needed her most. "Come inside. Let's get you all settled. Do you want coffee?"

"I would love some," Aiden said. "Thank you."

"Latte for me, please," Sara said. "Extra foam."

It felt amazing to have her here, and I would have caught the fish to make her sushi if she had asked me to. I put their bags in the guest room and went back to the kitchen to make everyone their drinks.

"Sara," my dad said, crossing the kitchen to give her a hug. "You made it!"

"Wait, you knew?" I asked.

"Of course I knew," he said. "I'm your father. I know everything."

I rolled my eyes and smiled. He was right about that.

"You must be Aiden," he said, extending his arm to shake his hand. "I know you just got here, but what do you say about coming into town with me and letting these two knuckleheads catch up?"

"That sounds great, Mr. Abernathy," Aiden responded.

"Call me Paul. Leah, why don't you put Aiden's coffee in a travel cup?"

"Sure, just a second," I said, giddy with excitement for this unexpected morning.

The second the front door closed, Sara bombarded me with questions.

"Spill it," she demanded. "I need to know everything."

"Goodness, how do you always know when I have something on my mind?" I shook my head at her.

"I think we both know that I'm amazing and know all," she said, playfully tossing her hair over her shoulder and fluttering her eyelashes. "You and Caleb clearly still love each other. Have you thought about just telling him? Hanging out as friends is great if that's all you want, but you're not going to get that sappy romance if you remain silent."

"I mean, when I fell over at the meadow, he helped me up but then walked right away like he didn't feel the same sparks that I did."

"You are the biggest overthinker I know," she told me. "Just talk to him and get it over with. Stop thinking of every scenario and how it might play out. You're only going to stress yourself out that way."

Full of Grace

"I know. You're right," I replied. "How is work? How's Cameron?"

"Work is good. We've been swamped, but I wouldn't want it any other way. Cameron seems much happier these days, too, so that makes everything easier."

"I miss it there, but I know I made the right choice," I told her. "I'm happier here. I feel . . . I don't know, I feel lighter almost."

"I get it," she said, reaching across the table to hold my hand. "You're my little country girl, and I love every bit of you."

No matter what I was going through, she was able to fix it. She was the definition of a sister, and I knew in my heart that she would be by my side for the rest of my life. In a lot of ways, our friendship reminded me of the one my mother had with Tammy and Becky. I had grown up with their example of trust, loyalty, and love, and it shaped who I am and what I felt I deserved out of life.

"So," she said, her eyebrows jumping up and down, "what are you going to wear tonight?"

"Oh, gosh," I said, panic slowly creeping up inside me. "I hadn't even thought of that. I just figured jeans and a T-shirt. But if he's going to be there . . ."

"Relax," Sara said. "I didn't mean to freak you out. It's just a carnival; jeans and a T-shirt are totally fine. Throw on some chucks and you're in business."

"What would I do without you?" I asked her.

My dad and Aiden came home a few hours later, and it looked like Aiden never wanted to leave Grace Valley. All he kept talking about was how nice the people were and how quaint the town was. I almost fell over laughing when he looked at Sara and said, "Love, pack your bags. We're buying a house in the country."

"We'll see," she said, blushing and leaning into him. "This would be a nice place to raise a family."

LAUGHTER FILLED the air as I stood staring at the lights on all the rides. The smell of the popcorn and fried dough made my stomach rumble. Aiden was an adrenaline junkie and wanted to ride the Spider, but Sara was adamant that she would not be joining him, so I decided to partner up with him. We went on the ride three times before deciding we should probably let some of the kids have a turn. I was having the time of my life.

And then I saw Caleb standing next to Dooley's old truck. He must have finished working on it. I watched intently as he walked alone from the parking lot toward the ring toss game, and memories of our childhood flooded my mind.

"Go talk to him," Sara said, nudging me. "You're going to regret it if you don't."

My palms started to sweat, and I felt dizzy. Both Aiden and Sara smiled softly at me and nodded toward the games, letting me know they had my back.

"You better be waiting if I crash and burn," I told them. "We'll be heading straight home."

"Go," Sara said again.

I'd practiced this scenario a million times, but I never thought it would actually happen. So, when I got closer to him, I almost turned around and walked the other way.

"Aww, I'm out of tickets," Caleb said to the man at the stand.

"Here, you can have mine," I said, walking up beside him.

"Leah," he said, his eyes soft and kind. "Thank you."

I watched as he handed the man his tickets and won his mother another teddy bear.

"Glad to see this tradition is still going strong." My eyes met his, and my heart began to thump loudly.

"I wasn't sure if you were going to come tonight." I could see the corners of his mouth turn up as he fought against his own

Full of Grace

smile. "The barn looks great, huh? I can't believe how much we were able to finish."

"Yeah, you should be proud of yourself. You really are good at that."

"Thanks." His eyes sparkled in the moonlight, and I waited for him to say something else. "What's up?"

Now was my chance. If I didn't ask him then, I never would, and I thought I owed it to the both of us to just do it.

"Do you want to go for a ride on the Ferris wheel?" I asked him. "I've still got some tickets, and the fireworks are going to start soon."

Caleb smiled widely and nodded. "I would love to."

We walked silently to the Ferris wheel and waited in line with the rest of the people who were desperate to see the fireworks display. The line started moving, and I felt Caleb's hand on the small of my back, gently guiding me forward, and I felt as though I might melt under his touch. It was just as strong as it was the other day. Fate was definitely on my side. I looked back at him and smiled.

"Caleb, I'm so sorry about everything," I blurted out. "I never meant to hurt you."

He didn't say anything. He just stood there, looking down at me quietly.

"Tickets," the girl said to us as we approached the ride.

I handed her our tickets and made my way into the car, making sure to buckle myself in, and she closed the door tightly behind us. There was no way out of this now that we were locked in and about to be forty feet off the ground.

"Leah," he said, grabbing ahold of my hands and placing them in his lap. "What happened after high school was so long ago. We were kids. It took me a long time to get over it, but I am. You don't have to apologize."

He's over it? What have I done?

The ride started moving, jolting us both forward, and we smacked into each other. My heart started racing and I began to panic. I needed to get out of there but I couldn't. I wasn't about to jump out. I needed to face my fears. I needed to be a grown up. And since there was nowhere for me to run, now was as good a time as any to start.

"I guess I just wish I hadn't made some of the choices that I made back then," I admitted.

"Yeah, but Leah," he said, "if you hadn't made those choices, you wouldn't be where you are now. And neither would I. We've both become successful in our own right, and I can only speak for myself here, but I'm happy with how life has treated me."

"I'm happy too," I agreed, looking longingly into his piercing blue eyes. "But I still feel bad."

The Ferris wheel stopped, and we were at the top. It was like a scene from a cheesy movie. The fireworks started shooting off into the sky, beautiful colors and shapes illuminating every part.

"Leah?" Caleb said, running his hand through his hair nervously.

"Yes, Caleb?" I replied, still looking at the fireworks.

"I could be happier," he said, causing me to spin around in the seat and look at him.

My breath caught in my throat, and I didn't know what to say. I wasn't entirely sure what was happening.

"You could?" I asked.

He nodded and licked his lips. He was so nervous. I had put us in this mess, and I should be the one to get us out of it.

"Caleb, I love you," I said, biting my lip. "I shouldn't have let you go then, and I shouldn't have waited so long to tell you I was back. It's always been you, and it will always be you. I'm sorry it took me so long to figure it all out."

"Shut up and kiss me," he said and smiled.

A soft chuckle slipped out of his mouth as it met mine. The connection was so strong, and it was as if the world had righted all of its wrongs. *Now, I am truly home.*

28

CALEB

SIX MONTHS LATER

WHAT SEEMED LIKE AN UNATTAINABLE FEAT TURNED OUT TO BE my future. I couldn't have been any happier with Leah. Tossing the few remaining folders I still needed to go through into my briefcase, I latched it, put my coat on, and flicked the light switch. I was exhausted and thankful to not have to return back to school for a few days.

Basketball season was in full swing and the beginning of the third quarter of classes had just begun. Everyone was busy and still reeling over the extra-long Christmas break thanks to all of the snow we had been getting. The kids loved their snow days, but I had a feeling they weren't taking into consideration all of the days that would be tacked on to the end of the school year in June.

I popped my trunk open and threw my briefcase inside next to the basketballs that had once again found their way outside of the mesh bag I had them in. I really needed to get a better setup for this stuff. As soon as I was in the driver's seat, I plugged my phone into the charger and started my car. Oh, how I wished I had remote start so I wouldn't have to wait for it to warm up. I dialed Leah's number while I waited.

"Hello, my love," she greeted me. "Are you heading over here?"

I would never get sick of hearing her voice. I could hear her rifling through papers and assumed she was still at the office. She could probably benefit from a relaxing night in too.

"Do you want to meet me at my place instead? We can order in and just relax. Today was long."

"Sure, I'll grab something on my way there. Any preference?"

"I could go for Italian."

"Works for me," she said. "I'll be there in about an hour and a half. I really need to get the rest of the project done so I won't have to work this weekend."

"All right. See you soon."

I spent the first seventeen years of my life loving Leah, but that was nothing compared to the way I felt about her now. As cliché as it sounded, she was a part of me that I couldn't live without. I didn't want to and I wouldn't. I'd been down that road before and while I was capable of being without her, I wasn't happy that way.

The car finally warmed up, and I was on the road home, grateful the day was over. The roads were fairly empty as everyone was probably home getting ready for their dinners and nightly routines. I found myself daydreaming of a life with Leah where we would be preparing and eating dinner with our kids before snuggling up to them and putting them to bed for the night.

I took a sharp left turn down the windy road where I was renting a small cottage from Mr. and Mrs. Kratzes' daughter and son-in-law. It was a tiny, two-bedroom, two-bathroom house, but it was perfect. There was plenty of room for me, plus enough space if Leah ever decided she wanted to move in. We hadn't discussed it yet, but the thought was always lingering in the back of my mind. And the way things were going, I could see that happening in the near to distant future. Hopefully, near.

I had enough time to shower and straighten up a bit before she arrived, and it was nice to be in my sweats on the couch and not wearing a suit in a stuffy office anymore. I heard Leah's key slide into the lock and got up to meet her in the kitchen.

"I got food from Franco's, that new place next to the coffee shop. I have no idea how good it is, but Jackie told me she went there a few nights ago and loved it." Her eyes sparkled with excitement over the discussion of food.

Man, I love this woman.

"Honestly, I'm so hungry right now that I would be fine with anything at this point." I rubbed my stomach, which was growling so loudly they could probably hear it the next town over.

"Well, we better get you good and fed then," she laughed, giving me a quick peck and unloading the take-out bag.

"Which would you prefer? Chicken piccata or chicken marsala?" she asked me, knowing damn well I knew that marsala was one of her favorite meals.

"I'm not falling for that one." I winked. "I'll take the piccata. Did it come with any bread?"

She smiled and pulled out another paper bag, revealing the dinner rolls. "You think I'd forget that?"

I pulled her close and held her against my beating heart for a few seconds before kissing her forehead. I stared into her eyes and slowly reached my arms back around her body, grabbing a garlic knot and popping it into my mouth.

"Let's eat," I said and grabbed the food off the table.

"You're such a tease, Caleb Patterson," she said, shaking her head and following me into the family room.

She was right, though. I loved to tease her in any way I could. I turned back and winked at her and then tripped over my own two feet and almost dropped the food on the floor.

Full of Grace

"See? God punished you," she teased right back, holding out a hand to make sure I didn't actually drop the food.

"I grabbed a bottle of red from the pantry earlier if you'd like some." I held the bottle out and picked up a glass from the coffee table.

She nodded and took the glass from my hand while I poured for her and then myself. I sat on the couch and got settled with my food. I didn't speak for five minutes while I inhaled as much food as I possibly could without a care in the world about how much I looked like a pig.

"How was your day?" I asked when I finally came up for air.

"Long and very busy," she said, carefully taking a bit of her chicken. "I can't wait until it slows down again. I'm burning out."

I wiped my mouth and put my food down on the coffee table. "Maybe you should hire someone for the entire year instead of just a temporary intern. Your business is continuing to grow, and I'm not sure it's healthy for you to carry on like this alone."

"I know," she said, nodding in agreement. "You're right, but I don't even know where to start."

"Try a temp agency. They have candidates with various backgrounds, and you can interview them yourself to see if you think they would be a good fit. I could also ask Sally if she knows anyone who might be looking for a part-time gig."

"Oh, that would be great! I didn't even think of Sally," she exclaimed.

Sally was one of the secretaries at Grace Valley School, and she knew just about everyone, including a slew of stay-at-home moms who were always looking for something to do. If she couldn't find someone to help Leah out, no one could.

"Hand me the garlic knots, please." She puffed out her bottom lip in the cutest pout. "I could eat those things all day."

I smiled and handed her the tray. We finished our dinner, and I refilled our wine glasses as she cleared the empty food containers and tossed them into the kitchen trash.

"Can we watch the cooking show competition? I've been trying to catch up, and I think the finale is tonight."

"Only if you promise to try to cook something from the show," I replied.

"Oh, you're so on." She laughed. "But we both have to."

"Deal."

I patted the couch next to me, and she scooted over. She picked up the remote to the gas fireplace and clicked the button to turn it on before grabbing a blanket that I had draped over the back of the couch. She brushed her hair off her neck and rested her head on my shoulder. I could have stayed like this forever.

About twenty minutes into the show, my phone started buzzing on the coffee table. Leah reached out to grab it and handed it to me. Her breath caught and she cleared her throat.

"Um, here," she said, handing the phone back to me.

Her nostrils flared, and I furrowed my brows in confusion. Looking down at the screen, I realized why she reacted the way she had.

"What the fuck?"

Brittany.

"Caleb, what's going on?" Leah asked me, slowly turning her body so it was no longer under the blanket.

I didn't know why she started calling me again, but I hadn't told Leah about her calling me before, and I wasn't ready for this conversation. I knew I should have told her, but we weren't together then, and I didn't really think I owed her anything at that point. I was kicking myself for not just being open and honest.

"Caleb, answer me," she said, flinging the rest of the blanket toward me and darting up.

"It's not what you think," I replied, immediately regretting my choice in words.

"Not what I think?" she yelled. "Well, then why don't you explain it? Because you don't even want to know what I'm thinking right now."

I rubbed my forehead and ran my hands down my face, stopping to close my eyes and try to figure shit out. I took a deep breath and stood up, maintaining eye contact the entire time. She wasn't going to like what I had to say, but I wasn't about to lie to her.

"She started calling and texting me last summer," I admitted. "I sent all calls to voicemail and deleted all text messages before I even had a chance to read them. Then one day, I answered and told her to never contact me again and almost threw my phone in the pond at the meadow. That's it."

Leah began to pace, and that's when I knew it was going to be a long night. She was a fairly patient person, but when she felt that someone was trying to play her, watch out. I knew I had to choose my words wisely because the bomb that stood in front of me could detonate at any second.

"Leah, I promise you." I walked across the room to where she was standing and reached my hand out to her.

I wanted her to know that she had full reign over what happened next.

She took a deep breath and placed her hand in mine, allowing me to gently pull her into my arms. I caressed her back and gently kissed her hair, hoping this was the end of the conversation, but knowing damn well it was only the beginning. I lifted her chin with my fingers and looked her in the eyes before bending down to kiss her.

"I really don't know what her problem is, but I want nothing to do with her. I haven't uttered a word to her since we broke up, with the exception of telling her to leave me alone."

She wrapped her arms around my neck and looked up at me, sadness filling her eyes. "I know. I just can't stand her."

I laughed at her declaration. Nobody could stand Brittany. I motioned for us to reclaim our spots on the couch when my phone buzzed for the second time. I looked at Leah and clicked the button to send the call to voicemail again.

"I should change my number."

I tossed my phone over to the loveseat and snuggled up next to Leah. Thankfully, that whole ordeal only lasted the length of the commercial break, and we were able to get back to the show without missing much. Leah's choice for chefs ultimately won the challenge, and we changed programs to watch old reruns of a sitcom. Just when we were getting ready to head to bed, my phone rang for the third time. I couldn't send it to voicemail because it was closer to Leah. She launched herself across the couch to the loveseat and snatched up the phone.

Shit.

"Hello? Hello?" She looked over at me and handed me my phone.

"She hung up," she said.

"Good," I replied, folding the blanket and grabbing the wine glasses. "Now, let's go to bed."

29

LEAH

It had been a little over a month since Brittany called Caleb, and while I was confident he wanted nothing to do with her, I couldn't shake the feeling that she would do anything to win him back. People like her don't just stop. I knew she was planning something. I could feel it.

I rolled over and propped myself up on my elbow, sinking into the pillow, but it gave me a better view of Caleb. The rhythmic pattern of his chest rising and falling soothed my anxious mind. I had already lost him once, and there was no way in hell I was losing him again.

The need for coffee hit me hard, so I carefully slid out of bed and stepped into my slippers. I grabbed a hoodie I had left draped on the end of Caleb's bed and threw it on. The wood-burning stove was blazing, so he must have woken up and filled it not too long ago. God, I loved that man. He pulled sixty-hour weeks at work and still got up in the middle of the night to make sure the fire didn't go out. I warmed my hands by the fire before heading into the kitchen. I would take too long to heat up the water for the French press, so I just made us two coffees from his single serve machine. I drank half of my cup before his was even done.

"Caleb?" I called out softly, sitting on the side of the bed holding both mugs.

"Hmm," he grumbled, pulling the covers tighter over his body.

"I made coffee," I told him, subtly bribing him to sit up.

It worked.

"Thank you." He readjusted himself and reached out to take the hot mug. "This tastes amazing."

My cheeks plumped as my smile grew wider. "You say that every time I make you coffee."

"That's because it's true." He leaned over to kiss me. "Mm, morning breath."

I playfully swatted at him. "Stop that!"

"Come back to bed where it's warmer," he said, rubbing the sheets next to him. "There's something I want to run by you."

I furrowed my brows but went back under the covers. He was right, I was freezing sitting there, but the coffee was helping. I had come to enjoy my weekends here with him. It was just what we needed after so many years apart. He placed his mug on the nightstand and turned to face me, looking at me with an expression I couldn't quite decipher.

"Leah, there's something I need to tell you." The words flew out of his mouth, and my heart dropped.

That was never a good thing to hear. In fact, it was usually began an admission of some sort, and I wasn't ready for anything on that level.

"Is everything okay?" I asked him, biting my bottom lip.

He held my hands and smiled, his cheeks changing to a pink tone. "I want you to move in."

My jaw dropped and my hands flew up to cover my face. "Oh my God."

"You okay over there?" His soothing voice brought me back, and I looked at him, my pout ever-present.

"I thought something was wrong," I said, shaking my head. "I'm glad you're okay, but for the record, please don't ever start a conversation with 'There's something I need to tell you' because that is the worst thing you could say."

Caleb laughed a little and squeezed my hands, his touch alone set fire to my entire body. "What do you say? You wanna move in here with me?"

His upper lip twitched. He was nervous, and it was so cute to watch it happening while he anxiously waited for my response. I let him suffer for a few seconds longer than I should have, but he deserved it. Of course I wanted to live with him. I had been spending every weekend here already and the occasional weeknight when we weren't too busy. It was the natural progression for the type of relationship we were in, and I was more than ready for the next step.

"I would love to move in with you," I answered him, my heart bursting with love and excitement.

"Great, let's go to your house and start packing now."

I leaned over and kissed him, wrapping my arms around his neck and nuzzling up tighter next to him. His warm breath on my neck sent shivers up and down my spine in the best possible way.

"I think we have some time before we need to do that. It's seven a.m."

"All right, I guess it can wait until tomorrow, then." He winked and grabbed the remote.

He turned on the television and flipped through the channels, stopping on the Weather Channel. More snow was coming, and it was getting to the point where we would be buried if it didn't stop soon. I love the snow, but when it snows every single day, it gets to be annoying. But I wouldn't mind being snowed in with the love of my life.

We sat in bed watching TV until we were too hungry to be lazy anymore.

"I don't feel like cooking anything," I said. "Do you want to get some food at the diner?"

"Definitely." He peeled off his sweatpants and replaced them with his jeans.

THERE WERE a handful of people in the diner. Not as many as most Saturdays, but enough to surprise me given the temperature outside. We sat in a booth in the back, and Tammy came right over to us with two mugs and a carafe of coffee.

"Freshly brewed." She smiled as she poured some into the mugs. "I'm surprised to see you two here this morning. Everything all right at the house?"

"Everything is fine, Mom," Caleb told her. "We just wanted to eat out."

"All right then. What can I get for you?"

"Pancakes, sausage, and scrambled eggs." Caleb winked after he placed his order.

"I'll just have a western omelet with home fries, please," I replied, handing her my menu.

I would have ordered a side of cardboard if it meant I would get to eat. I felt like I hadn't eaten in days.

"So"—Caleb ran his tongue across his bottom lip—"we're really going to do this?"

I smoothed my napkin across my lap and looked back up at him. "Yeah, we are."

"I've been waiting for this moment for a long time, Leah."

"Me too."

"Well, whenever you're ready, you let me know, and I'll come help you get whatever you need."

I was on cloud nine, and even though I had assumed that our relationship would naturally progress in this direction, I never expected it would happen so soon. But I wasn't complaining. This was the life I had dreamed of, and it was perfect. I looked across the table at Caleb and smiled at the man he had grown into. A part of me regretted not being able to witness the change, but the rest of me was so grateful to be able to be with him again. He locked his phone and gently placed it screen-side up on the table—a sign of trust that didn't go unnoticed.

"Leah, my dear." His eyes sparkled when he said my name. "What's going through that amazing mind of yours?"

I stretched my arms across the table and took his hands in mine. A single touch from him could still scatter goosebumps across my arms and make my heart skip a beat. I couldn't imagine being in a better place with him than where we were in that very moment.

"Here you go, love birds." Tammy placed our food in front of us and winked. "Enjoy."

I stabbed my fork into the home fries and shoved it into my mouth, savoring every bit of the diced peppers and onions that were mixed in.

"Classy," Caleb teased, reaching across the table with his napkin.

"I've got it, thanks." I laughed.

"Do you remember that barbecue we went to with Jess and Matt Homecoming Weekend our junior year?" he asked me out of the blue.

"Yeah, why?" I replied, taking another bite.

He placed his fork down, wiped his mouth, and sat straight up. *This is going to be good.*

"You refused to eat anything at the game because you wanted to make sure you had room for Matt's dad's famous burgers, and when we got to the barbecue, you were so hungry that you basically inhaled the burger." He paused to take a bit of his breakfast. "You were such a slob with the burger juices dripping down your arms, but you didn't care. You only cared about that burger."

I threw my head back and laughed. Cheeseburgers were in a food group of their own. I didn't know what Matt's dad did to his, but they were the best damn burgers I had ever eaten. I looked forward to any party at his house just for those burgers. It was even written in my likes section of the senior yearbook.

"Oh, that's such a good point." I picked up my phone to text Jess. "We should see if his dad will make us some for our next game night."

Caleb laughed and shook his head. "There are so many things I love about you, Leah Abernathy, but this one might take the cake."

I winked and raised my eyebrows. A little flirting in the local diner was harmless, but it did make me want to get out of there quickly and back home with Caleb. He looked back with at me with mischief in his eyes, and I could tell he was thinking the same thing. Our flame had fizzled out once before, but this second chance had set our hearts ablaze.

"Hey, Mom," Caleb called across the empty diner to the bar where Tammy was sitting. "You mind bringing us the bill when you get a chance?"

She nodded and disappeared into the back. Caleb and I played footsie under the table while we waited, trading smiles back and forth to each other. I brushed the hair out of my face, gently placing it behind my ear when I heard the voice that caused Caleb's entire demeanor to change. He clenched his jaw and his nostrils flared. *No way this is happening right now.*

"Hey, y'all." The shrill of a familiar southern twang pierced my eardrums.

"Oh, shit." Caleb leaned back in the booth. "Brittany, what are you doing here?"

I slowly turned around to see Brittany standing behind our

booth, dressed to the nines with a baby bouncing on her hip. For a brief second, I saw her expression change to shock when she saw that I was sitting with Caleb. She quickly regained her stance and adjusted the baby.

"Now is that any way to greet your fiancée, Caleb?"

"I am not your fiancé anymore, Brittany. What do you want?"

"I've been trying to reach you, and you weren't picking up your phone, so I decided to come to this little town to get some answers," she admitted, her bright red lips pouting with every word she uttered. "I went to your Mom's place first, but no one was there. I thought I'd come here to see if she could tell me how to find you."

Tammy walked out of the back with our bill and froze in her steps. I could see the confusion on her face as she realized who was standing behind me.

Caleb stood up and walked to the side of the booth, careful not to get too close to Brittany. I remained seated, conflicted between wanting to crawl under the table and cry and getting up and punching her in the face. But I couldn't hit a lady who was holding a baby so I just sat there. Whose baby was that, anyway?

30

CALEB

"What are you doing here?" I nodded to the baby in her arms. "And whose baby did you steal?"

I could feel my mom's and Leah's eyes on me as they both whipped their heads in my direction. I didn't care how rude I sounded.

"Oh, Caleb, silly." Brittany came closer to me and I instinctively backed up. "This precious little boy is Colt. He's our son."

Seeing her standing there with a child . . . thinking he could have been mine should have been my first thought. But I wasn't in the right frame of mind to think logically, and I wasn't thinking that I could be anyone's father. Brittany was so shady, that kid could have belonged to anyone, except he looked just like her but with my eyes. In a split second, I went from angry that she was there to full-blown panicking. I sat back down in the booth and stared at Leah, who was breathing heavy and looking at my mom.

"Excuse me, what did you just say?" my mom demanded.

"Tammy," Brittany started.

"Mrs. Patterson," my mother interrupted. "You may call me Mrs. Patterson."

Brittany sneered and subtly rolled her eyes. "Well, then, Mrs. Patterson. I hate to burst your little bubble, but this is your grandson. This is Caleb's son. And maybe if he picked up his phone when I called, he wouldn't be so shocked to find out about him now."

Her smirk was enough to make anyone want to slap her, but that wasn't how we did things here. There were already enough hotheads in this place, and the last thing this town needed was gossip about the assault of a new mom. I grabbed the closest glass of water to me and chugged it. I wasn't sure if I was going to pass out or explode, so I just sat there trying to absorb everything that was just thrown at me.

Brittany sauntered over to me, baby Colt still on her hip, and seductively leaned against the table, her back to Leah. Only Brittany could spring a baby on someone while they were having brunch with their girlfriend in their mother's restaurant and then continue to try to seduce them. I could only imagine what she would have been like had I actually went through with the marriage.

"Caleb, darling." She licked her lips and smiled at me. "Don't you want to hold your son?"

I looked up and across the table to Leah to see a lone tear trickle down her cheek. Her eyes met mine, and the look of devastation in them mirrored exactly how I had felt the night she broke up with me before leaving for college. Our world went from nearly perfect to completely shattered, again.

"Brittany, I don't know what kind of sick joke you think you're playing, but it isn't funny." I stood up and stared down at her. "Where are you staying? Let's get you out of here."

"We're staying with you, silly," she proclaimed as if she had control over everything.

That baby boy was beautiful. But was he mine? Could I really be someone's father? The more I looked at him, the more I saw myself in his little face. I stroked his little hand, and he firmly clutched onto my finger as if to say yes.

"No, you most certainly are not staying at our house," Leah finally spoke. "You are not welcome here." She stood up and looked at my mother—for guidance, maybe—and turned around. "Now, if you'll excuse me, I need to use the restroom."

My heart began to pound, and I had flashbacks of her leaving me when we were younger.

"Leah, wait," I called out to her.

She turned back toward me, her eyebrows pulled close together and her mouth tightly closed. "Get her out of here."

The slamming of the bathroom door caused me to close my eyes, and I was grateful that the only other person in the diner at that moment was Dante in the kitchen. The soap opera that had become my life was not a channel I needed to subscribe to any longer.

"Brittany, this is not the time or place to have this discussion. Is your car parked outside?"

"No, I took a bus to Virginia and then three different trains until we ended up here."

Dante walked out of the kitchen, wiping his hands on a towel he had tucked into his pocket. "Do you know how dangerous it is to travel that far of a distance alone with a baby that young? What were you thinking?"

"Save it, old man." Brittany's arrogant nature was on full display. "I don't need your two cents. Go back into the kitchen."

"Don't you dare talk to my staff that way. I will have your ass escorted out of here so fast your head will spin." My mother was searing.

"There is a bed and breakfast in Litchfield," I intervened, needing to halt this before it turned into a war. "I can call and see if there are any rooms available for you and the baby."

"His name is Colt. And, no, I will not be staying in some

stupid hick-town bed and breakfast. Just take me to your house so I can get some rest."

I needed to nip this in the bud, and quick.

"Let's go for a drive, get you guys settled, and we can talk there, okay?"

The thought of being alone with me and the baby seemed to please her because her appearance softened.

"Thank you." She reached out to grab my hand, and I pulled away quickly. "The car seat is over in the front entry."

"Wonderful," my mother sneered, still standing an arm's length away.

I dug into my pants pocket for my keys and clicked the remote start button. I wanted to make sure the car was warm enough for the baby. I still couldn't believe she was here. With a baby. That could be mine.

"Mom, could you let Leah know that I left?"

I didn't need to finish my question for her to read my thoughts. She closed her eyes and nodded, walking to the bathroom.

Poor Leah was still in the bathroom, probably falling apart at the seams, and I couldn't leave Brittany to go and check on her because I didn't know what kind of nonsense she would pull if I let her out of my sight.

I grabbed my coat while Brittany fastened the baby into his car seat. I glanced back across the diner just in time to see Leah exit the bathroom, her eyes puffy. When they met mine, she cried while slowly nodding, letting me know she understood. I mouthed, "I love you" as we exited the diner.

"My car is right over here." I motioned to the road. "I'll pull it up for you two to get in."

"Thank you," she said, struggling with the diaper bag and her overnight bag.

"Here, let me take the bags to the car for you," I offered.

"Don't forget the stroller," she called, motioning back toward the diner as I was headed toward the car.

Where had she hid that?

I brushed the snow off the windshield and drove over to the front of the diner. I hoped the flurrying would be the worst of it because I didn't want to get stranded, and I was not about to stay at the bed and breakfast with Brittany. She carefully placed the seat in the back and secured it tightly with the seat belt. I was shocked at the level of care she provided this little boy considering she was the most selfish person I had ever known.

"Do you need any help with that?" I offered.

She looked up and flashed her sparkling white smile. "No thanks, I'm used to this. Piece of cake."

Brittany wiped the snow off her shoulders and got into the passenger seat. After fastening her seat belt, she looked over at me and paused for a moment.

"I'm sorry, Caleb, but I tried to tell you."

Tried to tell me? She never tried to tell me. She sent a text message about clothes. And then when she tried calling, she never left a voicemail. I could be the father of this little boy and I'd missed out on, what, six months of his life already because she couldn't just own up to things in the very beginning?

Did she really think that backhanded apology was going to suffice? There was a baby in the back seat of my car that wasn't the child of my current girlfriend. Did she not see the problem there? I white-knuckled the steering wheel and pulled out onto the main road. Breathing out a long breath, I was finally ready to talk to her.

"Brittany, this is serious. And we definitely need to talk about it, but it's too much for me right now," I told her. "I'll book you a room at the bed and breakfast, and I'll pay for everything. But I need you to give me some space. This is freaking me out."

She smiled her Cheshire Cat grin and shrugged her shoulders.

Full of Grace

"He's yours, babe. Ain't nothing you can say to change that. Just take me back to your place."

"I don't live alone, Brittany. That isn't appropriate," I lied—sort of. Leah was going to move in, she just hadn't yet.

Luckily, that kept her quiet for the remainder of the drive and thirty minutes later, we pulled into the parking lot. "Stay here while I check to see if there's a room. Is there anything special you need for the baby?"

"Just a crib, if possible."

"Okay, I'll be right back."

I combed my fingers through my hair, not believing my actions were real life. It had to be a dream. No, a nightmare. The bed and breakfast was nearly empty, so I was able to secure a room for them without a problem. I got back to the car to see Brittany sitting in the back seat bottle feeding the baby, so I popped open the trunk and started taking their things out.

"Why don't you get him inside, and I'll bring everything in for you?"

"Okay," she said quietly, surprising me with her lack of fighting the issue.

I wanted to be inside of her head so badly. There were so many answers I needed, and I knew she wasn't going to give them freely. Everything with Brittany came with a cost. One too steep for me to pay. I got them settled into the room and sat on the edge of the bed while she finished feeding Colt. She soothed him and rubbed his cheek as he drank. Being a mother looked good on her, I had to admit. I just hoped she didn't screw up that little boy's life.

"Brittany, this is a lot to take in right now, and I need some time to process it all, but I will call you later to check up on you." I knew she wasn't going to like that, but if she wanted the outcome she desired, she was going to have to play by someone else's rules for the time being.

She lifted her finger and placed it in front of her lips. "Shh."

I watched in awe as she placed the baby in the crib and caressed his little cheek again before kissing her fingers and placing them on his forehead.

"I understand," she said in barely a whisper, standing over the suitcase she was preparing to unpack. "We'll be here if you change your mind and want to come back."

"I'll talk to you later, Brittany." I knew it was a dick move to leave and not discuss this, but I was so messed up in the head over it that I had to leave.

I looked at Colt sleeping peacefully, his tiny body looked even smaller in the large crib they provided. Even with his eyes closed, he was a spitting image of his mother. He was a beautiful baby, but he wasn't mine. Was he?

31
LEAH

As the door to the diner slammed shut, I crumbled into Tammy's arms, watching my future disappear with his past. The morning rush had started to trickle in, so I composed myself as best I could and gathered my belongings.

"I'm going to walk to my office, Tammy. I need a little air."

"Okay, dear. You know how to reach me if you need me." She rested her hand softly on my forearm.

I sucked in my lip and bit down, trying now to let any more tears escape my increasingly puffy eyes. It was hard not to feel so negative about things when they all came crashing down on you at once. I opened the door and the cold air stung my face as icicles formed on my eyelashes. It hurt so good. I could feel my phone vibrating in my pocket, and I scrambled to get it, hoping it would be Caleb telling me he was on his way back and this was all a cruel joke. My heart dropped when I saw Becky's name flash across the screen instead.

I wiped the tears away and tried to stand up tall. "Hello?"

"Leah, what the hell is going on? I just saw Caleb get into his car Brittany and a baby!" She spoke so fast I wasn't sure she even took a breath. "I'm across the street at the shop. Just come over and I'll fix you a coffee."

She hung up before I could protest, but everyone in this town knew they could reel me in with a promise of caffeine, so off I went. I felt like all I had been doing that morning was holding and releasing my breath, afraid of what might come next. If I held it long enough, maybe it would take away some of the pain.

Nope.

Becky flung her shop door so hard that it almost smacked me in the face. Although, that probably would have taken my mind off Caleb for at least five minutes. I jumped back, narrowly avoiding contact, and then scurried into the shop as if I were going to get swept away with the wind.

"Shit, Leah! I'm sorry," she apologized as she wiped the snow off my jacket. "Here, come sit down. I've got coffee and cookies."

I hung up my coat on the hook and looked back across the street to the diner. The pavement where Caleb's car was parked was starting to get covered with the snow, quickly erasing any trace of him being there. My bottom lip began to quiver, and I turned around to see Becky stand up, her arms outstretched, ready to envelop me in a much needed hug.

"Sweetie, what is going on?"

I cleared my throat and looked up at her, feeling grateful. "Brittany is back. She's back for Caleb and says the baby is his. I'm trying to be strong, but, Becky, I just got him back."

"Excuse me, what? Caleb has a baby? With Cruella de Vil? What is this world coming to?"

"Apparently, but I don't think the baby is his. I don't want to sound like 'that girl,' but something tells me Brittany knows that too." I shocked myself when I admitted that out loud, but it was the truth.

Becky released me from her maternal grip and slowly sat

down on her chair. I followed suit and watched as her expression went from shocked to confused to angry.

"What I don't understand is why she's bringing a child here to tell him now? Hasn't she ever heard of a phone?"

"She's tried contacting him quite a bit, and he's ignored her. So, I guess this was the next best thing," I explained.

She crossed her legs and then her arms, pursing her lips and sucking her teeth. "I don't believe a thing that comes out of that girl's mouth. I knew she was trouble the second she set foot in this shop."

"Becky!" I exclaimed. "I mean, I don't like her either, but geez."

Becky let out a quiet laugh and shrugged her shoulders. She was never one to keep her feelings quiet, and while I didn't agree with her terminology in that moment, I could appreciate her mama bear tendencies for me.

"I don't know what to do," I admitted. "I really thought the past was behind us, and we could fully move on. We were just talking about moving in together, and then she walked into the diner, crushing all of our plans. And who the hell is the father? I know it's not Caleb, Becky. I can feel it. Oh my gosh, what if he *is* the father? Is he going to leave me for her? I can't do this."

"Breathe, Leah." Becky held her hands up in front of me, signaling me to slow down. "You're going to make yourself sick over something that you can't control. I think you need to wait and see what he says when he gets back. Where is he anyway?"

"Caleb took them to a bed and breakfast so she would have a place to stay. Becky, I can't lose him. I can't."

Tears began streaming down my face, and my body shook uncontrollably. I had felt pain and hurt before, but not like this. This was mixed with fear, and I wasn't equipped to handle it. Normally, I would bury myself in my work, get so consumed with responsibilities that I wouldn't have to think about anything, but not this time. This time I needed to wallow in my sadness and let it get the best of me so that I would be able to talk to Caleb like a rational adult when—if—he came back.

"Becky, is Jackie here today? Can one of you please take me home? I really don't want to walk right now."

"It's slow, sweetheart." She stood up and pulled her coat off the hook behind the register. "I'll take you."

32

CALEB

I had left Brittany and all she encompassed back in Tennessee with the intent of never speaking to her again. So how did she end up back in Grace Valley with a kid.

"Anything she needs, just put it on the tab, and I'll pay it when they check out," I told the clerk at the front desk.

I buttoned up my coat and rushed out the door and to my car. The snow had really started coming down, but I needed to get home and back to Leah to fix this mess. There was nothing that could keep me from her, especially not this. The car was still warm from the drive over so just a quick brush off of the snow was enough, and then I was on my way. With the way the storm had hit, I knew it was going to take me at least an hour to get back, but she was worth it.

The roads were slick, and I had to be more cautious than I'd been in years. Living in Tennessee during winter was a blessing. I hadn't seen snow the entire time I had lived there, and I didn't miss it. But I'd always missed Leah.

Shit.

Trees were down everywhere. I downshifted just as my car started to slide toward the embankment, and I gripped the steering wheel, my car immediately fishtailing. I turned the wheel back and forth until I was safely back on the road again. In hindsight, I should have pulled over and relaxed my brain for a minute instead of haphazardly racing home. But I needed to be with her. I needed it more for her than for me, and that's how I knew every decision I made from there on out should be made with her in mind.

I needed to drown out the voices in my head, so I turned the radio on to the local rock station. I always listened to rock when I was working out or playing ball. The beating of the drums and strumming of the guitar got my mind right, and before I knew it, I was home. I didn't know what made me think she would be there waiting for me, but when I opened the front door and ran inside, it was dark and quiet, just as we'd left it.

I pulled my phone out of my pocket to check if she had left any messages, but there was nothing. The machine wasn't blinking either, so I knew she hadn't called the house phone. I sat on the couch with my head in my hands and thought about all of the places she might be. The snow had piled up to a good foot. I would back out for her in a heartbeat, but it wasn't safe. My mother had texted me while I was driving home that she was closing the diner early due to the storm, and she never closed early.

I started to dial her number to let her know I had made it home safe when my front door flew open, the wind blowing in snow at a rapid speed. I jumped off the couch and walked to the door to see Leah brushing the snow off her coat and kicking her boots to a corner of the mudroom.

"Holy crap, it's bad out there," she said, shaking her head, more snow falling to the floor.

"Leah, you should have called me. I would have picked you up on my way through town. Where were you?"

Her eyes were swollen, and I could tell she had been crying. Our beautiful morning had turned to shit, and I needed to fix it somehow. I cradled her in my arms, and she began to sob, a heavy, gut-wrenching sob. I felt like I had broken her. I silently rubbed her back and held her in my arms until she was ready to talk.

"I went home," she whispered. "I needed to be alone."

I held her hand, gently guiding her behind me into the kitchen, and I put a kettle of water on the stove.

We continued to hold hands until the water boiled, and I needed both to pour. It felt good to be needed and, ultimately, still wanted. She didn't say a word as I placed the mugs and tea bags on the kitchen table. In fact, she didn't do anything except sit down and stare off into space. I made her tea the way she liked and slid it across the table to her. She lifted her hands and wrapped them around the mug without moving her eyes. This was going to be harder than I thought.

"I love you, Leah—"

"Do you think he's yours?" she whispered, her eyes slowly looking up to meet mine.

I stood up and moved my chair until we were sitting right next to each other instead of across from one another. I placed my hands palms up and waited for her to hold them. I wanted her to know that she was in control of this conversation, and I was just there to make sure she knew I was listening.

"Leah, I love you, and I would never do anything to jeopardize what we have. I am not getting back with Brittany. I know that, she knows that—whether she chooses to believe it or not—and now you know it. Listen, I don't know if Colt is mine, and even if he is, that will not change a thing between us. I will do what's right, but I won't be a part of her life any more than I need to be."

Her eyes ceasefired, and her breathing slowed to a normal speed. I noticed she was picking at her fingers, so I cupped my hands over hers and waited for her to say something. She didn't.

"I got them a room. Told her they could stay as long as they needed, but that was it. Leah, you have to trust me."

When she finally looked back up at me again, she was almost hollow looking. I leaned over and kissed her hands, giving them a little squeeze. I had never seen her this way and was becoming worried about her. She licked her lips and bit her bottom lip, which had begun to quiver.

"I believe you; it's just really hard to process. That woman will stop at nothing to have you, and we all know it," she started. "Colt is a beautiful baby boy, and if he really is yours, we'll figure things out. I wouldn't expect you to not be in his life. But if I'm being honest, I feel like this is just another one of her games. Either way, you need to find out and you need to find out as soon as humanly possible."

Leah's intuition was unparalleled, and when she truly felt things were a certain way, she was always right. I didn't know how she did it or how she knew, but she always had. I was a disaster after she left for college, but even at seventeen years old, she knew what needed to be done in order to better her life. I admired that about her.

"You are a remarkable woman, Leah Abernathy, and I thought I couldn't love you anymore than I did, but you just keep proving me wrong."

She wiped her tears and smiled the first real smile I had seen since breakfast. "We weren't together. I can't get mad about something that happened before me, or after, whichever way you want to look at it. But I do think you should look into getting a paternity test."

"I know. I'm petrified. But I know it needs to happen. I just don't think she'll stick around long enough for that to happen," I told her, confident in my conclusions.

"Caleb, have you met her? She's the number one master manipulator. She will go to the ends of the earth to get what she wants, and she will pull out all the stops to make sure she has you back at the end of the day. Don't give her an inch because, I promise you, she will take a mile. I can almost guarantee that she will not leave here without you unless you take that test and prove otherwise. She knows how kind you are, and she's probably hoping you won't want to take one. That's how she's going to suck you back in. Don't fall for it."

"I appreciate you looking out, but it's not that serious."

She threw my hands back and flew off her chair. Her eyes widened and her nostrils flared, and out came the venom. "Are you delusional? Not that serious? I don't care if that is the Pope's baby, he's a baby! This isn't a joke, Caleb. You may not think she will stop at nothing to get what she wants, but you need to dot your i's and cross your t's because she will come at you with a vengeance if you don't take this seriously. And the sooner you do this, the sooner they're either back to Tennessee or you can start to have a relationship with your child."

I knew she was right, even though I wanted to wake up from this nightmare and move on with my life.

"I know. You're absolutely right. I was just letting my emotions get the best of me. You do realize that I'll need her permission to test the baby. God, why did she need to come back here?" I was so annoyed.

"Because she's a melodramatic psychopath, that's why. But I wouldn't worry about her anymore. We're going to get to the bottom of this, and hopefully, it will all be over soon and she will be on the next train back to Tennessee. I just hope for Colt's sake that she really does know who the father is."

Leah yawned, and I could tell that being in this kitchen discussing impossibilities wasn't going to change anything, so I suggested a movie. I shot Brittany a quick text to check in before we retreated to the couch. I was ready to sleep that entire day off.

33

CALEB

WHAT THE HELL IS THAT NOISE?

I rubbed my eyes, confused and still half asleep. I finally realized the sound was my cell phone. I rolled over to grab the phone off the nightstand and knocked it onto the floor. Ugh. Leah's phone started ringing as I reached down to grab my phone off the floor which was ringing again.

"What is going on right now?" Leah said from under the comforter. "What time is it?"

My eyes finally adjusted, and I could see the sun reflecting off the snow and peeking in through the sliver of space between the curtains.

"It's nine fifteen a.m.," I told her, shooting straight up. "Holy crap, we slept so late!"

"Who cares? It's Sunday, and we have nowhere to be." She turned her phone over and threw the comforter over her head.

I laughed at how cute she was. That girl could stay in bed all day if I'd let her. I followed suit and put my phone back on the nightstand, rolled over, and put my arms around her, pulling her close to me. I kissed her neck softly and held her tight. Then both of our phones went off at the same time and we had to answer.

Full of Grace

"Caleb." She shot up out of bed. "I have six missed calls from Becky. Did Dooley call you? I hope there's not an emergency."

"I don't know; I'm checking." I unlocked my phone and scrolled the notification screen. "Yep, and so did Becky. I'm going to call back now."

I pressed the button with his picture on it and waited for him to pick up. It was the longest ten seconds of my life.

"Caleb, what the hell is going on, man? Does Paul know about this? And where the hell is Leah? I swear, kid, you messed up big time," Dooley yelled at me through the phone.

I looked over to Leah, who hadn't called Becky yet, and she mouthed to me, "What's going on?"

"I don't know," I mouthed back.

"Dooley, what are you talking about? Leah is right here next to me."

"You might want to check your text messages," he said through short breaths.

I'd never heard him yell like this or even seen him mad—not that I could remember anyway. Whatever was going on must have been huge, but I couldn't figure out what he was talking about. Until I saw it: loads of messages from the townspeople congratulating me on the birth of my son. Some were from people who were confused about my relationship with Brittany and Leah, and wondering how this all happened. Some were just downright nasty. But the worst one was from Becky. She had taken a picture of Brittany outside of the bakery talking to Mrs. Kratz, who was doting over the baby.

"Dooley, what is she doing talking to Mrs. Kratz?"

"You tell me! Brittany was parading Colt around town, telling everyone and their mother that he's your son and that you two are back together. Care to explain?"

I was fuming. I jumped up out of bed and threw on my jeans

and a hoodie. I paced back and forth, debating between punching the wall and running into town to tell off Brittany.

"Shit! She got here yesterday and sprung this all on me. I really don't know anything other than that I might have a kid. But I can assure you that Leah and I are fine, and Brittany and I are never getting back together. That chick is so delusional and twisted!"

"I don't know, man. Some are saying he has your eyes. I wasn't there. Becky said she already knew about him but didn't tell me because she wanted me to hear it from you. Why didn't you call? Hell, I don't even want to know."

I had to get into town and get Brittany out of it, but I didn't want to run the risk of anyone seeing me with her again. I needed to put the rumors to rest, but how was I going to do that when everyone was out and about and probably keeping tabs on her like the hawks they were? I also didn't want to cause a scene, regardless of how mad I was. How did women watch this kind of stuff on TV? The drama was too much.

"I gotta go." I hung up the phone and threw it on the bed.

"What's going on?" Leah asked again.

"Go check the text from Becky in my phone."

I watched her reluctantly pick up the phone and type in my passcode. Her face turned multiple shades of red before she threw the phone back down and turned to look at me.

"You ready for that paternity test now?" She raised her eyebrows at me and got dressed.

"Where are you going?"

"I'm going to the office to get some work done while you figure out how to get Brittany out of this town. I think it'll be better for the town to see me before they see you."

"Are you sure, Leah? You can work here if you need to, or we can go to town together. I don't want you to be dragged through the mud for this."

"Oh, please, Caleb. I'm already knee-deep in mud, and I would gladly sink with you if I had to. We're going to get to the bottom of this one way or another. Let's just do it sooner rather than later."

She disappeared into the bathroom, and I could hear her turn the faucet on and brush her teeth. This entire weekend had been one disaster after another and, of course, it once again revolved around Brittany. It seemed like every argument we had was about her. How can the one person you try never see cause you so much pain and misery?

"Come on," she called from the door. "Let's go before I change my mind."

34

CALEB

As much as I didn't want to listen to her in that moment, I knew the best thing to do would be to listen to Leah. The only way to move past the baby-mama drama was to take a paternity test. I was hesitant on taking one initially because I honestly didn't think I could handle it if he was mine. I could have driven myself mad thinking about all of ways this child could or couldn't have been mine. For starters, Brittany had been so busy with work, and her newest clients had her traveling all over the country for the latest design trends. But also, I was always careful and we rarely had sex toward the end. The only reason I put a ring on her finger before Christmas was because I thought that was the natural next step. On the other hand, anything was possible, and I couldn't count my chickens before they hatched.

I dropped Leah off at her office and kissed her goodbye. Parking in the side lot so I wouldn't be seen, I began to scour the streets, desperate to find Brittany and haul her ass back to the B&B. The crowd must have gone home for lunch because there were barely any people out then. I wasn't in the mood to go inside of each and every store, but I wanted—no, I needed—to find her.

I was so angry that she would show up in my town and pull a

stunt like this. I wanted to ask myself who she thought she was but that would have gotten me nowhere. I knew who she was. A manipulative little bitch since the moment I met her but was too blind to see it until it was almost too late.

I went into the bakery for a coffee to fuel my search and ran into my mother. I loved her, but she was the last person I wanted to see that day. The amount of questioning that she was known for was not on my list of things to do, and I wasn't sure I could handle the added stress.

"Well, look what the cat dragged in." She kissed me on the cheek and nodded over to Mrs. Kratz and then back at me.

Mrs. Kratz winked and retreated to the coffee station. I loved the silent language everyone in this town spoke.

"Hey, Mom."

"You look like hell, Caleb. Let me buy you lunch too."

"Coffee is fine, Mom. Thanks. I'm good."

Mothers knew their children better than they knew themselves, and my mother could see right through me. I thanked Mrs. Kratz for the coffee when she handed it to me across the counter and sat in the corner booth with my mom. I would rather just get the conversation over with so I could get on with my day. But she surprised me once again and didn't hover or try to get involved.

"She went back to the bed and breakfast," she said, sipping her coffee and looking out the window. "The baby needed to take a nap."

"When?" was all I could get out.

She put her coffee down and looked at her watch, taking her time to watch me suffer. "About an hour ago."

I relaxed a bit knowing that it took at least thirty minutes to get to Litchfield, and I could take my time before heading over there. I didn't want to barge in guns blazing, so taking some extra time was a smart idea. I felt my body calm down, and my shoulders released the tension they had been carrying since she'd arrived. It was a feeling I wasn't sure I would feel again, and it was nice. My mother noticed it too.

"Just be kind; whatever you end up saying to her. At the end of the day, there is still a baby in the picture."

"I will."

"And for the record, we will welcome that little boy with open arms if he is yours," she said, stroking the back of my hand reassuringly. "So, don't you even worry about that."

We finished our coffee in silence and waved to Mrs. Kratz when we left. Even though she knew what was going on, she didn't mention anything, and I loved that level of privacy she gave to everyone. In a town as small as Grace Valley, everyone knew your business. But every once in a while, I was pleasantly surprised by someone not running their mouth.

"Does Leah know you're here?" My mother raised her eyebrows.

"Yes, we came here together. She's at her office if you want to go see her. She could probably use another friendly face right about now."

We said our goodbyes and I got on the road. I wasn't sure how long the baby napped, but I had hoped that I wouldn't disturb him when I arrived. Lord knows whatever Brittany had up her sleeve was enough of a disturbance as is. Pulling into the B&B's parking lot made my stomach drop. I didn't know which version of her was going to greet me.

The sun was shining brightly against the snow and was an exact contrast to how I was feeling. What a joke. I waved to the concierge and went up to her room. My knock was as light as I could make it so as to not wake Colt, just in case.

"Come in," Brittany called sweetly from the other side.

She was the picture of style and grace sitting in the armchair, feeding Colt a bottle. I was surprised at how natural and maternal she looked with him. This was the only time that I had seen her without her façade on, and her love for him truly surpassed anything I had known of her.

"Hi, Brittany." I tried to sound as normal as possible and masked any anger by looking straight at that little boy.

Man, he really was a beautiful little thing, the spitting image of his mother. And the more I looked at him, the more I saw my eyes in him. I was in no position to co-parent, but he could have a great life with me here in Grace Valley. I began to fantasize about being a father and how wonderful Leah would be as a stepmother. No doubt she would take that role seriously and provide him with everything he could ever want or need. I stopped myself before things got too crazy.

Brittany carefully shifted her body to look at me while trying to stay comfortable for Colt. "Just a second; he's almost finished."

I watched in awe as he finished the bottle and she lifted him up to her shoulder to burp him. He let out a wallop of a belch, but she patted him again.

"Always burp him twice, or he will spit up while he's napping," she instructed, as if I were there to babysit him and not have an important conversation with her.

Still, I admired her level of care with him, something she only showed to her work and certainly never to me. She placed him gently on the bed and wrapped him tightly in something that made him look like a blue and green burrito and then snuggled him in the crook of her neck, softly humming. Once he was safely nestled in his crib, she sat down on the bed, patting next to her for me to come sit.

"I'll stand." No way I was getting any closer to her. "Why did you come here, Brittany? And what the hell were you thinking going around my town telling them that Colt was my son? Do you have any idea of the damage you could have caused?"

She licked her lips and looked at me, her eyes desperately trying to lure me over to her. "I only told them the truth, my love.

I knew you'd come back to me, Caleb. It was only a matter of time before you realized our family is all that matters."

"Cut the shit, Brittany. I'm here because of the baby and because I need to know if he's really mine. You were never around at the end of our relationship."

A slap that could have been heard clear across the country left a sting worse than any hornet. She was pissed. And quite frankly, I didn't blame her. I wasn't treating her with the respect that I was taught to, but I also didn't care. She wasn't the only one allowed to be upset by this ordeal. I lifted my hand to touch the cheek that moments before had connected with the palm of her right hand.

"Shit, Caleb, I'm so sorry. I shouldn't have done that." She put her palms on the sides of my face and tried to pull me down toward her.

Is this chick really trying to kiss me after she just slapped me?

"I want a paternity test, Brittany. Immediately. I'm making an appointment at the clinic first thing tomorrow morning."

I expected World War III to begin, but instead, she pulled me closer to her, my shirt crumpling in her fists.

"Caleb, look at him; you know he's yours. You don't need a paternity test to tell you that. Just forget your mousey little girlfriend and come back home with us."

I took her wrists in my hands and pulled them away from my body, trying to be as gentle with her as possible so I didn't detonate the bomb that was Brittany. I took a few steps back, creating space between us, and looked between her and the baby.

"Listen, if Colt is mine, I will make him a priority. I will spend time with him and get to know him and raise him as he should be raised. But I will do it from here while you are still in Tennessee. We will never be together again; I can promise you that. So whatever little game you're continuing to play needs to end now because you're not going to get the outcome you want."

Bomb activated.

"How dare you?" She seethed with a clenched jaw. "After everything I've been through trying to get ahold of you and getting back here to you, you're going to treat me this way? You'll pay, Caleb. Oh, you'll pay. And you want to stay here with that little prudish brat? Fine! But I promise YOU that your life will never be as good as it would have been with me."

Cause that definitely sounds like the type of woman who would make me happy.

I rolled my eyes and braced myself for another slap, but I was saved by the baby's little whimper. Brittany went to check on him and soothed him back to sleep, her face contorting as she looked back toward me. How I dated, let alone almost married, this woman was beyond me.

"Fine, Caleb," she barked. "You want a paternity test? You got it! But just so you know, I'll be retaining a lawyer to make sure I take you for every single penny you're worth. Child support ain't cheap, bud."

"You are insane." I scowled. "I'll text you tomorrow when I have the time and address for the appointment. And once we receive the results—regardless of what they say—I'm gonna need you to get the hell out of here and never come back."

I wanted to slam that door as hard as I could, but I couldn't bear the thought of waking Colt. Mine or not, he didn't need to suffer for his mother's indiscretions. I could hear Brittany crying on the other side of the door, and a part of me wanted to go back in and console her because that's how I was raised, but I was also taught to just let sleeping dogs lie. And that's exactly what Brittany did best.

35

LEAH

What a week. Between the whole Brittany bullshit and two new clients, I was over everything and ready for the weekend. Honestly, I would have been fine with just curling up with a good book and not leaving my bed the entire weekend with the exception of getting something to eat. I needed to recharge.

Caleb took a paternity test on Monday that was horrific. Brittany was the type of person who just couldn't help but make every situation about her regardless of who it could hurt. People like that are the absolute worst. She spent the entire visit telling the doctor what to do and making demands left and right. Finally, they asked her to take the baby and leave, and they finished Caleb's swab without her. She was a real piece of work considering Caleb had paid for everything she needed since she arrived last week.

The bell on my office door dinged, alerting me that my client had arrived. It was just the welcomed distraction that I needed.

"Hello, Margaret. Thank you so much for meeting me today. I know how busy your schedule is."

Margaret smiled as she hung her coat on the rack and joined

me at the table. "Not a problem at all. Any time away from the office is time well spent."

"Wonderful. Shall we begin?" I had been prepping for this meeting all week and was nervous to present her with my idea.

"Absolutely." She exuded an aura of professionalism that I aspired to attain.

"Taking your numbers into consideration, as well as the location, I think your best bet would be to add an indoor waterpark instead of placing it outdoors. Given the fact that we only have a few months of hot weather each year, you're better off with it inside. I think this will bring a different crowd and keep your business running at a constant speed all year long." I spoke as though my life depended on it, and in a sense, it did.

"I'll be honest with you, Leah. After finding out this was a young company, I wasn't sure if this would be a partnership that would benefit us both. However, I am pleasantly surprised to hear your ideas and observations. I never would have thought of that."

"I appreciate that. Growing up in New England opens your eyes to things that many people would normally overlook. I would have loved a local place for my parents to have taken me when I was younger. We always stayed local, but everything revolved around winter activities. I tend to look at things with a childlike lens when working on projects such as this."

The bell on the door dinged again, startling me because I wasn't expecting anyone, and I knew Caleb was at work for the rest of the day. Imagine my surprise when I looked up to see Brittany standing in the doorway glaring at me.

I put on my most professional face and gave her my winning smile. "Good afternoon, ma'am. Why don't you take a seat over there? I'll be with you momentarily."

She smirked and rolled her eyes. She fingered the pamphlets that were carefully placed on a table across the side wall. The smacking of her bubblegum was like daggers to my ears, but I had to maintain my composure. I couldn't risk losing my patience and ultimately losing this client. I did my best to drown her out while I finished the meeting, and as soon as Margaret left, I retreated back into fight mode. Earrings out, hair up, gloves off. Not literally, but in my mind, I had just walked into the octagon and—ding!—fight started. *I have got to stop watching MMA with Caleb.*

"What do you want, Brittany?"

"Is that any way to speak to the woman who is about to take your man away from you?" She swiped her tongue across her teeth and smirked at me again.

What I wouldn't give to wipe that smirk off her face.

Wow! The claws are out today. Who am I? Breathe. Just breathe. She is not worth it.

I sucked in my bottom lip and prepared to start the long speech I had practiced in case this moment ever arose, but I realized something.

"Brittany, where is Colt?" I asked, concerned.

"Oh, he's with his grandmother right now at the diner. I figured they ought to spend some quality time together before we all head back."

Caleb had told me how delusional of a person she was, but I didn't believe him. His stories sounded overexaggerated, and to be honest, kind of untrue, but now that I saw it firsthand, I was dumbfounded. I loved Caleb with everything that I had, but I would never take things to this level just to win him back. If for whatever reason he decided one day that he no longer wanted to be with me, I would be devastated. But I would never—and I really mean never—try to force him to stay with me. Why would I ever want to be with someone who didn't love me and want to be with me?

"Brittany, let me ask you something." All of a sudden, I was filled to the brim with confidence. "Why are you trying so hard to force someone to be with you? You do realize that, even if this child is Caleb's, which I think we all know isn't true, he isn't leaving here. He isn't leaving his family, his life, or his job. And he sure as shit is not leaving me. So why don't you just pack up your things and get out of our town?"

"I think it's so cute that you think you have a future with him." Her smile suddenly transformed into a look I could only describe as the devil's daughter.

She pursed her lips and glared at me. Her squinting eyes and heavy breathing would have scared me if I wasn't so confident that her bite was not as big as her bark. She would be too afraid to break a nail to ever hit me.

"Leah, dear, Caleb is mine. He's always been mine, and he will always be mine. If I were you, I would bow out gracefully before you really get hurt."

She licked her bright red lips and let out a long breath. Her hands were strategically placed on her hips, and I walked right past her, grabbed her coat off the rack, and flung it at her, accidentally whipping her across the face with the waist buckle.

Oops.

"Just leave."

As soon as she was out the door, I stood up and locked it behind her. I wasn't planning on having any other clients come into the office so it didn't matter if I closed up shop or not. I raced back over to my desk and grabbed my phone to FaceTime Sara, even though I knew she was out of town on business.

"Hey, girl!" she exclaimed, sitting under a cabana sipping a beverage. "What's going on?"

"I thought you were out of town for work."

"This is," she told me. "I'm in Arizona."

"Must be nice." I glowered at her. "Well, I guess I'll let you go then."

She sat up and placed her drink on the table next to her. "What's going on, love?"

I broke down in front of her and spilled tears all over my desk, frantically pushing my paperwork aside so it didn't get ruined. "I didn't want to bother you with it because I know how busy you are, but Brittany is here and she has a baby with her that she says is Caleb's."

"Oh my gosh, Leah. The hits just keep coming with that one, don't they? What's he going to do?"

"He took a paternity test, so we just have to wait and see. I trust that we will be okay, but this is taking such a toll on me. I feel guilty because he's the one who might have a child, not me. His life could potentially be turned upside down, and I'm more concerned over what will happen to us as a couple."

"Oh, honey. You can't let get to you. I know you're scared, but you're doing nothing wrong by worrying about your future. That's a normal reaction to something like this. I promise you, anyone would be thinking and feeling the same way you are right now."

As always, Sara swooped in to save the day, forcing me out of my thoughts and back into reality. Reality. What a word for everything that was going on in such a short amount of time. I couldn't imagine this being anyone's reality, but I would rather it be mine than have anyone else have to go through something as painful and confusing as this.

"Thank you, Sara," I said through my lingering sniffles. "I'm sorry to bother you on your business trip."

"You, my love, are never a bother. I'll be back in the city tomorrow, and I will call you once I'm back at the apartment."

My heart felt far lighter when we hung up the phone than it had when the call began. I mean, I was still unbelievably pissed at

Brittany, but I was a little calmer. I was ready to hear what the results were now, whichever way the tide turned. I made a promise to Caleb when we were kids that I would never leave him, and I broke it when I was seventeen. God gave us a second chance, and I wasn't about to mess up a second time.

36

CALEB

I sank into the driver's seat of my car and leaned my head back, waiting for the heat to kick in. It was only five p.m., but I was exhausted. The weight of the world was crushing me, and a part of me was ready to let it. I closed my eyes, and Leah's face flashed through my mind. She was the part worth fighting for. I fastened my seat belt and set off to meet her at her office, hopeful that once I had her in my arms, my mood would change.

"Figure out what you want to eat because I am not cooking tonight," Leah snapped at me as she unlocked the door to her office to let me in.

"Whoa, killer. What's with the attitude?"

"I know. I'm sorry. I thought I was over it, but clearly I'm not," she said, walking over to kiss me hello. "Brittany was here today. Totally threw me for a loop and made me want to punch her in the face."

"She came here? What did she want?"

Leah kissed me again and led me to the table she had set up for clients. "Sit."

"Ugh, that bad?" I draped my jacket and scarf across the back of one of the chairs and sat down while Leah leaned up against her desk.

"Long story short: you're hers and not mine, Colt is one hundred percent yours, and she's taking you back to Tennessee to wait on her hand and foot until the day you die." She rolled her eyes.

"That's dramatic," I winked.

"She's a shitshow. Can we go to your place now?"

"Of course. We can get settled and order something later. Come on." I stood up and reached my hand to hers, gently pulling her toward me and kissing her deeply. "And for the record, you're stuck with me for life, love."

She smiled, and for the first time in days, I felt like all was right in the world. I helped her with her jacket and then buttoned mine up. I paid close attention to her as she closed up shop and locked the door. She had given everything she had to run this place, and I couldn't have been prouder of her.

The sidewalk was icy from the rapid change in temperature since the sun had set, so I guided her to my car and opened the passenger door for her. Placing my hand at the small of her back was such a simple gesture, but one that I would always make sure I did. Once she was safely in the car, I made my way around and slid into the driver's seat. I leaned over and held her hands in mine, blowing warm air on them to keep her from getting too cold. Man, I loved that woman.

Leah kissed my hands and turned on the radio. The local station always played love songs at night, and she was notorious for listening to it every single night growing up. It made me happy to see that some things truly didn't change. I pressed my foot to the gas and started the quick drive to our home. Well, soon it would be ours.

We pulled in and walked hand in hand to the mailbox like we had when we were teenagers, not wanting to waste a second of our time not loving on each other. Our time apart had allowed us an opportunity to relive all of these moments again, and while we had missed out on so much, it was well worth the wait. I opened the mailbox and pulled out the mail—bills, catalogs, a random flyer for driveway paving, and the test results.

I whipped my head back over to where Leah was standing and watched as the color drained from her face.

"Here, take this. I can't look at it." I tossed the mail to her, half of it floating to the snow-covered ground. "Sorry."

"It's okay," she said sweetly, picking up the mail and taking my hand. "Let's do this in the house."

We usually wasted no time getting inside, but tonight, we took our time. I was in no rush to open the envelope that would seal my fate. Our fate, essentially

"Um, should we order some food while we wait to open this?" Leah asked me at the same time her stomach let out a bellowing rumble.

Leave it to her to make me laugh in a time of crisis.

"Are you cool with Mexican tonight? I could go for some enchiladas."

"Mmm, yes! Definitely." She licked her lips and rubbed her belly.

"You're so weird." I laughed.

"You okay if I go change?" she asked.

"Yeah, I won't be opening that for a while. I'll order while you change. The usual?"

"Yes, please."

It was pointless to take Leah to a new restaurant because she always ordered the same things wherever she went. She would be creative in her own kitchen but never dared to leave her comfort zone when someone else was cooking.

That damn envelope stared at me while I placed our order, and it took everything I had not to throw it in the wood-burning stove.

I had no idea what was going to be on the inside, and there was a huge part of me that believed she could be telling the truth.

Leah came back a few short minutes later dressed in her signature attire: baggy sweats, one of my hoodies, and fuzzy slippers. "When will the food be here?"

"Twenty minutes."

I was shocked the first time we ordered from that restaurant because the food was delivered so fast I was afraid they didn't cook it enough. I got that trait from my mother.

We had just stocked the fridge with our favorite beer so I grabbed two bottles and handed one to Leah. "I'm gonna change. Try not to snoop, little nosey."

She scrunched up her nose at me and took a long sip of her beer, savoring every drop. She playfully reached over to grab the envelope, but I snatched it away from her and took it with me to go change. She was getting a second beer by the time I was back, so I quickly caught up with her and got myself another too. The envelope once again laid on the counter, still unopened.

The doorbell rang, letting us know that our dinner had arrived, and at that point, I could have kissed the delivery man. "Fuel up before we open?"

"Your call." She always left things that I didn't want to deal with up to me.

After a beer and a half and about five bites of my dinner, I was ready to open the envelope—well, I was ready to see the results, but I had Leah open it for me.

"Are you sure you want me to open this, Caleb?"

I nodded and shoved another forkful of enchilada into my mouth. I wiped it away and continued to eat. If I occupied myself with food, maybe it wouldn't be so hard to swallow the truth—assuming it was one that I didn't want to hear.

I held my breath as she slowly slid her finger across the top of the envelope, careful not to rip it. She paused before taking the results out and looked up at me. I nodded for her to continue, and she pulled the paper out and flattened it on the counter. Her face went from nervous and hopeful to sad.

"Caleb, I'm sorry—"

"No, Leah, I am. I promise you, this won't change anything between us," I interrupted.

"Oh, no, Caleb. You are not the father of Colt," she finished. "I'm just sorry that he won't have a man as wonderful as you raising him."

"Come here." I held her close as soon as she rounded the corner of the counter and fell into my arms. "You're amazing."

"Let's finish eating before we go to the B&B. I think this is something we should tell Brittany in person."

I honestly never wanted to see her face again, but Leah was a far better person than I was, and she was right. We ate quickly, changed again, and drove through the snow to Brittany. We made it there in record time, and if all went well, we would be able to make it back home before it was too late. I wanted to enjoy at least an hour of alone time with Leah before bed.

"Oh, hi, I didn't realize you would be tagging along," Brittany snapped at Leah.

Leah ignored her attitude and walked inside before I did. "Is Colt awake?"

Brittany softened a bit at the mention of her son. "Yes, he's just lying in the crib."

"May I hold him?" Leah asked, a sparkle in her eyes.

Brittany cleared her throat, and I knew her well enough to know she was thinking of something snarky to reply with. Surprising us all, she just nodded a yes. Leah gently pulled Colt out of his crib and snuggled him, his head gently resting in the crook of her left elbow as he let out a little whimper. A baby looked good on her.

"I can feed him his bottle if you'd like," Leah offered.

Brittany seemed to be taken aback. "Um, okay, thank you. I just made him a bottle. It's sitting on the counter in the bathroom."

Leah smiled and took Colt with her to get the bottle. As soon as she sat in the chair and began to feed him, I started the conversation with Brittany.

"The results came in today. Would you like to sit down for this?"

"Do I want to know?" she asked, a single tear traveling down her cheek, stopping right above her top lip.

"That all depends on your outlook."

I pulled the chair that was nestled under the desk in the corner and turned it around. Sitting backward in a chair was something I hadn't done since high school, and my body was feeling it. Nonetheless, I ignored the physical discomfort and braced myself for the rest.

"Why don't you just tell me that he's not yours, Caleb?" she snapped at me. "I think we all know how much pleasure you're taking from this."

"I'm taking no pleasure whatsoever in this whole situation. Are you sure you don't want to see for yourself?"

There was massive part of me that thought I really would relish in this information, but between Leah's comment about Colt not having a good father, and me just not being that type of man, I was genuinely sincere with my feelings.

"I'm sorry, Brittany, but I am not Colt's father."

Brittany began to sob on the bed, and tears quickly poured down her face. I looked at Leah, worried, and she rushed around the bed to hand me Colt and his bottle. I finished feeding him while she lay down next to Brittany and held her as she sobbed. The amount of love that girl could hold in her heart, even after someone deliberately did her dirty, was admirable. I'd always thought myself a good man, but I would never be to the level of her.

"Come on, sit up," Leah instructed Brittany. "It's going to be okay."

She looked at me. "Would you hand me that box of tissues and grab her a water bottle out of the mini fridge, please?"

I did as I was told, and Leah continued to comfort Brittany. Rubbing her back and brushing her still perfectly styled hair away from her tears.

"What can we do for you?" Leah asked her kindly. "Do you have anyone at home?"

Brittany took the tissues and patted her mascara-stained cheeks. "I am so sorry. I knew there was a possibility that Caleb wasn't the father, and I put you all through this. I'm so embarrassed."

I had never seen Brittany take ownership of her actions before, and I could honestly say that I was really sad this was the turning point for her. No one should have to go through the fear of telling the truth or going through hard times alone.

"I'm sorry to ask this, but do you know who the father is?" Leah moved slightly away from Brittany when she asked her that question, almost as if she were afraid of what Brittany might do.

Brittany blew her nose and took a sip of the water, looking closely at Colt and waving me over to her so she could have him back. "I know who it is, but I can't raise a baby with him. He's not a good man, and it was a really big mistake."

She looked up at me as though that were her way of apologizing. A year ago, I might have been hurt by the admission, but it didn't bother me now.

"I don't ever want him to know. He didn't know I was pregnant, and Colt doesn't have his last name. I've been taking care of him by myself for this long, and I will continue to do so," she told us proudly. "Oh god, I am so sorry I did this you, Caleb. And to you, Leah. I was so jealous of everything that you and Caleb had. I knew I couldn't compete and I just wanted what was best for Colt."

"Brittany." Leah took her hands and placed them on Brittany's. "What's best for Colt is a happy, healthy, and present mother. That's all he needs, and he's all you need. Look, what you did wasn't right, and it could have cost a lot of people a lot of things, but we forgive you. I know how hard this must be for you, but you're a strong woman and you'll be okay. That I can promise you."

Brittany began to cry again, and I watched the two women hug as if they were old friends instead of semi-mortal enemies.

"Thank you," Brittany said to Leah, and then to me, "Please let me know what I owe you for all of this."

"Nothing," I said, holding out a hand to help her up off the bed. "Don't worry about it. Just get a good night's rest and have a safe trip home tomorrow."

"I don't know how you two are so kind after everything I put you through but thank you. I hope that I can one day repay you for your kindness."

Leah stood up and kissed baby Colt on the forehead and smiled at Brittany. I gave her one final hug goodbye and gently stroked Colt's cheek. We walked to the door in unison, Leah leaving in silence while I followed and Brittany cradled her son in her arms.

"Caleb?" Brittany quietly called over to me.

"Yeah?"

"If you ever change your mind about that little mouse of a girlfriend you have, you know where to find me." She winked.

I shook my head and walked out of the door. We were so close. So close. But some things never change.

37

LEAH

It had been a full month since Caleb received the results of the paternity test and Brittany and Colt had gone back to Tennessee. She checked in a couple of times and seemed to be doing well last we spoke. It was an odd feeling for me to be in contact with my boyfriend's ex-fiancée, but life was funny, and stranger things had happened. We would never be friends, but it gave me comfort knowing they were both safe and happy.

"I don't understand how you have so much stuff, pumpkin," my dad said, waving a hand across the disaster that was once my bedroom floor.

I laughed and tossed a balled-up sock at him. "I did move an entire apartment worth of stuff back here."

"True. So you're really doing this, huh?"

It was bittersweet, packing with my dad. The last time I did this was over a decade ago. and I was supposed to come home after college. This time it was to move in with the love of my life. I looked over at him, his face beaming with pride, but I was falling apart on the inside. Caleb lived less than five minutes away from my dad, so it wasn't like I'd never see him, but I was still sad about moving out.

"What's on your mind?"

"You. And leaving you alone."

"You know, when you were a little girl, I couldn't fathom living in any place where you weren't. Then you got a bit older and started high school, and I knew you would be applying to colleges. Your mother wanted you to stay local. She was always so afraid she would lose you to a big city, but I secretly wished that you'd spread your wings and soar like I knew you were meant to do. And guess what? You did. And it was the single proudest moment of my life as a father. Even more so when you graduated and then when you started your own company. Leah, you have always been the type to take the bull by the horns and live the life you've dreamed for yourself. So while I'm sad to see you go, I couldn't be happier to watch you in this next step of your journey."

He remained silent for quite a while, and we packed up my room and started to load my bins in the back of his pickup. Gnocchi hopped into the bed of the pickup and rubbed around on all of the bins.

"Oh, ol' boy. I'm gonna miss you so much."

I scooped him up and nuzzled him against my face. His purr echoed as he moved his little head down toward my neck. His claws stuck to my shirt, but I didn't care. I loved every second of being with him, which I felt had been less and less lately.

"Bring him with you," my dad told me. "You'll both be happier."

I looked up at my dad while Gnocchi looked up at me. "I couldn't. You'd be all alone if I took him. I'm close. I can come visit him every day."

He reached over and scratched Gnocchi on the top of his head, causing his purr to grow louder. "He's your cat and you're his person. Please, I want you two to be together."

I kissed Gnocchi and nuzzled him again. "You hear that, boy? You're coming with me."

He jumped out of my arms and back into the house, returning moments later with his little toy. It was as if he had understood us and was packing for himself.

"I'll bring him with me when I come over for dinner. Every night."

My dad rolled his eyes and smiled, knowing I was being serious. Who wouldn't want a cat as a dinner guest? We finished loading up the pickup and dropped off the first load to Caleb's house. Only the furniture was left, but that wouldn't take long to bring down. I would officially be changing my address in only a few short hours, and I was feeling all sides of the coin.

The day flew by, and before we knew it, we were sitting in Caleb's—I mean our—kitchen and reminiscing about old times. All of the Sundays at the meadow, running around and collecting flowers, eating Tammy's amazing lunches. Our homecoming dances, proms, graduation. The front door flew open during one of dad's retellings of my play junior year when I was inches away from being clobbered by a falling light fixture.

"Hello!" Tammy's voice rang through the hallway. "I've brought reinforcements!"

"We're in the kitchen," Caleb called back to her. "What did you bring?"

"Just a little dinner for us. Chicken parmigiana, penne, garlic bread, and tiramisu. I figured this was an important day, and since your mom can't be here with us, I would bring a little bit of who she was instead."

That was when my dad lost it. He was such strong and emotional man, and he was never afraid to show how he felt about any situation. I reached over and touched his shoulder, to which he brought his hand up and placed it on top of mine.

Full of Grace

"These are happy tears, pumpkin. This is exactly how your mother would have celebrated."

"Let's eat!" Tammy unloaded all of the food while Caleb set the table and I poured us all wine.

A new version of Sunday supper had been born. When we finished our dinner, my dad and Tammy cleaned up the kitchen while Caleb reloaded the wood stove. I followed him into the family room and waited while he finished before wrapping my arms around his waist, still not believing this was real life.

"All right, you two," my dad said, interrupting our little moment. "We're going to head out and let you enjoy your first night together in your home as a couple."

He walked over and held his hand out for Caleb to shake and then pulled me in for a tight hug. He kissed the top of my head and whispered in my ear.

"Not a day will ever go by that you don't make me proud. I love you, pumpkin."

"I love you, too, daddy," I whispered back, not loosening up on my hug.

When we finally parted, he kissed me again, this time on my cheek, and Tammy came in for a hug. Hers was much shorter and the only words exchanged were "Lock the door behind us" as she pulled the front door shut.

"So, Ms. Abernathy, now that you're all settled, what should we do first?" Caleb winked and grabbed my hands.

"I can think of a few things," I replied, looking into his eyes.

"I love you." His words wrapped around me, and I was caught in his spell again.

"I love you too. Forever."

38

CALEB

FOURTH OF JULY, ONE YEAR LATER

The air was so thick that I was covered in sweat two seconds after I got out of the shower. I hated nights like these and couldn't wait to buy a house with central air. There wasn't a window in the bathroom, so we couldn't put an air conditioning unit in there, and I died a little during summer. I prayed that would be our last summer in the rental. I wrapped a towel around my waist and crossed the hallway to the bedroom, ripping it off me and tossing it on the floor as soon as I was standing in front of the cool air. I lifted my arms out to my sides and tilted my head back. It was so nice.

"Hey, are you almost ready?" Leah burst out laughing as soon as she entered the room. "What are you doing?"

I whipped my head around to look at her, not expecting her to be home until a bit later. "It's so hot in that damn bathroom."

She continued to laugh, bending over to pick the wet towel up off the floor and hanging it on the rack in the bathroom. Still shaking her head at me, she sat on the corner of the bed and waited for me to get dressed.

"Well, hurry up. Jess and Matt are already on their way there. What took you so long anyway?"

"Nothing. I was just working on something and lost track of time. Can you do me a favor and grab me a bottle of water from the fridge, please?" I reached over to the chair to grab my clothes and winked at her.

Her cheeks turned a shade of rose as she left the room. I quickly got my clothes on and stuffed my pockets with all of the essentials. I was fully dressed by the time she returned and pounded the water she brought me, crumpling the bottle and tossing it into the garbage can.

"Now I'm ready."

I draped my arm over her shoulder, and she replied by wrapping her tiny arm around my waist, and we headed to the carnival.

"Park at the farm so we don't get stuck trying to leave later," Leah instructed me.

"Oh, good call."

I parked and we walked down the hill to the bottom of the meadow where the carnival was held every year. My palms were sweating so badly holding onto her hands that I thought she might slip right out of them.

"Hey, guys!" Jess called out to us through the sea of people who had already congregated.

"Sup, man." Matt held a fist out to give me dap. "Hey, Leah."

"I'm so excited for this." Leah grinned from ear to ear. "I don't think I'll ever get sick of coming to this carnival."

"Well, I heard this was the last year they were having it, so you better get all your rides in tonight," Matt teased her.

"What? What are you talking about? Who told you that? Caleb, can you talk to Bill about this? No, this cannot happen. Oh my gosh." Leah paced back and forth, hand to her head as she speed talked.

I don't know how Matt held a straight face through this whole ordeal, but he was good. Jess broke down first and told her he was just messing with her.

"I hate you," Leah said as she walked right past them to the ring toss booth.

"She's kidding," I told him as they continued to laugh, knowing damn well she didn't hate them one bit.

They followed me to the booth, and I surprisingly was able to win my mom a teddy bear on the first try. Leah had been my good luck charm for so many years, and my sappy self loved that she still was.

We traveled through the carnival, riding on everything we were able to and playing so many games that I felt like we were back in high school again. The only difference was that we were a decade older, and Jess and Matt were married now. Their wedding was the coolest I'd ever been to. Matt played the bagpipes as Jess walked down the aisle, and it was truly breathtaking. I hadn't heard him play since St. Patrick's Day our senior year, and I had missed it.

I looked at my watch and noticed it was nearing nine. If we wanted the best seat in the house for the fireworks show, we'd better get to the Ferris wheel quickly. Leah handed over our tickets, and we hopped into the cart as the ride began to spin us slowly, up and down and up again. Eventually, we stopped at the top, and Leah was shocked that, once again, we were able to watch the show from the highest point.

"I can't believe it stopped with us again. I can't wait!"

Well, I had paid the kid twenty bucks to make sure of it.

She leaned over and kissed me and then snuggled up tightly against my chest. I wrapped my left arm around her as she looked up in delight, waiting for the first sparkle to flash across the sky. I laid my right hand on my pocket, feeling for the box I knew was still there and would finally be opened. I'd kept that box in my sock drawer since the summer she left me. I don't know how I'd known, but I knew one day she would be wearing it. I slowly reached into my pocket, not wanting to draw any attention and have her notice prematurely.

As if on cue, the show started, and the sky lit up with the most beautiful colors—a true testament to the love and camaraderie of this town. I held the box in my hand and waited until the moment was perfect. And then, it was. In giant letters, the words, *Will you marry me?* miraculously painted the night sky.

"Aww, Caleb look!" she exclaimed, looking over to me. "Someone is proposing!"

I let go of her and held the box open between us. Her jaw dropped and she burst into tears.

"Leah, I have loved you for as long as I can remember. You are the best thing that has ever happened to me, and I can't imagine having adventures with anyone else. Will you marry me?"

She lifted her hands to wipe the tears off her face and cupped my face in her palms.

"Yes!" she shouted. "A million times, yes."

I placed the ring on her finger, and the cheering began to roar from all around us. The Ferris wheel began moving again, and we were quickly off the ride and back on solid ground. Our parents and the world's best friends were all waiting for us, and it felt like we were still on top of the world.

Everyone was exchanging hugs and congratulations and saying, "Let me see the ring" when Paul came over to me. He put his hands on my shoulders and looked at me, pulling me in for a bear hug and slapping me on the back.

"I always knew you'd be my son someday. I couldn't have picked a better man for my girl."

And then he started crying. I was glad I wasn't the only sap in the group.

"Get together, you two. I want to take a picture of you." My mom pushed Leah and I together and pulled her phone out of her pocket to capture the moment.

I pulled Leah in as close as I could and kissed her. I couldn't wait to marry my girl.

THE END

Enjoy this book? I'd love to hear about your thoughts and reactions. Please leave a review using the link below. Stay tuned for book three of the *Grace Valley* series, *Saving Grace*.

https://amzn.to/2SpwNU4

ACKNOWLEDGMENTS

First and foremost, thank you to everyone who is reading this right now. Your support throughout this journey, and what's to come, is incredible. It means more to me than I can ever put into words.

Dave. My husband, my best friend, my #1 supporter. I couldn't do any of this without you. I love you. And I promise to fold the laundry now.

Sabrina and Alexandria. My little magical babies. You are the world's greatest story. I love you the most.

Mom and Dad. Thank you for being my biggest fans. I love you times infinity.

Nacolle. You're next!

Adelya and Kimberly. There isn't even enough space on this page for me to tell the world how much I adore you both. This book would not be here today if not for you. And a shit ton of coffee!

Jessica. I hope Chris doesn't mind that I married you off to another man! Love you!

Cheryl. Thank you for being such a bright light at the end of a sometimes very dark tunnel. Your support means the world to me!

Melanie Cherniak. AKA Elsa Kurt. There will never be a book where I don't mention you in the acknowledgements. Ever. You've forever changed my life.

Amanda Cuff. I cannot believe book two is done! Thank you for everything!

Carmen Richter. You swooped in and saved me in so many ways. I am forever grateful to you.

Marie Force. I will never forget all of the advice you have given me and I thank you times a billion.

The Martin Family. All one million of you! The amount of love and support you have shown me is proof that love is thicker than water. I love all of you so much and I am so grateful to be your blood.

And last but certainly not least, The Hallmark Channel. I'm still waiting on that book/movie deal …

And to anyone I missed, thank you for everything! Writing this series has brought me so much joy and I owe it to each and every one of you.

ALSO BY BETHANY SURREIRA

GRACE VALLEY SERIES:

1. *Return to Grace:* https://amzn.to/39TdXuY
2. *Full of Grace:* https://amzn.to/2SpwNU4

ABOUT THE AUTHOR

Bethany is an author, wife and mother to two little girls. When she isn't writing or spending time with her family, you can find her whipping up something in the kitchen, enjoying a hot cup of coffee, or with her nose stuck in a book.

Website :www.bethanysurreira.com

Newsletter: http://eepurl.com/hvQCGn

Facebook: https://www.facebook.com/BethanySurreira

Instagram: https://www.instagram.com/bethanysurreira/

Goodreads: https://www.goodreads.com/author/show/20888348.Bethany_-Surreira

Amazon: https://www.amazon.com/BethanySurreira/e/B08N5FLQF3

Made in the USA
Las Vegas, NV
10 January 2022